V.L

Val McDermid gr
coast of Scotland, then read English at Oxford. She was a journalist for sixteen years, spending the last three years as Northern Bureau Chief of a national Sunday tabloid. Now a full-time writer, she divides her time between Cheshire and Northumberland.

Common Murder is the second of six novels featuring journalist-sleuth Lindsay Gordon (the fifth, *Booked for Murder*, was shortlisted for the Lambda award). Val is also the author of the Kate Brannigan series and four tense psychological thrillers featuring criminal profiler Tony Hill. The first of these *The Mermaids Singing*, was awarded the 1995 Gold Dagger Award for Best Crime Novel of the Year while the second, *The Wire in the Blood*, lends its name to the acclaimed ITV series featuring Robson Green as Tony Hill. She has also written three stand-alone thrillers: *A Place of Execution*, *Killing the Shadows* and *The Distant Echo*.

For more information see Val's website
www.valmcdermid.com

By the same author

The Distant Echo
Killing the Shadows
A Place of Execution

TONY HILL NOVELS

The Torment of Others
The Last Temptation
The Wire in the Blood
The Mermaids Singing

KATE BRANNIGAN NOVELS

Star Struck
Blue Genes
Clean Break
Crack Down
Kick Back
Dead Beat

LINDSAY GORDON NOVELS

Hostage to Murder
Booked for Murder
Union Jack
Final Edition
Report for Murder

NON-FICTION

A Suitable Job for a Woman

V.L. McDERMID

Common Murder

HarperCollins*Publishers*

This novel is entirely a work of fiction.
The names, characters and incidents portrayed in it are the work of the author's imagination. Any resemblance to actual persons, living or dead, events or localities is entirely coincidental.

HarperCollins*Publishers*
77–85 Fulham Palace Road
London W6 8JB

The HarperCollins website address is:
www.harpercollins.co.uk

First published in Great Britain by
The Women's Press Ltd 1989

This paperback edition published 2004

1

The author asserts the moral right to be identified as the author of this work

ISBN: 978-0-00-787980-9

Set in Meridien by Palimpsest Book Production Limited, Polmont, Stirlingshire

Printed and bound by Clays Ltd, St Ives plc

For my father

ACKNOWLEDGEMENTS

Thanks to: Helen for keeping us laughing at Greenham; Andrew Wiatr for advice on computers (any errors are mine); Diana for all the constructive criticism; Lisanne and Jane for their hard work; John and Senga, Laura and Ewan for their hospitality at the crucial point; Sue Jackson for her inimitable skills; Henry the lawyer for letting me pick his brains; and Linzi.

1

'This is murder,' Lindsay Gordon complained, leaning back in her chair and putting her feet up on the desk. 'I can't bear it when there's nothing doing. Look at us. Eight p.m. on the dynamic news-desk of a national daily. The night news editor's phoning his daughter in Detroit. His deputy's straining his few remaining brain cells with the crossword. One reporter has escaped to the pub like a sensible soul. Another is using the office computer to write the Great English Novel . . .'

'And the third is whingeing on as usual,' joked the hopeful novelist, looking up from the screen. 'Don't knock it, Lindsay, it's better than working.'

'Huh,' she grunted, reaching for the phone. 'I sometimes wonder. I'm going to do a round of calls, see if there's anything going on in the big bad world outside.'

Her colleague grinned. 'What's the problem? Run out of friends to phone?'

Lindsay pulled a face. 'Something like that,'

she replied. As she opened her contacts book at the page with the list of police, fire and ambulance numbers she thought of the change in her attitude to unfettered access to the office phone since she'd moved from her base in Glasgow to live with her lover Cordelia in London. She had appreciated quiet night shifts in those days for the chance they gave her to spend half the night chattering about everything and nothing with Cordelia. These days, however, it seemed that what they had to say to each other could easily be accommodated in the hours between work and sleep. Indeed, Lindsay was beginning to find it easier to open her heart to friends who weren't Cordelia. She shook herself mentally and started on her list of calls.

On the newsdesk, Cliff Gilbert the night news editor finished his phone conversation and started checking the computerised newsdesk for any fresh stories. After a few minutes, he called. 'Lindsay, you clear?'

'Just doing the calls, Cliff,' she answered.

'Never mind that. There's a bloody good tip just come in from one of the local paper lads in Fordham. Seems there's been some aggro at the women's peace camp at Brownlow Common. I've transferred the copy into your personal desk. Check it out, will you?' he asked.

Lindsay sat up and summoned the few paragraphs on to her screen. The story seemed straightforward enough. A local resident claimed he'd been assaulted by one of the women from the peace camp. He'd had his nose broken in the incident, and the woman was in custody. Lindsay was instantly sceptical. She found it hard to believe that one of a group pledged to campaign for peace would physically attack an opponent of the anti-nuclear protest. But she was enough of a professional to concede that her initial reaction was the sort of knee-jerk she loved to condemn when it came from the other side.

The repercussions unfolding outside Fordham police station made the story interesting from the point of view of the *Daily Clarion* newsdesk. The assaulted man, a local solicitor called Rupert Crabtree, was the leader of Ratepayers Against Brownlow's Destruction, a pressure group dedicated to the removal of the peace women from the common. His accusation had provoked a spontaneous demonstration from the women, who were apparently besieging the police station. That in its turn had provoked a counter-demonstration from RABD members outraged at the alleged attack. There was a major confrontation in the making, it appeared.

Lindsay started making phone calls, but soon hit a brick wall. The police station at Fordham were referring all calls to county headquarters. Headquarters were hiding behind the old excuse: 'We can make no statement yet. Reports are still coming in.' It was not an unusual frustration. She walked over to Cliff's desk and explained the problem. 'It might be worth taking a run down there to see what the score is,' she suggested. 'I can be there in an hour at this time of night, and if it is shaping up into a nasty, we should have someone on the spot. I don't know how far we can rely on the lad that filed the original copy. I've got some good contacts at the peace camp. We could get a cracking exclusive out of it. What do you think?'

Cliff shrugged. 'I don't know. It doesn't grab me.'

Lindsay sighed. 'On the basis of what we've got so far, we could be looking at a major civil disturbance. I'd hate the opposition to beat us to the draw when we've got a head start with my contacts.'

'Give your contacts a bell, then.'

'There are no phones at the camp, Cliff. British Telecom have shown an incomprehensible reluctance to install them in tents. And besides, they'll probably all be down the copshop protesting. I might as well go. There's sod all else doing.'

He grinned. 'Okay, Lindsay, go and take a look. Give me a check call when you get there. I'll see if we can get any more information over the phone. Remember your deadlines – there's no point in getting a good exclusive if we can't get it in the paper.'

'What about a pic man?'

'Let me know if you need one when you get there. I seem to remember there's a local snapper we've used before.'

Five minutes later, Lindsay was weaving through the London traffic in her elderly MG roadster. She drove on automatic pilot while she dredged all she knew about the peace camp to the surface of her mind.

She'd first been to the camp about nine months before. She and Cordelia had made the twenty-mile detour to Brownlow Common one sunny May Sunday after a long lunch with friends in Oxford. Lindsay had read about the camp in one of the Sunday papers, and had been intrigued enough by the report to want to see it for herself. Cordelia, who shared Lindsay's commitment to opposing the nuclear threat, had been easily persuaded to come along on that initial visit, though she was never to share Lindsay's conviction that the camp was an effective form of protest. For Cordelia, the channels of dissent that came easiest were the traditional ones of letters to the *Guardian* and MPs. She had never felt comfortable with the ethos of the camp. Cordelia always felt that she was somehow being judged and found wanting by the women who had made that overwhelming commitment to the cause of peace. So she seldom accompanied Lindsay on later visits, preferring to confine her support to handing cash over to Lindsay to purchase whatever necessities the camp was short of, from lentils to toilet chemicals. But for that first visit, she suspended her instinctive distrust and tried to keep her mind open.

The peace camp had started spontaneously just over a year before. A group of women had marched from the West Country to the American airbase at Brownlow Common to protest at the siting of US cruise missiles there. They had been so fired by anger and enthusiasm at the end of their three-week march that they decided to set up a peace camp as a permanent protest against the nuclear colonisation of their green unpleasant land.

Thinking back to that early summer afternoon, Lindsay found it hard to remember what she'd expected. What she had found was enough to shatter her expectations beyond recall. They had turned off the main road on to a leafy country lane. After about a mile and a half, the trees on one side of the road suddenly stopped. There was an open clearing the size of a couple of football pitches, bisected by a tarmac track that led up to a gate about 250 yards from the road. The gate was of heavy steel bars covered with chain-link fencing and surmounted by savage angled spikes wrapped with barbed wire. The perimeter fence consisted of ten-foot tall concrete stanchions and metal-link fencing, topped by rolls of razor wire. More razor wire was laid in spirals along the base of the fence. The gate was guarded by four British soldiers on the inside and two policemen on the outside. A sign declared 'USAF Brownlow Common'.

In the distance, the long low humps of the

missile silos broke the skyline. Three hundred yards inside the perimeter fence were buildings identifiable as servicemen's quarters – square, concrete blocks with identical curtains. From beyond the wire, they looked like a remand centre, Lindsay had thought. They provided a stark contrast to the other human habitation visible from the car. Most of the clearing outside the forbidding fence had been annexed by the peace women. All over it were clusters of tents – green, grey, orange, blue, brown. The women were sitting out in the warm sunshine, talking, drinking, cooking, eating, singing. The bright colours of their clothes mingled and formed a kaleidoscope of constantly changing patterns. Several young children were playing a hysterical game of tig round one group of tents.

Lindsay and Cordelia had been made welcome, although some of the more radical women were clearly suspicious of Lindsay's occupation and Cordelia's reputation as a writer who embodied the establishment's vision of an acceptable feminist. But after that first visit Lindsay had maintained contact with the camp. It seemed to provide her with a focus for her flagging political energies, and besides, she enjoyed the company of the peace women. One in particular, Jane Thomas, a doctor who had given up a promising career as a surgical registrar to live at the camp, had become a close and supportive friend.

Lindsay had come to look forward to the days

she spent at Brownlow Common. The move to London that had seemed to promise so much had proved to be curiously unsatisfying. She had been shocked to discover how badly she fitted in with Cordelia's circle of friends. It was an upsetting discovery for someone whose professional success often depended on that mercurial quality she possessed which enabled her to insinuate herself virtually anywhere. Cordelia, for her part, clearly felt uncomfortable with journalists who weren't part of the media arts circus. And Cordelia was no chameleon. She liked to be with people who made her feel at home in the persona she had adopted. Now she was wrapped up in a new novel, and seemed happier to discuss its progress with her friends and her agent than with Lindsay, who felt increasingly shut out as Cordelia became more absorbed in her writing. It had made Lindsay feel uncomfortable about bringing her own work problems home, for Cordelia's mind always seemed to be elsewhere. Much as she loved and needed Cordelia, Lindsay had begun to sense that her initial feeling that she had found a soulmate with whom she occasionally disagreed was turning into a struggle to find enough in common to fill the spaces between the lovemaking that still brought them together in a frighteningly intense unity. Increasingly, they had pursued their separate interests. Brownlow Common had become one of Lindsay's favourite boltholes.

But the camp had changed dramatically since

those heady summer days. Harassment had sprung up from all sides. Some local residents had formed Ratepayers Against Brownlow's Destruction in an attempt to get rid of the women who created in the camp what the locals saw as an eyesore, health hazard and public nuisance. The yobs from nearby Fordham had taken to terrorising the camp in late-night firebomb attacks. The police were increasingly hostile and heavy-handed in dealing with demonstrations. What media coverage there was had become savage, stereotyped and unsympathetic. And the local council had joined forces with the Ministry of Defence to fight the women's presence through the civil courts. The constant war of attrition coupled with the grim winter weather had changed the camp both physically and spiritually. Where there had been green grass, there was now a greasy, pot-holed morass of reddish-brown clay. The tents had vanished, to be replaced with benders – polythene sheeting stretched over branches and twine to make low-level tepees. They were ugly but they were also cheap, harder to burn and easier to reconstruct. Even the rainbow colours the women wore were muted now that the February cold had forced them to wrap up in drab winter plumage. But more serious, in Lindsay's eyes, was the change in atmosphere. The air of loving peace and warmth, that last hangover from the sixties, had been heavily overlaid with the pervading sense of something harder. No one was in any doubt that this was no game.

It was typically ironic, she thought, that it needed crime to persuade the *Clarion* that the camp was worth some coverage. She had made several suggestions to her news editor about a feature on the women at the peace camp, but he had treated the idea with derision. Lindsay had finally conceded with ill grace because her transfer to the job in London was a relatively recent achievement she couldn't afford to jeopardise. The job hadn't quite turned out the way she'd expected either. From being a highly rated writer who got her fair share of the best assignments, she had gone to being just another fish in the pool of reporters. But she remembered too well the years of hard-working, nail-biting freelancing before she'd finally recovered the security of a wage packet, and she wasn't ready to go back to that life yet.

Jane Thomas, however, encouraged her to use her talents in support of the camp. As a result, Lindsay had rung round her magazine contacts from her freelance days and sold several features abroad to salve her conscience. Thanks to her, the camp had had extensive magazine coverage in France, Italy and Germany, and had even featured in a colour spread in an American news magazine. But somewhere deep inside, she knew that wasn't enough. She felt guilty about the way she had changed since she'd decided to commit herself to her relationship with Cordelia. She knew she'd been seduced as much by Cordelia's comfortable lifestyle as by her lover's charm. That had made it hard to sustain the political commitment that had once been so important to her. 'Your bottle's gone, Gordon,' she said aloud as she pulled off the motorway on to the Fordham road. Perhaps the chance for redemption was round the next corner.

As she reached the outskirts of the quiet market town of Fordham, her radiopager bleeped insistently. Sighing, she checked the dashboard clock. Nine fifteen. Forty-five minutes to edition time. She wasted five precious minutes finding a phone box and rang Cliff.

'Where are you?' he said officiously.

'I'm about five minutes away from the police station,' she explained patiently. 'I'd have been there by now if you hadn't bleeped me.'

'Okay, fine. I've had the local lad on again. I've said you're *en route* and I've told him to link up with you. His name's Gavin Hammill, he's waiting for you in the lounge bar of the Griffon's Head, in the market place, he says. He's wearing a Barbour jacket and brown trousers. He says it's a bit of a stalemate at present; anyway, suss it out and file copy as soon as.'

'I'm on my way,' Lindsay said.

Finding the pub was no problem. Finding Gavin Hammill was not so simple. Every other man in the pub was wearing a Barbour jacket and half of them seemed to be alone. After the second failure, Lindsay decided to buy a drink and try again. Before she could down her Scotch, a gangling youth with mousy brown hair and a skin problem inadequately hidden by a scrubby beard tapped her on the shoulder and said, 'Lindsay Gordon? From the *Clarion*? I'm Gavin Hammill, *Fordham Weekly Bugle*.'

Far from relieved, Lindsay smiled weakly. 'Please to meet you, Gavin. What's the score?

'Well, both lots are still outside the police station but the police don't seem to know quite how to play it. I mean, they can't treat the ratepayers the way they normally treat the peace women, can they? And yet they can't be seen to be treating them differently. It's kind of a stand-off. Or it was when I left.'

'And when was that?'

'About ten minutes ago.'

'Come on then, let's go and check it out. I've got a deadline to meet in twenty minutes.'

They walked briskly through the market place and into the side street where a two-storey brick building housed Fordham police station. They could hear the demonstration before they saw the demonstrators. The women from the camp were singing the songs of peace that had emerged over the last two years as their anthems. Chanting voices attempted to drown them out with 'Close the camp! Give us peace!'

On the steps of the police station, sat about

forty women dressed in strangely assorted layers of thick clothing, with muddy boots and peace badges fixed to their jackets, hats and scarves. The majority of them looked remarkably healthy, in spite of the hardships of their outdoor life. To one side, a group of about twenty-five people stood shouting. There were more men than women, and they all looked as if they ought to be at home watching 'Mastermind' instead of causing a civil disturbance outside the police station. Between the two groups were posted about a dozen uniformed policemen who seemed unwilling to do more than keep the groups apart. Lindsay stood and watched for a few minutes. Every so often, one of the RABD group would try to push through the police lines, but not seriously enough to warrant more than the gentlest of police manhandling. These attempts were usually provoked by jibes from one or two of the women. Lindsay recognised Nicky, one of the camp's proponents of direct action, who called out, 'You're brave enough when the police are in the way, aren't you? What about being brave when the Yanks drop their bombs on your doorstep?'

'Why aren't the cops breaking it up?' Lindsay asked Gavin.

'I told you, they don't seem to know what to do. I think they're waiting for the superintendent to get here. He was apparently off duty tonight and they've been having a bit of bother getting hold of him. I imagine he'll be able to sort it out.'

Even as he spoke, a tall, uniformed police officer with a face like a Medici portrait emerged from the station. He picked his way between the peace women, who jeered at him. 'That him?' Lindsay demanded.

'Yeah. Jack Rigano. He's the boss here. Good bloke.'

One of the junior officers handed Rigano a bull-horn. He put it to his lips and spoke. Through the distortion, Lindsay made out, 'Ladies and gentlemen, you've had your fun. You have five minutes to disperse. If you fail to do so, my officers have orders to arrest everyone. Please don't think about causing any more trouble tonight. We have already called for reinforcements and I warn you that everyone will be treated with equal severity unless you disperse at once. Thank you and goodnight.'

Lindsay couldn't help grinning at his words. At once the RABD protesters, unused to the mechanics of organised dissent, began to move away, talking discontentedly among themselves. The more experienced peace women sat tight, singing defiantly. Lindsay turned to Gavin and said, 'Go after the RABD lot and see if you can get a couple of quotes. I'll speak to the cops and the peace women. Meet me by that phone box on the corner in ten minutes. We'll have to get some copy over quickly.'

She quickly walked over to the superintendent and dug her union Press Card out of her pocket.

'Lindsay Gordon. *Daily Clarion,*' she said. 'Can I have a comment on this incident?'

Rigano looked down at her and smiled grimly. 'You can say that the police have had everything under control and both sets of demonstrators were dispersed peacefully.'

'And the assault?'

'The alleged assault, don't you mean?'

It was Lindsay's turn for the grim smile. 'Alleged assault,' she said.

'A woman is in custody in connection with an alleged assault earlier this evening at Brownlow Common. We expect to charge her shortly. She will appear before Fordham magistrates tomorrow morning. That's it.' He turned away from her abruptly as his men began carrying the peace women down the steps. As soon as one woman was carried into the street and the police returned for the next, the first would outflank them and get back on to the steps. Lindsay knew the process of old. It would go on until police reinforcements arrived and outnumbered the protesters. It was a ritual dance that both sides had perfected.

When she saw a face she recognised being dumped on the pavement, Lindsay quickly went over and grabbed the woman's arm before she could return to the steps. 'Jackie,' Lindsay said urgently. 'It's me, Lindsay, I'm doing a story about the protest, can you give me a quick quote.'

The young black woman grinned. She said, 'Sure. You can put in your paper that innocent women are being victimised by the police because we want a nuclear-free world to bring up our children in. Peace women don't go around beating up men. One of our friends has been framed, so we're making a peaceful protest. Okay? Now I've got to get back. See you, Lindsay.'

There was no time for Lindsay to stay and watch what happened. She ran back to the phone box, passing a police van loaded with uniformed officers on the corner of the market-place. Gavin was standing by the phone box, looking worried.

Lindsay dived into the box and dialled the office copytakers' number. She got through immediately and started dictating her story. When she had finished, she turned to Gavin and said, 'I'll put you on to give your quotes in a sec, okay? Listen, what's the name of this woman who's accused of the assault? The lawyer will kill it, but I'd better put it in for reference for tomorrow.'

'She comes from Yorkshire, I think,' he said. 'Her name's Deborah Patterson.'

Lindsay's jaw dropped. 'Did you say . . . Deborah Patterson?'

He nodded. Lindsay was filled with a strange sense of unreality. Deborah Patterson. It was the last name she expected to hear. Once upon a time it had been the name she scribbled idly on her notepad while she waited for strangers to answer their telephones, conjuring up the mental image of the woman she spent her nights with. But that had been a long time ago. Now her ghost had come back to haunt her. That strong, funny woman who had once made her feel secure against the world was here in Fordham.

2

Lindsay stroked the four-year-old's hair mechanically as she rocked her back and forth in her arms. 'It's okay, Cara,' she murmured at frequent intervals. The sobs soon subsided, and eventually the child's regular breathing provided evidence that she had fallen asleep, worn out by the storm of emotions she'd suffered. 'She's dropped off at last,' Lindsay observed to Dr Jane Thomas, who had taken charge of Cara after her mother's dramatic arrest.

'I'll put her in her bunk,' Jane replied. 'Pass her over.' Lindsay awkwardly transferred the sleeping child to Jane, who carried her up the short ladder to the berth above the cab of the camper van that was Deborah's home at the peace camp. She settled the child and tucked her in then returned to sit opposite Lindsay at the table. 'What are your plans?' she asked.

'I thought I'd stay the night here. My shift finishes at midnight, and the boss seems quite happy for me to stop here tonight. Since it looks as if Debs won't be using her bed, I thought I'd take advantage of it and keep an eye on Cara at the same time if that sounds all right to you. I'll have to go and phone Cordelia soon, though, or she'll wonder where I've got to. Can you stay with Cara while I do that?'

'No sweat,' said Jane. 'I was going to kip down here if you'd had to go back to London, but stay if you like. Cara's known you all her life, after all. She knows she can trust you.'

Before Lindsay could reply, there was a quiet knock at the van's rear door. Jane opened it to reveal a redheaded woman in her early thirties wearing the standard Sloane Ranger outfit of green wellies, needlecord jeans, designer sweater and the inevitable Barbour jacket.

'Judith!' Jane exclaimed, 'Am I glad to see you! Now we can find out exactly what's going on. Lindsay, this is Judith Rowe, Deborah's solicitor. She does all our legal work. Judith, this is Lindsay Gordon, who's a reporter with the *Daily Clarion*, but more importantly, she's an old friend of Deborah's.'

Judith sat down beside Lindsay. 'So it was you who left the note for Deborah at the police station?' she asked briskly.

'That's right. As soon as I found out she'd been arrested, I thought I'd better let her know I was around in case she needed any help,' Lindsay said.

'I'm glad you did,' said Judith. 'She was in a

bit of a state about Cara until she got your message. She seemed calmer afterwards. Now, tomorrow, she's appearing before the local magistrates. She's been charged with breach of the peace and assault resulting in actual bodily harm on Rupert Crabtree. She's going to put her hand up to the breach charge, but she wants to opt for jury trial on the ABH charge. She asked me to tell you what happened before you make any decisions about what I have to ask you. Okay?'

Lindsay nodded. Judith went on. 'Crabtree was walking his dog up the road, near the phone box at Brownlow Cottages. Deborah had been making a call and when she left the box, Crabtree stood in her path and was really rather insulting, both to her and about the peace women in general. She tried to get past him, but his dog started growling and snapping at her and a scuffle developed. Crabtree tripped over the dog's lead and crashed face first into the back of the phone box, breaking his nose. He claims to the police that Deborah grabbed his hair and smashed his face into the box. No witnesses. In her favour is the fact that she phoned an ambulance and stayed near by till it arrived.

'It's been normal practice for the women to refuse to pay fines and opt for going to prison for non-payment. But Deborah feels she can't take that option since it would be unfair to Cara. She'll probably be fined about twenty-five pounds on the breach and won't be given time to pay since she'll also be looking for bail on the assault charge and Fordham mags can be absolute pigs when it comes to dealing with women from the camp. She asked me to ask you if you'd lend her the money to pay the fine. That's point one.'

Judith was about to continue, but Lindsay interrupted. 'Of course I will. She should know that, for God's sake. Now, what's point two?'

Judith grinned. 'Point two is that we believe bail will be set at a fairly high level. What I need is someone who will stand surety for Deborah.'

Lindsay nodded. 'That's no problem. What do I have to do?'

'You'll have to lodge the money with the court. A cheque will do. Can you be there tomorrow?'

'Provided I can get away by half past two. I'm working tomorrow night, you see. I start at four.' She arranged to meet Judith at the magistrates' court in the morning, and the solicitor got up to leave. The night briefly intruded as she left, reminding them all of the freezing February gale endured by the women outside.

'She's been terrific to us,' said Jane, as they watched Judith drive away. 'She just turned up one day not long after the first court appearance for obstruction. She offered her services any time we needed legal help. She's never taken a penny from us, except what she gets in legal aid. Her family farms on the other side of town and her mother comes over about once a month with fresh vegetables for us. It's really heartening when you get support from people like that, people you'd always vaguely regarded as class enemies, you know?'

Lindsay nodded. 'That sort of thing always makes me feel ashamed for writing people off as stereotypes. Anyway, I'd better go and phone Cordelia before she starts to worry about me. Will you hold the fort for ten minutes?'

Lindsay jumped into the car and drove to the phone box where the incident between Deborah and Crabtree had taken place though it was too dark to detect any signs of the scuffle. A gust of wind blew a splatter of rain against the panes of the phone box as she dialled the London number and a sleepy voice answered, 'Cordelia Brown speaking.'

'Cordelia? It's me. I'm down at Brownlow Common on a job that's got a bit complicated. I'm going to stay over. Okay?'

'What a drag. Why is it always you that gets stuck on the out-of-towners?'

'Strictly speaking, it's not work that's the problem.' Lindsay spoke in a rush. 'Listen, there's been a bit of bother between one of the peace women and a local man. There's been an arrest. In fact, the woman who's been arrested is Deborah Patterson.'

Cordelia's voice registered her surprise. 'Deborah from Yorkshire? That peace camp really is a small world, isn't it? Whatever happened?'

'She's been set up, as far as I can make out.'

'Not very pleasant for her, I should imagine.'

'You've hit the nail on the head. She's currently locked up in a police cell, so I thought I'd keep an eye on little Cara till Debs is released tomorrow.'

'No problem,' Cordelia replied. 'I can get some more work done tonight if you're not coming back. It's been going really well tonight, and I'm reluctant to stop till my eyes actually close.'

Lindsay gave a wry smile. 'I'm glad it's going well. I'll try to come home tomorrow afternoon before I go to work.'

'Okay. I'll try to get home in time.'

'Oh. Where are you off to? Only, I thought you were going to be home all week.'

'My mother rang this evening. She's coming up tomorrow to do the shops and I promised I'd join her. But I'll try to be back for four.'

'Look, don't rush your mother on my account. I'll see you tomorrow in bed. I should be home by one. Love you, babe.'

A chill wind met her as she stepped out of the phone box and walked quickly back to the car. She pictured her lover sitting at her word processor, honing and refining her prose, relieved at the lack of distraction. Then she thought of Deborah, fretting in some uncomfortable, smelly cell. It wasn't an outcome Lindsay had anticipated all those years before when, a trainee journalist on a local paper in Cornwall, she had encountered Deborah at a party. For Lindsay, it had been lust at first sight, and as the evening progressed and drink had been taken, she had contrived to make such a nuisance of herself that Deborah finally relented for the sake of peace and agreed to meet Lindsay the following evening for a drink.

That night had been the first of many. Their often stormy relationship had lasted for nearly six months before Lindsay was transferred to another paper in the group. Neither of them could sustain the financial or emotional strain of separation, and soon mutual infidelities transformed their relationship to platonic friendship. Not long after, Lindsay left the West Country for Fleet Street, and Deborah announced her intention of having a child. Deborah bought a ruined farmhouse in North Yorkshire that she was virtually rebuilding single-handed. Even after Lindsay moved back to Scotland, she still made regular visits to Deborah and was surprised to find how much she enjoyed spending time with Deborah's small daughter. She felt comfortable there, even when they were joined for the occasional evening by Cara's father Robin, a gay man who lived near by. But Lindsay and Deborah never felt the time was right to revive their sexual relationship.

After she had fallen for Cordelia, Lindsay's visits had tailed off, though she had once taken Cordelia to stay the night. It had not been a success. Deborah had been rebuilding the roof at the time, there was no electricity and the water had to be pumped by hand from the well in the yard.

Cordelia had not been impressed with either the accommodation or the insouciance of its owner. But Lindsay had sensed a new maturity in Deborah that she found appealing.

Deborah had clearly sensed Cordelia's discomfort, but she had not commented on it. She had a willingness to accept people for what they were, and conduct her relationships with them on that basis. She never imposed her own expectations on them, and regarded her reactions to people and events as entirely her responsibility. It would be nice, thought Lindsay, not to feel that she was failing to come up to scratch. Time spent with Deborah always made her feel good about herself.

Back at the van, she brought in a bottle of Scotch from the car and poured a nightcap for herself and Jane.

'Are you all right, Lindsay?' Jane asked.

Lindsay's reply was drowned out by a roar outside louder, even, than the stormy weather. It was a violent sound, rising and falling angrily. Lindsay leapt to her feet and pulled back the curtain over the van's windscreen. Fear rose in her throat. The black night was scythed open by a dozen brilliant headlamps whose beams raked the benders like prison-camp searchlights. The motor bikes revved and roared in convoluted patterns round the encampment, sometimes demolishing benders as they went. As Lindsay's eyes adjusted to the night, she could make out pillion riders on several of the bikes, some wielding stout sticks, others swinging heavy chains at everything in their path. It was clearly not the first time the women had been raided in this way, for everyone had the sense to stay down inside the scant shelter the benders provided.

Lindsay and Jane stood speechless, petrified by the spectacle. The van's glow seemed to exert a magnetic effect on three of the bikers and their cyclops lamps swung round and lit it up like a follow-spot on a stage.

'Oh shit,' breathed Lindsay as the bikes careered towards the van. She leaned forward desperately and groped round the unfamiliar dashboard. What felt like agonising minutes later she found the right switch and flicked the lights on to full beam. The bikes wavered in their course and two of them peeled off to either side. The third skidded helplessly in the mud and slithered into a sideways slew on the greasy ground. The rider struggled to his feet, mouthing obscenities, and dragged himself round to his top-box. Out of it he pulled a large plastic bag which he hurled at the van. The women instinctively dived for the floor as it slammed into the windscreen with a squelching thud. Lindsay raised her head and nearly threw up. The world had turned red.

All over the windscreen was a skin of congealing blood with lumps of unidentifiable material slowly slithering down on to the bonnet. Jane's head appeared beside her. 'Oh God, not the pigs' blood routine again,' she moaned. 'I thought they'd got bored with that one.'

As she spoke, the bikes revved up again, then their roar gradually diminished into an irritated buzz as they left the camp and reached the road.

'We must call the police!' Lindsay exclaimed.

'It's a waste of time calling the police, Lindsay. They just don't want to know. The first time they threw blood over our benders, we managed to get the police to come out. But they said we'd done it ourselves, that we were sensation seekers. They said there was no evidence of our allegations. Tyre tracks in the mud don't count, you see. Nor do the statements of forty women. It doesn't really matter what crimes are perpetrated against us, because we're sub-human, you see.'

'That's monstrous,' Lindsay protested.

'But inevitable,' Jane retorted. 'What's going on here is so radical that they can't afford to treat it seriously on any level. Start accepting that we've got any rights and you end up by giving validity to the nightmares that have brought us here. Do that and you're half-way to accepting that our views on disarmament are a logical position. Much easier to treat us with total contempt.'

'That's intolerable,' said Lindsay.

'I'd better go and check that no one's hurt,' Jane said. 'One of the women got quite badly burned the first time they fire-bombed the tents.'

'Give me a second to check that Cara's okay

and I'll come with you,' Lindsay said, getting up and climbing the ladder that led to Cara's bunk. Surprisingly, the child was still fast asleep.

'I guess she's used to it by now,' Jane said, leading the way outside.

It was a sorry scene that greeted them. The headlights of several of the women's vehicles illuminated half a dozen benders now reduced to tangled heaps of wreckage, out of which women were still crawling. Jane headed for the first aid bender while Lindsay ploughed through the rain and wind to offer what help she could to two women struggling to salvage the plastic sheeting that had formed their shelter. Together all three battled against the weather and roughly re-erected the bender. But the women's sleeping bags were soaked and they trudged off to try and find some dry blankets to get them through the night.

Lindsay looked around. Slowly the camp was regaining its normal appearance. Where work was still going on, there seemed to be plenty of helpers. She made her way to Jane's bender, fortunately undamaged, and found the doctor bandaging the arm of a woman injured by a whiplashing branch in the attack on her bender.

'Hi, Lindsay,' Jane had said without pausing in her work. 'Not too much damage, thank God. A few bruises and cuts, but nothing major.'

'Anything I can do?'

Jane shook her head. 'Thanks, but everything's under control.'

Feeling slightly guilty, but not wanting to leave Cara alone for too long, Lindsay returned to the van. She made up the double berth where Jane had shown her Deborah normally slept.

But sleep eluded Lindsay. When she finally dropped off, it was to fall prey to confusing and painful dreams.

Cara woke early, and was fretful while Lindsay struggled with the unfamiliar intricacies of the van to provide them both with showers and breakfast. Luckily, the night's rain had washed away all traces of the pigs' blood. Of course, the keys of the van were with Deborah's possessions at the police station, so they had to drive into town in Lindsay's car.

Fordham Magistrates Court occupied a large and elegant Georgian town house in a quiet cul-de-sac off the main street. Inside, the building was considerably less distinguished. The beautifully proportioned entrance hall had been partitioned to provide a waiting room and offices and comfortless plastic chairs abounded where Chippendale furniture might once have stood. The paintwork was grubby and chipped and there was a pervasive odour of stale bodies and cigarette smoke. Lindsay felt Cara's grip tighten as they encountered the usual odd mixture of people found in magistrates' courts. Uniformed policemen bustled from room to room, up and down stairs. A couple of court ushers in robes like

Hammer Horror vampires stood gossiping by the WRVS tea stand from which a middle-aged woman dispensed grey coffee and orange tea. The other extras in this scene were the defeated-looking victims of the legal process, several of them in whispering huddles with their spry and well-dressed solicitors.

For once, Lindsay felt out of her element in a court. She put it down to the unfamiliar presence of a four year old on the end of her arm, and approached the ushers. They directed her to the café upstairs where she had arranged to meet Judith. The solicitor was already sitting at a table, dressed for business in a black pinstripe suit and an oyster grey shirt. She fetched coffee for Lindsay and orange juice for Cara, then said, 'I'd quite like it if you were in court throughout, Lindsay. How do you think Cara will cope if we ask a friendly policeman to keep an eye on her? Or has she already acquired the peace women's distrust of them?'

Lindsay shrugged. 'Best to ask Cara.' She turned to her and said, 'We're supposed to go into court now, but I don't think you're allowed in. How would it be if we were to ask a policeman to sit and talk to you while we're away?'

'Are you going to get my mummy?' asked Cara.

'In a little while.'

'Okay, then. But you won't be long, will you, Lindsay?'

'No, promise.'

They walked downstairs to the corridor outside the courtroom and Judith went in search of help. She returned quickly with a young policewoman who introduced herself to Cara.

'My name's Barbara,' she said. 'I'm going to sit with you till Mummy gets back. Is that all right?'

'I suppose so,' said Cara grudgingly. 'Do you know any good stories?'

As Lindsay and Judith entered the courtroom, they heard Cara ask one of her best questions. 'My mummy says the police are there to help us. So why did the police take my mummy away?'

The courtroom itself was scarcely altered from the house's heyday. The parquet floor was highly polished, the paintwork gleaming white. Behind a table on a raised dais at one end of the room sat the three magistrates. The chairwoman, aged about forty-five, had hair so heavily lacquered that it might have been moulded in fibreglass and her mouth, too, was set in a hard line. She was flanked by two men. One was in his late fifties, with the healthy, weatherbeaten look of a keen sailor. The other, in his middle thirties, with dark brown hair neatly cut and styled, could have been a young business executive in his spotless shirt and dark suit. His face was slightly puffy round the eyes and jowls and he wore an air of dissatisfaction with the world.

The court wound up its summary hearing of a drunk and disorderly with a swift £40 fine and moved on to Deborah's case.

Lindsay sat down on a hard wooden chair at the back of the room as Deborah was led in looking tired and dishevelled. Her jeans and shirt looked slept in, and her hair needed washing. Lindsay reflected, not for the first time, how the law's delays inevitably made the person in police custody look like a tramp.

Deborah's eyes flicked round the courtroom as a uniformed inspector read out the charges. When she saw Lindsay she flashed a smile of relief before turning back to the magistrates and answering the court clerk's enquiry about her plea to the breach of the peace charge. 'Guilty,' she said in a clear, sarcastic voice. To the next charge, she replied equally clearly, 'Not guilty.'

It was all over in ten minutes. Deborah was fined £50 plus £15 costs on the breach charge, and remanded on bail to the Crown Court for jury trial on the assault charge. The bail had been set at £2500, with the conditions that Deborah reported daily to the police station at Fordham, did not go within 200 yards of the Crabtree home, and made no approach to Mr Crabtree. Then, the formalities took over. Lindsay wrote a cheque she fervently hoped would never have to be cashed which Judith took to the payments office. Lindsay returned to Cara, who greeted her predictably with, 'Where's my mummy? You said you'd get her for me.'

Lindsay picked up the child and hugged her. 'She's just coming, I promise.' Before she could put Cara down, the child called, 'Mummy!' and struggled out of Lindsay's arms. Cara hurtled down the corridor and into the arms of Deborah who was walking towards them with Judith. Eventually, Deborah disentangled herself from Cara and came over to Lindsay. Wordlessly, they hugged each other.

Lindsay felt the old electricity surge through her, and pulled back from the embrace. She held Deborah at arms' length. 'Hi,' she said.

Deborah smiled. 'I didn't plan a reunion like this,' she said ruefully.

'We'll do the champagne and roses some other time,' Lindsay replied.

'Champagne and roses? My God, you've come up in the world. It used to be a half of bitter and a packet of hedgehog-flavoured crisps!'

They laughed as Judith, who had been keeping a discreet distance, approached and said, 'Thanks for all your help, Lindsay. Now you'll just have to pray Deborah doesn't jump bail!'

'No chance,' said Deborah. 'I wouldn't dare. Lindsay's motto used to be 'don't mess with the messer', and I don't expect that's changed.

Lindsay smiled. 'I've got even tougher,' she said. 'Come on, I'll drop you off at the camp on my way back to London.'

They said goodbye to Judith and headed for the car park. Deborah said nonchalantly to Lindsay. 'You can't stay, then?'

Lindsay shook her head. 'Sorry. There's nothing

I'd rather do, but I've got to get back to London. I'm on the night shift tonight.'

'You'll come back soon, though, won't you, Lin?'

Lindsay nodded. 'Of course. Anyway, I'm not going just yet. I expect I can fit in a quick cup of coffee back at the van.'

They pushed through the doors of the courthouse and nearly crashed into two men standing immediately outside. The taller of the two had curly greying hair but his obvious good looks were ruined by a swollen and bruised nose and dark smudges beneath his eyes. He looked astonished to see Deborah, then said viciously, 'So you're breaking your bail conditions already, Miss Patterson. I could have you arrested for this, you know. And you wouldn't get bail a second time.'

Furious, Lindsay pushed forward as Deborah picked up her daughter protectively. 'Who the hell do you think you are?' she demanded angrily.

'Ask your friend,' he sneered. 'I'm not a vindictive man,' he added. 'I won't report you to the police this time. When the Crown Court sentences you to prison, that will be enough to satisfy me.'

He shouldered his way between them, followed by the other man, who had the grace to look embarrassed.

Deborah stared after him. 'In case you hadn't guessed,' she said, 'that was Rupert Crabtree.'

Lindsay nodded. 'I figured as much.'

'One of these days,' Deborah growled, 'someone is going to put a stop to that bastard.'

3

The alarm clock went off at a quarter to six. Lindsay rolled on to her side, grunting 'Drop dead, you bastard,' at the voice-activated alarm Cordelia had bought her to replace the Mickey Mouse job she'd had since university. She curled into a ball and considered going back to sleep. The early Saturday morning start to her weekend at the peace camp that had seemed such a good idea the night before now felt very unappealing.

But as she hovered on the verge of dozing off, she was twitched into sudden wakefulness as Cordelia's finger ends lightly traced a wavy line up her side. Cordelia snuggled into her and kissed the nape of her neck gently. Lindsay murmured her pleasure, and the kisses quickly turned into nibbles. Lindsay felt her flesh go to goose pimples; thoroughly aroused she twisted round and kissed her lover fiercely. Cordelia pulled away and said innocently, 'I thought you had trouble waking up in the morning?'

'If they could find an alarm clock that did what you do to me, there would be no problem,' Lindsay growled softly as she started to stroke Cordelia's nipples. Her right hand moved tentatively between Cordelia's legs.

Cordelia clamped her thighs together, pinning Lindsay's hand in place. 'I've started so I'll finish,' she murmured, moving her own fingers unerringly to the warm, wet centre of Lindsay's pleasure.

The feeling of relaxation that flooded through Lindsay afterwards was shattered by the alarm clock again. 'Oh God,' she groaned. 'Is that the time?'

'What's your hurry?' Cordelia asked softly.

'I promised I'd be at Brownlow really early. There's a big action planned for today,' Lindsay replied sleepily.

'Oh, for Christ's sake, is that all you think about these days,' Cordelia complained, pulling away from Lindsay. 'I'm going for a bloody shower.' She bounced out of bed before Lindsay could stop her.

'I wasn't finished with you,' Lindsay called after her plaintively.

'I'll wait till your mind's on what you're doing, if it's all the same to you,' came the reply.

It was just after seven when Lindsay parked alongside the scruffy plastic benders. She had tried to make her peace with Cordelia, but it had been fruitless. Now Cordelia was on her way to spend the weekend with her parents, and Lindsay was keeping the promise she'd made to Deborah three weeks before. She parked her MG between a small but powerful Japanese motor bike and a 2CV plastered with anti-nuclear stickers. If they ever stopped making 2CVs, she mused, the anti-nuclear sticker makers would go out of business. She cut her engine and sat in silence for a moment.

It was a cool and misty March morning, and Lindsay marvelled at the quiet stillness that surrounded the encampment. The only sign of life was a thin trickle of smoke coming from the far side of the rough circle of branches and plastic. She got out of the car and strolled over to Deborah's van. The curtains were drawn, but when Lindsay tried the door, she found it unlocked. In the gloom, she made out Deborah's sleeping figure. Lindsay moved inside gingerly and crouched beside her. She kissed her ear gently and nearly fell over as Deborah instantly woke, eyes wide, starting up from the bed. 'Jesus, you gave me a shock,' she exploded softly.

'A pleasant one, I hope.'

'I can't think of a nicer one,' said Deborah, sitting up. She pulled Lindsay close and hugged her. 'Put the kettle on, there's a love,' she said, climbing out of bed. She disappeared into the shower and toilet cubicle in the corner of the van, leaving Lindsay to deal with the gas rings.

Lindsay thought gratefully how easy it was to

be with Deborah. There was never any fuss, never any pressure. It was always the same since they had first been together. They slipped so easily into a comfortable routine, as if the time between their meetings had been a matter of hours rather than months or weeks. Lindsay always felt at home with Deborah, whether it was in a Fordham courtroom or a camper van.

Deborah reappeared, washed and dressed, towelling her wavy brown shoulder-length hair vigorously. She threw the towel aside and settled down with a mug of coffee. She glanced at Lindsay, her blue eyes sparkling wickedly.

'You picked the right weekend to be here,' she remarked.

Lindsay leaned back in her seat. 'Why so?' she asked, 'Jane told me it was just a routine blockade of the main gate.'

'We're going in. Through the wire. We think it should be possible to get to the bunkers if we go in between gates three and four. The security's not that wonderful over there. I suppose any five-mile perimeter has to have its weak spots. The only exposed bit is the ten yards between the edge of the wood and the fence. So there will be a diversion at the main gate to keep them occupied while the others get through the wire. And it just so happens that there's a Channel 4 film crew coming down anyway today to do a documentary.' Deborah grinned broadly and winked complicity at Lindsay.

'Good planning, Debs. But aren't you taking a hell of a risk with the assault case already hanging over you? Surely they'll bang you up right away if they pick you up inside the fence?'

'That's exactly why we've decided that I'm not going in. I'm a very small part of the diversion. Which is why it's good that you're here. Left to my own devices, I'd probably find myself carried along with the flow. Before I knew it, I'd be back in clink again.' Deborah smiled ruefully. 'So, since I presume you're also in the business of keeping a low profile, we'll have to be each other's minder. Okay?'

Lindsay lit a cigarette and inhaled deeply before she replied. 'Okay. I'd love to go along with the raiding party to do an "I" piece, but given my bosses' views on peace women, I guess that's right out of the question.'

'You can help me sing,' said Deborah. She leaned across the table to Lindsay, grasped her hand tightly and kissed her. 'My, but it's good to be with you, sister,' she said softly.

Before Lindsay could reply, Cara's dark blonde head and flushed cheeks suddenly appeared through the curtains. As soon as she realised who was there, she scrambled down the ladder to hurl herself on Lindsay, hugging her fiercely before turning to Deborah. 'You didn't tell me Lindsay was coming,' she reproached her.

'I didn't tell you because I wasn't sure myself and I didn't want both of us to be disappointed if she couldn't make it. Okay?'

The child nodded. 'What are we having for breakfast? Have you brought bacon and eggs like you promised last time?'

'I managed to smuggle them past the vegetarian checkpoint on the way in,' Lindsay joked. 'I know you're like me, Cara, you love the things that everybody tells you are bad for you.'

'You really are a reprobate, aren't you,' Deborah said, amused. 'I know you like taking the piss out of all the vegetarian nonsmokers, but don't forget that a lot of us are veggies from necessity as much as choice. I love the occasional fry-up, but beans are a hell of a lot cheaper than bacon. Not everyone has the same sense of humour about it as I do.'

'Don't tell me,' Lindsay groaned. 'Cordelia never stops telling me how people like me who love red meat are causing the distortion of world agriculture. Sometimes I feel personally responsible for every starving kid in the world.'

Impatient with the conversation, Cara interrupted. 'Can we have breakfast, then?'

By the time they had eaten the bacon, eggs, sausages and mushrooms that Lindsay had brought, the camp had come to life again. Women were ferrying water from the standpipe by the road in big plastic jerry cans while others cooked, repaired benders or simply sat and talked. It was a cold, dry day with the sun struggling fitfully through a haze. Lindsay went off to see Jane and found her sitting on a crate, writing in a large exercise book. She looked tired and drawn.

'Hi, Doc. Everything fine with you?'

Jane shrugged. 'So so. I think I'm getting too close to all this now. I'm getting so wrapped up in the logistics of the camp I'm forgetting why I'm here. I think I'm going to have to get away for a few days to put it back into perspective.'

'There's always a bed at our place if you need a break.' Jane nodded as Lindsay went on, 'Debs says you can fill me in with the details of today's invasion plan.'

Jane outlined the intended arrangements. Nicky was leading a raiding party of a dozen women armed with bolt-cutters. They would be waiting in the woods for a signal from the look-out post that the diversion at the main gate was attracting enough attention from camp security to allow them to reach the fence and cut through the wire. What followed their entry into the base would be a matter for their own judgment but it was hoped that they'd make it to the missile silos. The diversion was timed for noon, the main attraction for fifteen minutes later.

'You should keep out of the front line,' she concluded. 'Help Deborah with the singing. Keep an eye on her too. We don't want her to get arrested again. It would be just like her to get carried away and do something out of order. I imagine that a few of the local coppers know perfectly well who she is and wouldn't mind the chance to pick her up and give her a hard time. Crabtree is pretty buddy-buddy with the local police hierarchy according to Judith. Understandably enough, I suppose. So do us all a favour unless you desperately want to take on Cara full-time – keep the lid on Deborah.'

By late morning there was an air of suppressed excitement around the camp. The television crew had arrived and were shooting some interviews and stock background shots around the benders. It wasn't hard for Lindsay to suppress her journalistic instincts and avoid them. She was, after all, off duty, and since the *Clarion* had no Sunday edition, she felt no guilt about ignoring the story. She noticed Jane and a couple of other long-standing peace campers having a discreet word with the crew, which had included a couple of unmistakable gestures towards the long bunkers that dominated the skyline.

At about midday, Deborah came looking for her. Leaving Cara and three other children in the van with Josy, one of the other mothers living at the camp, they joined the steady surge of women making for the main gate. About forty women were gathered round. A group of half a dozen marched boldly up to the sentry boxes on either side of the gate and started to unwind the balls of wool they carried with them. They wove the wool around the impassive soldiers and their sentry boxes, swiftly creating a complex web. Other women moved to the gates themselves and began to weave wool strands in and out of the heavy steel mesh to seal them shut. Deborah climbed on top of a large concrete litter bin just outside the gates and hauled Lindsay up beside her. Together they started to sing one of the songs that had grown up with the camp and soon all the women had joined in.

Inside the camp the RAF police and behind them the USAF guards came running towards the gate. On the women's side, civil police started to appear at the trot to augment the pair permanently on duty at the main gate. The film crew were busy recording it all.

It looked utterly chaotic. Then one of the women let out an excited whoop and pointed to the silos. There, silhouetted against the grey March sky, women could be seen dancing and waving. Alerted by her cries, the film crew ran off round the perimeter fence, filming all the while. Inside the wire, the military turned and raced across the scrubby grass to the bunkers constructed to house the coming missiles.

Outside the base the women calmly dispersed, to the frustration of the police who were just getting into the swing of making arrests. Lindsay, feeling as high as if she'd just smoked a couple of joints, jumped down from the litter bin and swung Deborah down into her arms. Like the other women around them they hugged each other and jumped around on the spot, then they bounced away from the fence and back towards the main road. A tall man stood at the end of the camp road. On the end of a lead was a fox-terrier. A sneer of scorn spoiled his newly healed features.

'Enjoy yourself while you can. Miss Patterson. It won't be long before I have you put some place where there won't be much to rejoice over.' His threat uttered, Crabtree marched on down the main road away from the camp. Lindsay looked in dismay at Deborah's stunned face.

'Sadistic bastard. He can't resist having a go every time he sees me,' said Deborah. 'He seems to go out of his way to engineer these little encounters. But I'm not going to let him get the better of me. Not on a day like today.'

4

The women had gathered in the big bender that they used for meeting and talking as a group. Lindsay still couldn't get used to the way they struggled to avoid hierarchies by refusing to run their meetings according to traditional structures. Instead, they sat in a big circle and each spoke in turn, supposedly without interruption. The euphoria of the day's action was tangible. The film crew were still around, and not even the news that the dozen women who had made it to the silos had been charged with criminal damage and trespass could diminish the high that had infected everyone.

But there was a change in attitude since Lindsay had first encountered the peace women. It was noticeable that far more women were advocating stronger and more direct action against what they perceived as the forces of evil. She could see that Jane and several other women who'd been with the camp for a long time were having a struggle to impress upon others like the headstrong Nicky the need to keep all action non-violent and to minimise the criminal element in what they did. Eventually, the meeting was adjourned without a decision till the following afternoon.

The rest of the day passed quickly for Lindsay who spent her time walking the perimeter fence and picking up on her new friendships with women like Jackie. Lindsay appreciated the different perspectives the women gave her on life in Thatcher's Britain. It was a valuable contrast with the cynical world of newspapers and the comfortably well-off life she shared with Cordelia. Jackie and her lover Willow, both from Birmingham, explained to Lindsay for the first time how good they felt at the camp because there was none of the constant pressure of racial prejudice that had made it so difficult for them to make anything of their lives at home. By the time Lindsay had eaten dinner with Cara and Deborah, she knew she had made a firm decision to stay. By unspoken consent, Deborah took Cara off to spend the rest of the night with her best friend Christy in the bender she shared with her mother Josy. When she returned, she found Lindsay curled up in a corner with a tumbler of whisky.

'Help yourself,' said Lindsay.

Deborah sensed the tension in Lindsay. Carefully she poured herself a small drink from the bottle on the table and sat down beside her.

She placed a cautious hand on her thigh. 'I'm really glad to be with you again,' she said quietly. 'It's been a long time since we had the chance to talk.'

Lindsay took a gulp of whisky and lit a cigarette. 'I can't sleep with you,' she burst out. 'I thought I could, but I can't. I'm sorry.'

Deborah hadn't forgotten the knowledge of Lindsay that six hectic months had given her. She smiled. 'You haven't changed, have you? What makes you think I wanted to jump into bed with you again?' Her voice was teasing. 'That old arrogance hasn't deserted you.'

Outrage chased incredulity across Lindsay's face. Then her sense of humour caught up with her and she smiled. 'Touché. You never did let me get away with anything, did you?'

'Too bloody true I didn't. Give you an inch and you were always half-way to the next town. Listen, I didn't expect a night of mad, passionate lovemaking. I know your relationship with Cordelia is the big thing in your life. Just as Cara is the most important thing in my life now. I don't take risks with that, and I don't expect you to take risks with your life either.'

Lindsay looked sheepish. 'I really wanted to make love with you. I thought it would help me sort out my feelings. But when you took Cara off, I suddenly felt that I was contemplating something dishonest. You know? Something that devalued what there is between you and me.'

Deborah put her arm round Lindsay's tense shoulders. 'You mean, you'd have been using me to prove something to yourself about you and Cordelia?'

'Something like that. I guess I just feel confused about what's happening between me and her. It started off so well – she made me feel so special. I was happy as a pig. Okay, it was frustrating that I was living in Glasgow and she was in London. But there wasn't a week when we didn't spend at least two nights together, often more, once I'd got a job sorted out.

'We seemed to have so much in common – we liked going to the same films, loved the theatre, liked the same books, all that stuff. She even started coming hill-walking with me, though I drew the line at going jogging with her. But it was all those things that kind of underpinned the fact that I was crazy about her and the sex was just amazing.

'Then I moved to London and it seemed like everything changed. I realised how much of her life I just hadn't been a part of. All the time she spent alone in London was filled with people I've got the square root of sod all in common with. They patronise the hell out of me because they think that being a tabloid hack is the lowest form of pond life.

'They treat me like I'm some brainless bimbo that Cordelia has picked up. And Cordelia just tells me to ignore it, they don't count. Yet she still spends great chunks of her time with them. She doesn't enjoy being with the people I work with, so she just opts out of anything I've got arranged with other hacks. And the few friends I've got outside the business go back to Oxford days; they go down well with Cordelia and her crowd, but I want more of my life than that. And it never seems the right time to talk about it.

'About once a fortnight at the moment I seriously feel like packing my bags and moving out. Then I remember all the good things about her and stay.

Lindsay stopped abruptly and leaned over to refill her glass. She took another long drink and shivered as the spirit hit her. Deborah slowly massaged the knotted muscles at the back of her neck. 'Poor Lin,' she said. 'You do feel hard done by, don't you? You never did understand how compromise can be a show of strength, did you?'

Lindsay frowned. 'It's not that. It just seems like me that's made all the compromises – or sacrifices, more like.'

'But she has too. Suddenly, after years of living alone, doing the one job where you really need your own space, she's got this iconoclast driving a coach and horses through her routines, coming in at all hours of the day and night, thanks to her wonderful shift patterns, and hating the people she has to be nice to in order to keep a nice high profile in the literary world. It can't be exactly easy for her either. It seems to me that she's got the right idea – she's doing what she needs to keep herself together.'

Lindsay looked hurt. 'I never thought I'd hear you taking Cordelia's side.'

'I'm not taking sides. And that reaction says it all, Lin,' Deborah said, a note of sharpness creeping into her voice. 'I'm trying to make you see things from her side. Listen, I saw you when the two of you had only been together six months, and I saw you looking happier than I'd ever seen you. I love you like a sister, Lin, and I want to see you with that glow back. You're not going to get it by whingeing about Cordelia. Talk to her about it. At least you're still communicating in bed – build on that, for starters. Stop expecting her to be psychic. If she loves you, she won't throw you out just because you tell her you're not getting what you need from her.'

Lindsay sighed. 'Easier said than done.'

'I know that. But you've got to try. It's obviously not too late. If you were diving into bed with me to prove you still have enough autonomy to do it, I'd say you were in deep shit. But at least you're not that far down the road. Now, come on, drink up and let's get to bed. You can have Cara's bunk if you can't cope with sharing a bed with me and keeping your hands to yourself.'

'Now who's being arrogant?'

Lindsay stood by the kettle waiting for it to boil, gazing at Deborah who lay languidly in a shaft of morning sunlight staring into the middle distance. After a night's sleep, the clarity she had felt after the conversation with Deborah had grown fuzzy round the edges. But she knew deep down she wanted to put things right between her and Cordelia, and Deborah had helped her feel that was a possibility.

She made the coffee, and brought it over to Deborah. Lindsay sat on the top of the bed and put her arms round her friend. Lindsay felt at peace for the first time in months. 'If things go wrong when it comes to court, I'd like to take care of Cara, if you'll let me,' she murmured.

Deborah drew back, still holding Lindsay's shoulders. 'But how could you manage that? With work and Cordelia and everything?'

'We've got a crèche for newspaper workers' kids from nine till six every day. I can swap most of my shifts round to be on days and I'm damn sure Cordelia will help if I need her to.'

Deborah shook her head disbelievingly. 'Lindsay, you're incredible. Sometimes I think you just don't listen to the words that come out of your mouth. Last night, you were busily angsting about how to get your relationship with Cordelia back on an even keel. Now today you're calmly talking about dumping your ex-lover's child on her. What a recipe for disaster that would be! Look, it's lovely of you to offer, and I know she'd be happy with you, but I hope that won't be necessary. We'll look at the possibilities nearer the time and I'll keep it in mind. What counts is what's going to be best for her. Now, let's go and get Cara, eh? She'll be wondering where I am.' They found Cara with Jane, and after a bread and cheese lunch the four of them went for a walk along the perimeter fence. Lindsay and Cara played tig and hide-and-seek among the trees while Jane and Deborah walked slowly behind, wrangling about the business of peace and the problems of living at Brownlow.

They made their way back to the camp, where the adults settled down in the meeting bender for a long session. Three hours later, it had been agreed that the women charged the day before should, if they were willing, opt for prison for the sake of publicity and that a picket should be set up at the gate of Holloway in their support. Jane offered to organise the picket. Lindsay thought gratefully that at least that way her friend could make a small escape without offending her conscience. It had been a stormy meeting and Lindsay was glad when it was over. Even though she had by now experienced many of these talking-shops, she never failed to become slightly disillusioned at the destructive way women could fight against each other in spite of their common cause.

Deborah went off to collect Cara and put her to bed and Lindsay joined Willow and Jackie and their friends in their bender. There were a couple of guitars and soon the women were singing an assortment of peace songs, love songs and nostalgic pop hits. Deborah joined them and they sat close. Lindsay felt she couldn't bear to wrench herself away from the sisterhood she felt round her. Sentimental fool, she thought to herself as she joined in the chorus of 'I Only Want To Be With You.'

Just after ten the jam session began to break up. Most of the women left for their own benders. Lindsay and Deborah followed. 'I'm going to have a word with Jane about the Holloway picket,' said Lindsay. 'You coming?'

'No, I'll see you at the van.'

'Okay, I'll not be long.'

Deborah vanished into the darkness beyond the ring of benders to where the van was parked near the road. Lindsay headed for Jane's makeshift surgery and found the harassed doctor sorting through a cardboard box of pharmaceutical samples that a sympathetic GP had dropped off that evening. She stopped at once, pleased to see Lindsay in spite of her tiredness, and began to explain the picket plans. Although Lindsay was itching to get back to Deborah, it was after eleven when she finally set off to walk the fifty yards to the van.

The first thing that caught her eye as she moved beyond the polythene tents was bright lights. Now that the army had cleared the ground round the perimeter fence, it was possible to see the temporary arc lights from quite a distance. That in itself wasn't extraordinary as workmen occasionally sneaked in a night shift to avoid the picketing women.

She stopped dead as she caught sight of three figures approaching the camp, silhouetted against the dim glow from the barracks inside the fence. Two were uniformed policemen, no prizes for spotting that. The third was a tall, blond man she had noticed in the area a couple of times before. Her journalistic instinct had put him down as Special Branch. She was gratified to find that instinct vindicated. She glanced around, but the only other women in sight were far off by a campfire. Most of them had already gone to bed.

Lindsay had no idea what was going on, but she wanted to find out. The best way to do that was to stay out of sight, watch and listen. She crouched down against the bender nearest her and slowly worked her way round the encampment, trying to outflank the trio who were between her and the lights. When she reached the outer ring of tents, she squatted close to the ground while the three men passed her and headed for Jane's bender with its distinctive red cross. Lindsay straightened up and headed for the lights, keeping close to the fringes of woodland that surrounded the base. As she neared the lights, she was able to pick out details. There were a couple of police Landrovers pulled up on the edge of the wood. Near by, illuminated by their headlamps and the arc lights, were a cluster of green canvas screens. Beyond the Landrovers were three unremarkable saloon cars. A handful of uniformed officers stood around. Several people in civilian clothes moved about the scene, vanishing behind the screens from time to time.

Lindsay moved out of the shelter of the trees and approached the activity. She had only gone a few yards when two uniformed constables moved to cut off her progress. Her hand automatically moved to her hip pocket and she pulled out the laminated yellow Press Card which in theory granted her their co-operation. She flashed it at the young policemen and made to put it away.

'Just a minute, miss,' said one of them. 'Let's have a closer look if you don't mind.'

Reluctantly, she handed the card over. He scrutinised it carefully; then he showed it to his colleague who looked her up and down, noting her expensive Barbour jacket, corduroy trousers and muddy walking boots. He nodded and said, 'Looks okay to me.'

'I'm here writing a feature about the camp,' she said. 'When I saw the lights, I thought something might be doing. What's the score?'

The first constable smiled. 'Sorry to be so suspicious. We get all sorts here, you know. You want to know what's happening, you best see the superintendent. He's over by the Landrover nearest to us. I'll take you across in a minute, when he's finished talking to the bloke who found the body.'

'Body?' Lindsay demanded anxiously. 'What is it? Accident, murder? And who's dead?

'That's for the super to say,' the policeman replied. 'But it doesn't look much like an accident at this stage.'

Lindsay looked around her, taking it all in. The scene of the murder was like a three-ring circus. The outer ring took the form of the five vehicles and a thinly scattered cordon of uniformed police constables. Over by one of the Landrovers, a policewoman dispensed tea from a vacuum flask to a nervous-looking man talking to the uniformed superintendent whom Lindsay recognised from the demonstration outside the police station. She crossed her fingers and hoped the victim was no one from the camp.

The temporary arc lights the police had rigged up gave the scene the air of a film set, an impression exaggerated by the situation, part of a clear strip about fifteen yards wide between a high-chain link fence and a belt of scrubby woodland. It was far enough from any gates to be free of peace campers. The lamps shone down on the second ring, a shield of tall canvas screens hastily erected to protect the body from view. Round the screen, scene-of-crime officers buzzed in and out, communicating in their own form of macabre shorthand.

But the main attraction of the circus tonight was contained in the inner circle. Here there were more lights, smaller spotlights clipped on to the screens. A photographer moved round the periphery, his flash freezing for ever the last public appearance of whoever was lying dead on the wet clay. Could it be one of the women from the camp lying there? Superintendent Rigano said a few words to the man, then moved back towards the scene of the crime. The constable escorted Lindsay across the clearing, being careful, she noted, to keep between her and the tall canvas screens. Once there, he secured the attention of the superintendent, whom Lindsay recognised from their earlier encounter outside Fordham police station. 'Sir, there's a journalist here wants a word with you,' the constable reported.

He turned to Lindsay, fine dark brows scowling over deep-set eyes. 'You're here bloody sharpish,' he said grudgingly. 'Superintendent Rigano, Fordham Police.'

'Lindsay Gordon. *Daily Clarion*. We met at the demonstration after Deborah Patterson's arrest. I happened to be at the camp,' she replied. 'We're doing a feature comparing the peace camps at Brownlow and Faslane,' she lied fluently. 'I saw the lights and wondered if there might be anything in it for me.'

'We've got a murder on our hands,' he said in a flinty voice. 'You'd better take a note. It would be a pity to screw up on a scoop.' Lindsay obediently pulled out her notebook and a pencil.

'The dead man is Rupert Crabtree.' The familiar name shocked Lindsay. Suddenly this wasn't some impersonal murder story she was reporting. It was much closer to home. Her surprise obviously registerd with Rigano, who paused momentarily before continuing. 'Aged forty-nine. Local solicitor. Lives up Brownlow Common Cottages. That's those mock-Georgian mansions half a mile from the main gate of the camp. Bludgeoned to death with a blunt instrument, to wit, a chunk of drainage pipe which shattered on impact. Perhaps more to the point, from your side of things, is the fact that he was chairman of the local ratepayers' association who were fighting against that scruffy lot down there. It looks as if there was a struggle before he was killed. Anything else you want to know?'

Lindsay hoped her relationship with 'that scruffy lot down there' was not too obvious and that she was putting up a sufficiently good performance in her professional role as the single-minded news reporter in possession of a hot exclusive. 'Yes. What makes you think there was a struggle?'

'The mud's churned up quite a bit. And Crabtree had drawn a gun but not had the chance to fire it.'

'That suggests he knew his life was at risk, doesn't it?'

'No comment. I also don't want the gun mentioned just yet. Any other questions?'

She nodded vigorously. 'Who found the body?'

'A local resident walking his dog. I'm not

releasing a name and he won't be available for interview in the foreseeable future.'

'Any suspects? Is an arrest likely within the next few hours? And what was he doing on the common at this time of night?'

Rigano looked down at her shrewdly. 'No arrest imminent. We are actively pursuing several lines of enquiry. He was walking the bloody dog. He usually did this time of night. Well-known fact of local life.'

'Any idea of the time of death?' she asked.

Rigano shrugged expressively. 'That's for the doctors to tell us. But without sticking my neck out, I can tell you it was probably some time between ten and eleven o'clock. I hope you've got an alibi,' he said, a smile pulling at the corners of his mouth. 'Come and have a quick look.' He strode off, clearly expecting her to follow. She caught up with him at the entrance to the screens.

'I'd rather not, if you don't mind,' she said quickly.

His eyebrows shot up. 'Happy to dish the dirt, not so happy to see the nastiness?'

Lindsay was stung by his sardonic tone. 'Okay,' she said grimly. He led her through the gap in the screens.

She would not have recognised Rupert Crabtree. He lay on his front, the wet March ground soaking the elegant camel hair coat and the pinstripe trousers. His wellingtons were splashed with vivid orange mud, as were his black leather gloves. The back of his head was shattered. Blood matted his hair and had spattered over the fragments of a two-foot-long piece of earthenware water pipe which had clearly broken under the force with which it had been brought down on the skull. A few feet away, a handgun lay in the mud. Lindsay felt sick. Rigano took her arm and steered her away. 'You'll be wanting to get to a phone,' he said, not unkindly. 'If you want to check up on our progress later on, ring Fordham nick and ask for the duty officer. He'll fill you in with any details.' He turned away, dismissing her.

Slowly, Lindsay turned her back on the depressing camouflage of death. And at once, her mind was torn away from murder. Across the clearing, the trio she had seen earlier were returning. But now there were four people in the group. She felt a physical pain in her chest as she recognised the fourth. As their eyes met Lindsay and Deborah shared a moment of pure fear.

5

For a moment, Lindsay stood stock still, the journalist fighting the friend inside her. This was an important story, she had the edge on the pack and she needed to call the office as soon as possible. Logically, she knew there was little she could do for Deborah as the police Landrover carried her off. That didn't stop her feeling an overwhelming rage that translated itself into the desire for action. Abruptly, she turned back to the scene of the crime and found Rigano. Forcing herself to sound casual she elicited the information that Deborah had not been arrested but was assisting police with their enquiries. End message. Lindsay turned and started to run back to the van.

Once out of the circle of light, she was plunged into darkness. Tripping over tree roots and treacherous brambles, she stumbled on, her only guide the distant glow of the campfire and the dim light from a few of the benders. At one point she plunged headlong over a rock and grimly picked herself up, covered in mud. Cursing, she ran on till she reached the camp. As she reached the benders, she realised that several knots of women had gathered and were talking together anxiously. Ignoring their questioning looks, she made straight for the van, where she burst in, gasping for breath, to find Jane sitting over a cup of coffee. She took one look at Lindsay and said, 'So you know already?'

'How's Cara? Where is she? Lindsay forced out.

'Fast asleep. The coppers were very quiet, very civil. But the van mustn't be moved till they've had a chance to search it.' She was interrupted by a knock on the door. Lindsay leaned over and opened it to find a policewoman standing on the threshold.

'Yes?' Lindsay demanded roughly.

'I've been instructed to make sure that nothing is removed from this van until our officers arrive with a search warrant,' she replied.

'Terrific,' said Lindsay bitterly. 'I take it you've no objection to me moving a sleeping child to where she won't be disturbed?'

The policewomen looked surprised. 'I don't see why you shouldn't move the child. Where is she?'

Lindsay pointed up to the curtained-off bunk. She turned to Jane and said, 'I'll take Cara to Josy's bender. She'll be all right there.'

Jane nodded and added, 'I'll stay here to make sure everything's done properly.'

Lindsay smiled. 'Thanks. I've got to get to the

phone.' Then, with all the firmness she could muster, she said to the police officer, 'I'm a journalist. I've got the details of the story from Superintendent Rigano, and I intend to phone my office now. I'll be back shortly. Till then, Dr Thomas is in charge here.'

She climbed the ladder and folded Cara into her arms. The child murmured in her sleep but did not wake. Lindsay carried her to Josy, then ran as fast as she could to the phone box. She glanced at her watch and was amazed to see it was still only half past midnight. Her first call was to Judith Rowe. When the solicitor surfaced from sleep, she promised to get straight round to the police station and do what she could.

Next, Lindsay took a deep breath and put in a transfer charge call to the office. The call was taken by Cliff Gilbert himself. 'Listen,' she said. There's been a murder at Brownlow Common. I've checked it out with the cops locally and the strength of it is that the leader of the local opposition to the women's peace camp has been found with his head stoved in. I've got enough to file now, which I'll do if you put me on to copy. I'll also get stuck in to background for tomorrow if you think that's a good idea.'

Cliff thought for a moment. Lindsay could almost hear the connections clicking into place to complete the mental circuit. 'You've got good contacts among the lesbian beanburger brigade down there, haven't you?'

'The best. The prime suspect seems to be an old pal of mine.'

'What shift are you on tomorrow?'

'Day off.'

'Fine. Take a look at it if you don't mind and check in first thing with Duncan. I'll leave him a note stressing that I've told you to get stuck in. And Lindsay – don't do anything daft, okay?'

'Thanks, Cliff. How much do you want now?'

'Let it run, Lindsay. All you've got.'

There followed a series of clicks and buzzes as she was connected to the copytaker. She recited the story off the top of her head, adding in as much as she knew about Crabtree and his connection with the camp. 'A brutal murder shocked a women's peace camp last night,' she began.

Then, at nearly two o'clock she made her final call. Cordelia's sleepy voice answered the phone. 'Who the hell is it?'

Lindsay swallowed the lump that had formed in her throat at the sound of the familiar voice. She struggled with herself and tried to sound light. 'It's me, love. Sorry I woke you. I know you'll be tired after driving back from your parents', but I'm afraid I've got a major hassle on my hands. There's been a murder down here. Rupert Crabtree the guy whose face Debs is supposed to have rearranged – he's been killed. The cops have pulled Debs. I don't think they're going to charge her. I know I said I'd be home tomorrow lunchtime, but I don't know when the hell I'll make it now.'

'Do you want me to come down?'

Lindsay thought for a moment. The complication seemed unnecessary. 'Not just now, I think,' she replied. 'There's nothing either of us can really do till I know more precisely what's happening. I simply wanted to tell you myself so you wouldn't panic when you heard the news or saw the papers. I'll ring you later today, all right?'

'All right,' Cordelia sighed. 'But look after yourself, please. Don't take any chances with a murderer on the loose. I love you, don't forget that.'

'I love you too,' Lindsay replied. She put the phone down and walked back to the camp. She opened the door to the van, forgetting momentarily about the police. The bulky presence of two uniformed men searching the van startled her.

'What the hell are you doing?' she demanded angrily.

'We'll be as quick as we can,' said the older of the two, a freckle-faced, grey-haired man with broad shoulders and a paunch. 'We have a warrant. Your friend said it was all right,' he added, nodding towards Jane.

'I'd forgotten you'd be doing this.' Lindsay sighed as she collapsed into the comfortable armchair-cum-driver's seat.

True to the constable's word, they departed in about fifteen minutes with a bundle of clothing. Lindsay poured a large whisky for Jane and herself.

'I could do without another night like this,' Lindsay said. 'I don't know what it is about my friends that seems to attract murder.'

Jane looked puzzled. 'You mean this happens often?'

'Not exactly often. About two years ago, a friend of mine was arrested for a murder she didn't commit. Cordelia and I happened to be on the spot and got roped in to do the Sam Spade bit. That's when the two of us got together – a mutual fascination for being nosey parkers.'

'Well, I hate to say it, but I'm glad you've had the experience. I think you could easily find yourself going through the same routine for Deborah.'

Lindsay shook her head. 'Different kettle of fish. They've not even arrested Debs, never mind charged her. I'm pretty sure they don't have much to go on. It's my guess that Debs will be back here by lunchtime tomorrow if Judith's got anything to do with it. Let's face it, we all know Debs is innocent and I'm sure the police will find a more likely suspect before the day's out. They've just pulled her in to make it look good to anyone who's got their beady eyes on them. Now I'm going to bed, if you'll excuse me.'

In spite of Lindsay's exhaustion she did not fall asleep at once. Crabtree's murder had set her thoughts racing in circles. Who had killed him? And why? Was it anything to do with the peace camp, or was Debs' connection with him purely coincidental? And what was going to happen to

Debs? Lindsay hated being in a position where she didn't know enough to form reasonable theories, and she tossed and turned in Debs' bed as she tried to switch off her brain. Finally she drifted into a deep and dreamless sleep, which left her feeling neither rested nor refreshed when she awoke after nine.

After a quick shower, she emerged into a mild spring day with cotton-wool clouds scudding across the sky to find the camp apparently deserted. Puzzled, Lindsay glanced over at the big bender used for meetings; it seemed that was where the women had gathered. She decided to take advantage of the quiet spell by phoning the office and checking the current situation with the police.

Her first call was to the police HQ in Fordham. She asked for Rigano and was surprised to be put straight through to him. 'Superintendent Rigano? Lindsay Gordon here, *Daily Clarion*. We met last night at Brownlow . . .'

'I remember. You were quick off the mark. It's been hard to get away from your colleagues this morning. Now, what can I do for you?'

'I wondered where you were up to. Any imminent arrest?'

'You mean, are we going to charge your friend? The answer is, not at the moment. Off the record, we'll be letting her go later this morning. That's not to say I'm convinced of her innocence. But I can't go any further till I've got forensics. So you can say that at present good old Superintendent Rigano is following several lines of enquiry, but that the woman we have been interviewing is being released pending the outcome of those enquiries. Okay?'

'Fine. Do you mind if I drop in on you later today?'

'Please yourself,' he said. 'If I'm in, I'll see you. But I don't know what my movements will be later, so if you want to take a chance on missing me, feel free.'

Lindsay put the phone down, thoughtful. Her experience with the police during the Paddy Callaghan case had fuelled her ingrained mistrust of their intelligence and integrity. But in her brief encounter with Rigano she had felt a certain rapport which had not been dispelled by their telephone conversation. She had surprised herself by her request to call in on him and now she felt slightly bewildered as to what on earth she would find to discuss with him once Debs was released.

But that was for later. Right now she had the unpleasant task of talking to Duncan Morris, the *Daily Clarion*'s news editor and the man responsible for her move to London. She put the call in and waited nervously to be connected to her boss. His voice boomed down the line at her. 'Morning, Lindsay,' he began. 'I see from the overnight note that you're back in that nest of vipers. Still, you did a good job last night. We beat everyone else to the draw and that's the way I want to keep it.

It's of interest for us in terms of the link with the peace camp, okay, so let's keep that in the front of our minds. What I want from you by noon is a good background piece about the camp, a few quotes from the loony lefties about this man Crabtree and his campaign. I don't have to spell it out to you?' Lindsay fumed quickly as the venom of his prejudices ran over her. 'I also want to be well up on the news angles too. Try for a chat with the widow and family or his colleagues. And try to overcome your natural prejudices and stay close to the cops. Now, what's the score on all that?'

Lindsay somehow found her tongue. She was aware that she should know better than to be surprised by Duncan's about-turn when faced with a strong news story, but she still couldn't help being a little taken aback that he was now hassling her for a background piece on the camp. She stammered, 'The cops are releasing the woman they held for questioning. She's Deborah Patterson, the woman charged with assaulting him last month. I don't know what the legal implications are as yet – I should imagine that with his death the prosecution case automatically falls, but whether that releases us immediately from *sub judice* rules, I don't know.

'As far as the news feature's concerned, no problem. Also, I'm hoping to see the copper in charge of the case again this afternoon, so I can let you have whatever he says. I'll try the family but I don't hold out much hope. They're a bit too well clued-up about Her Majesty's gutter press to fall for the standard lines. But leave it with me.'

'Fine. Normally on one this big, I'd send someone down to help you out, but you're the expert when it comes to the lunatic fringe, so I'll leave you to it.' Patronising shit, she thought, as he carried on. 'We've got a local snapper lined up, so if you've got any potential pics, speak to the picture desk. Don't fall down on this one, Lindsay. File by noon so I can see the copy before I go into morning conference. And get a good exclusive chat with this woman they're releasing. If the lawyers say we can't use it, we can always kill it. Speak to you later.'

The phone went dead. 'Just what I love most,' Lindsay muttered. 'Writing for the wastepaper bin.' She walked back to the van and made herself some coffee and toast before she sat down and began to put her feature together. She had only written a few paragraphs when there was a knock at the van door.

'Come in,' she called. Jane entered, followed by Willow and another woman whom Lindsay knew only by sight.

'The very people I wanted to see,' she exclaimed. 'My newsdesk has said I can do a piece about the camp reaction to Crabtree's campaign. So I need some quotes from you about how you are here for peace and while you didn't have any sympathy for his organisation, you wouldn't ever have stooped to violence, etc., etc. Is that all right?'

Willow grinned. 'We'll have to see about that,' she replied. 'But first, we've got something to ask you. We've just had a meeting to discuss this business. We've decided we need to safeguard our interests. Already there have been reporters round here and we don't like the attitude they've been taking. That leaves us with a bit of a problem. We need someone who can help us deal with the situation. It's got to be someone who understands why none of us could have done this, but who also knows the way the system works. It looks like you're the only one who fits the bill.'

The third woman chimed in. 'It wasn't a unanimous decision to ask you. Not by a long chalk. But we're stuck. Personally, I don't feel entirely happy about trusting someone who works for a paper like the *Clarion*, but we don't have a lot of choice. Deborah's already been picked up, and even if she's released without charges, the mud's been slung and it will stick unless we can get our point of view across.'

Lindsay shrugged. 'I do know how the media works. But it sounds more like you're looking for a press spokeswoman, and that's not a job I can really do. It gives me a serious conflict of interest.'

The third woman looked satisfied. 'I thought you'd say that,' she said triumphantly. 'I knew that when the chips were down you'd know which side your bread was buttered.'

Needled, Lindsay said, 'That's really unfair. You know I want to do everything I can. Deborah's been my friend for years. Look, I can help you project the right kind of image. But don't expect miracles. What I do need if I'm going to do that is total co-operation. Now I know there are women here who would die before they'd help a tabloid journo, but from those of you who are willing to help I need support.'

Jane replied immediately. 'Well, I for one am willing to trust you. The articles you've written abroad about the camp have been some of the most positive pieces I've seen about what we're doing here. You're the only person capable of doing what we need that we can any of us say that about.'

'I'll go along with that,' Willow added. 'I'll pass the word around that you're on our side.'

'Care to supply some quotes before you go?' Lindsay asked as Willow and the other woman seemed about to leave.

'Jane can do that. She's good with words,' Willow said over her shoulder as they went out, closing the van door on Jane and Lindsay.

'There was something else I wanted to discuss with you,' Jane said hesitantly. 'I know a lot of the women would disagree with me, so I didn't raise it at the meeting. But I think we need someone to investigate this on our behalf. We are going to be at the centre of suspicion over this, and while they've got us as prime candidates, I don't think the police will be looking too hard for other possible murderers. Will you see what you can find out?'

For the second time that morning, Lindsay was taken aback. 'Why me?' she finally asked. 'I'm not any kind of detective. I'm a journalist, and there's no guarantee that my interests aren't going to clash with yours.'

Jane parried quickly. 'You told me you'd cleared a friend of a murder charge. Well, I figure if you did it once, you can do it again. Those features you wrote for the German magazine seem to have a feel for the truth, even if you don't always choose to report it. You can talk to the cops, you can talk to Crabtree's family and friends. None of us can do that. And you're on our side. You can't believe Deborah's guilty. You of all people can't believe that.'

Lindsay lit a cigarette and gazed out of the window. She really didn't want the hassle of being a servant of two masters. Jane sat quiet but Lindsay could feel the pressure of her presence. 'All right,' she said, 'I'll do what I can.'

By noon Lindsay had dictated her story and spoken to Duncan who, never satisfied, started to pressurise her about an interview with Deborah. Disgruntled, she was walking back from the phone box when a car pulled up alongside.

Suddenly Lindsay found herself enveloped in a warm embrace as Deborah jumped out of the car. Nothing was said for a few moments. Judith leaned over from the driver's seat and called through the open door, 'I'll see you up at the camp,' before driving off.

'Oh, Lin,' Deborah breathed. 'I was so afraid. I didn't know what was going on. The bastards just lifted me, I couldn't even do anything about Cara. I've been so worried. I haven't slept, haven't eaten – Thank God you had the sense to get Judith on to it straight away. God knows what I wouldn't have confessed to otherwise, just to get out of there. There was a big blond Special Branch bloke, but he was no big deal, they're always too busy playing at being James Bond. But the superintendent is so fucking clever. Oh Lin . . .' And the tears came.

Lindsay stroked her hair. 'Dry your eyes, Debs. Come on, Cara will be wanting you.'

Deborah wiped her eyes and blew her nose on Lindsay's crumpled handkerchief then they walked back to the camp arm in arm. As soon as they came into view, Cara came charging towards them. Behind her, to Lindsay's astonishment, came Cordelia, looking cool and unflustered in a designer jogging suit and green wellies, her black hair blowing in the breeze.

As mother and daughter staged a noisy and tearful reunion, Cordelia greeted Lindsay with a warm kiss. 'I couldn't sit in London not knowing what was happening,' she explained. 'Even if there's nothing I can do, I had to come.'

Lindsay found a smile and said, 'It's good to see you. I appreciate it. How long can you stay?'

'Till Wednesday lunchtime. Jane's filled me in on what's been happening. What's the plan now that you've been appointed official Miss Marple to the peace women? Do I have to rush off and buy you a knitting pattern and a ball of fluffy wool?'

'Very funny. I'm not entirely sure what I'm supposed to be doing. But I'll have to speak to Debs about last night. I've already warned her not to talk to anyone else. Of course, Duncan wants me to do the chat with her, but the lawyer will never let us use a line of it. I suppose I should have a crack at the family too. I've got a good contact, the copper who's handling things at the moment, a Superintendent Rigano. I'm going to see him this afternoon. Let's go and have a pint and I'll fill you in.'

Lindsay swallowed the emotional turmoil triggered off by Cordelia's appearance and told her lover all she knew about the murder over a bowl of soup in the nearest pub that accepted peace women customers – nearly three miles away. Cordelia was fired with enthusiasm and insisted that they set off immediately in her car for Brownlow Common Cottages which, in spite of their humble name, were actually a collection of architect-designed mock-Georgian mansions.

There could be no mistaking the Crabtree residence. It was a large, double-fronted two-storey house covered in white stucco with bow windows and imitation Georgian bottle-glass panes. A pillared portico was tacked on to the front. At the side stood a double garage. with a fifty-yard drive leading up to it. In front of the house was a neatly tended square lawn which had been underplanted with crocuses, now just past their best. The road outside was clogged on both sides by a dozen cars, the majority new. At the wrought-iron gate in the low, white-painted wall stood a gaggle of men in expensive topcoats. A few men and women stood around the cars looking bored. Every few minutes, one reporter peeled off from a group and ambled up the drive to ring the door bell. There was never any reply, not even a twitch of the curtains that hid the downstairs rooms from view.

'The ratpack's out in force,' Lindsay muttered as she climbed out of the car and headed for her colleagues. She soon spotted a familiar face, Bill Bryman, the crime man from the *London Evening Sentinel*. She greeted him and asked what was happening.

'Sweet FA,' he replied bitterly. 'I've been here since eight o'clock, and will my desk pull me off? Will they hell! The son answered the door the first time and told us nothing doing. Since then it's a total blank. If you ask me, they've disconnected the bell. I've told the office it's a complete waste of time, but you know news editors. Soon as they get promoted, they have an operation on their brains to remove all memory of what life on the road is all about.'

'What about the neighbours?'

Bill shook his head wearily. 'About as much use as a chocolate chip-pan. Too bloody "okay yah" to communicate with the yobbos of the popular press. Now if you were to say you were from the *Tatler* – though looking at the outfit, I doubt you'd get away it.' Lindsay looked ruefully at her clothes which still bore the traces of her headlong flight the night before, in spite of her efforts to clean up. 'You been down the peace camp yet?' he added. 'They're about as much help as this lot here.'

'So I'd be wasting my time hanging around here, would I?'

'If you've got anything better to do, do it. I'd rather watch an orphanage burn,' Bill answered resignedly with the cynicism affected by hard-boiled crime reporters the world over. 'I'll be stuck here for the duration. If I get anything, I'll file it for you. For the usual fee.'

Lindsay grinned to herself as she returned to the BMW. As they pulled away, Lindsay noticed the tall blond man she'd tagged as Special Branch when she'd seen him at the camp. He was leaning against a red Ford Fiesta on the fringes of the press corps, watching them.

'To Fordham nick,' she said to Cordelia. 'And stop at the first public toilet. Desperate situations need desperate remedies.'

6

Lindsay emerged from the public toilet on the outskirts of Fordham a different woman. Before they left the camp she had retrieved her emergency overnight working bag from the boot of her car, and she was now wearing a smart brown dress and jacket, chosen for their ability not to crease, coupled with brown stilettos that would have caused major earth tremors at the peace camp. Cordelia wolf-whistled quietly as her lover got back into the car. 'You'll get your lesbian card taken away, dressing like that,' she teased.

'Fuck off, she quipped wittily,' Lindsay replied. 'If Duncan wants the biz doing, I will do the biz.'

At the police station, Lindsay ran the gauntlet of bureaucratic obstacles and eventually found herself face to face with Superintendent Rigano. They exchanged pleasantries, then Lindsay leaned across his desk and said, 'I think you and I should do a deal.'

His face didn't move a muscle. He would have

made a good poker player if he could be been bothered with anything so predictable, thought Lindsay. When he had finished appraising her, he simply said, 'Go on.'

Lindsay hesitated long enough to light a cigarette. She needed a moment to work out what came next in this sequence of unplanned declarations. 'You had Deborah Patterson in here for twelve hours. I imagine she wouldn't even tell you what year it is.

'They'll all be like that,' she continued. 'They've gone past the "innocents abroad" stage down there, thanks to the way the powers that be have used the police and manipulated the courts. Now, they have a stable of sharp lawyers who don't owe you anything. Several of the peace women have been in prison and think it holds no terrors for them. They all know their rights and they're not even going to warn you if your backside is on fire.

'So if you want any information from them, you're stymied. Without me, that is. I think I can deliver what you need to know from them. I'm not crazy about the position I find myself in. But they trust me, which is not something you can say about many people who have a truce with the establishment. They've asked me to act as a sort of troubleshooter for them.'

He looked suspicious. 'I thought you were a reporter,' he said. 'How have you managed to earn their trust?'

'The women at the camp know all about me. I've been going there for months now.'

He could have blustered, he could have threatened, she knew. But he just asked, quietly, 'And what's the price?'

Glad that her first impression of him hadn't been shattered, Lindsay replied, 'The price is a bit of sharing. I'm a good investigative reporter. I'll let you have what I get, if you'll give me a bit of help and information.'

'You don't want much, do you?' he complained.

'I'm offering something you won't get any other way,' Lindsay replied. She doubted she could deliver all she had promised, but she reckoned she could do enough to keep him happy. That way, she'd get what she and the women wanted.

He studied her carefully and appeared to come to a decision. 'Can we go off the record?' he asked. Lindsay nodded. His response at first appeared to be a diversion. 'He was an influential man, Rupert Crabtree. Knew most of the people that are supposedly worth knowing round these parts. Didn't just know them to share a pink gin with – he knew them well enough to demand favours. Being dead seems to have set in motion the machinery for calling in the favours. I'm technically in charge of the CID boys running this at local level. But CID are avoiding this one like the plague. And other units are trying to use their muscle on it.

'Our switchboard has been busy. I'm under a lot of pressure to arrest your friend. You'll understand that, I know. But I'm old-fashioned enough to believe that you get your evidence before the arrest, not vice versa. That wouldn't have been hard in this case, if you follow me.

'I happen to think that she didn't kill him. And I'm not afraid to admit I'll need help to make that stick. You know I don't need to make deals to achieve that help. Most coppers could manage it, given time and a bit of leaning. But I don't have time. There are other people breathing down my neck. So let's see what we need for a deal.'

Lindsay nodded. 'I need access to the family. You'll have to introduce me to them. Suggest that I'm not just a newspaper reporter. That I'm working on a bigger piece about the Brownlow campaign for a magazine that will feature an in-depth profile of Crabtree – a sort of tribute.'

'Are you?'

'I can be by teatime. Also point out to them that it will get the pack off their back and end the siege. I'll be taping the conversation and transcribing the tapes. You can have full access to the tapes and a copy of the transcripts.'

'Are you trying to tell me you think it was a domestic crime?'

'Most murders are, aren't they? But I won't know who might have killed him till I've found out a lot more about his life. That means family, friends, colleagues and the peace women will all have to open up to me. In return, any of the peace women you want to talk to, you tell me honestly what it's about and I'll deliver the initial information you need. Obviously, you'll have to take over if it's at all significant, but that's got to be better for you than a wall of silence.'

'It's completely unorthodox. I can't run an investigation according to the whim of the press.'

'Without my help, I can promise you all you'll find at the camp is a brick wall. Anyway, you don't strike me as being a particularly orthodox copper.'

He almost smiled. 'When do you want to see the family?' he asked.

'Soon as possible. It really will get the rest of the press off the doorstep. You'll have to tell my colleagues at the gate that the family asked expressly to talk to a *Clarion* reporter or you'll get a load of aggravation which I'm sure you could do without.'

'Are you mobile?'

'The BMW cabriolet outside.'

'The fruits of being a good investigative reporter seem sweeter than those of being a good copper. Wait in the car.' He rose. The interview was over.

Slightly bewildered by her degree of success, Lindsay found her way through the labyrinthine corridors to the car park, feeling incongruous in her high heels after days in heavy boots, and slumped into the seat beside Cordelia, who looked at her enquiringly.

'I think perhaps I need my head examined,' Lindsay said. 'The way I've been behaving today, I think it buttons up the back. I've just marched into a superintendent's office and offered to do a deal with him that will keep Debs out of prison, get me some good exclusives and might possibly, if we all get very lucky indeed, point him in the right direction for the real villain. Talk about collaborating with the class enemy. Mind you, I expected him to throw me out on my ear. But he went for it. Can you believe it?'

Lindsay outlined her conversation with Rigano. When she'd finished, Cordelia asked, 'Would he be the one who looks like a refugee from a portrait in the Uffizi?'

'That's him. Why?'

'Because he's heading this way,' she said drily as Rigano's hand reached for Lindsay's door. Lindsay sat bolt upright and wound down the window.

'Open the back door for me, please,' said Rigano. 'I believe we may be able to do a deal.'

Lindsay did as she was told and he climbed in. A shadow of distaste crossed his face as his eyes flicked round the luxurious interior. 'Drive to Brownlow Common Cottages,' he said. 'Not too fast. There will be a police car behind you.'

Cordelia started the car, put it in gear, then, almost as an afterthought, before she released the clutch, she turned round in her seat and said, 'I'm Cordelia Brown, by the way. Would it be awfully unreasonable of me to ask your name?'

'Not at all,' he replied courteously. His face showed the ghost of a smile. 'I am Superintendent Giacomo Rigano of Fordham Police. I'm sorry I didn't introduce myself. I've grown so accustomed to knowing who everyone is that I forget this is not a two-way process. Because I knew who you were, I assumed you knew me too.'

'How did you know who I was?' she demanded, full of suspicion. She never seemed to remember that, as the writer of several novels and a successful television series, she was a minor celebrity. It had often amused Lindsay.

As usual, Rigano took his time in replying. 'I recognised you from your photographs.' He paused, and just before Cordelia could draw again on her stock of paranoia, he added, 'You know, on your dust jackets. And, of course, from television.'

Fifteen love, thought Lindsay in surprise. They drove off and Lindsay swivelled round in her seat. 'What's the deal, then?'

'I've just spoken to Mrs Crabtree. She wasn't keen, but I've persuaded her. I'll take you there and introduce you to her. Then I'll leave you to it. On the understanding that I can listen to the tapes afterwards and that you will give me copies of the transcript as agreed. In return, I need to know who was at the peace camp last night and where each woman was between ten and eleven. If you can give me that basic information, then I know who I need to talk to further.'

'Okay,' Lindsay agreed. 'But it'll be tomorrow before I can let you have that.'

'Then tomorrow will have to do. The people who want quick results will have to be satisfied with the investigation proceeding at its own pace. Like any other investigation.'

'Yes, but to people round here, he's not quite like any other corpse, is he?' Cordelia countered.

'That's true,' Rigano retorted. 'But while this remains my case, he will simply be a man who was unlawfully killed. To me, that is the only special thing about him.'

That must endear you to your bosses, Cordelia thought. Just what is Lindsay getting into this time? Maverick coppers we don't need.

Cordelia steered carefully through the crowd of journalists and vehicles that still made the narrow road in front of Brownlow Cottages a cramped thoroughfare. Lindsay noticed the blond watcher was no longer there. At the end of the Crabtrees' drive, Rigano wound down the window and shouted to the constable on duty there, 'Open the gate for us, Jamieson!'

The constable started into action, and as they drove inside, Lindsay could see the looks of fury on the faces of her rivals. As soon as the car stopped, Rigano got out and gestured to Lindsay to follow him. He was immediately distracted by journalists fifty yards away shouting their demands for copy, Lindsay took advantage of the opportunity to lean across and say urgently to

Cordelia, 'Listen, love, you can't help me here. I want us to work as a team like we did before. Would you go back to the camp and see if you can get Jane to help you sort out this alibi nonsense that Rigano wants? And make it as watertight as possible. Okay?'

'We have a deal,' said Cordelia, with a smile. 'As the good superintendent says.'

'Great. See you later,' Lindsay replied as she got out of the car and joined Rigano standing impatiently on the doorstep.

'Mrs Crabtree's on her own,' he remarked. 'There were some friends round earlier but she sent them away. The son, Simon, is out. He apparently had some urgent business to see to. So you should have a chance to do something more than ask superficial questions to which we all know the answers already.'

He gave five swift raps on the door knocker. Inside, a dog barked hysterically. As the door opened Rigano insinuated himself into the gap to block the view of the photographers at the end of the drive. Using his legs like a hockey goalkeeper he prevented an agitated fox-terrier taking off down the drive to attack the waiting press eager to snatch a picture of Rupert Crabtree's widow. Lindsay followed him into a long wide hallway. Rigano put his hand under Mrs Crabtree's arm and guided her through a door at the rear of the hall. The dog sniffed suspiciously at Lindsay, gave a low growl and scampered after them.

Lindsay glanced quickly around her. The occasional tables had genuine age, the carpet was dark brown and deep, the pictures on the wall were old, dark oils. This was money, and not *arriviste* money either. Nothing matched quite well enough for taste acquired in a job lot. Half of Lindsay felt envy, the other half contempt, but she didn't have time to analyse either emotion. She reached into her bag and switched on her tape recorder, then entered the room behind the other two.

She found herself in the dining room, its centrepiece a large rosewood drum table, big enough to seat eight people comfortably. Against one wall stood a long mahogany sideboard. The end of the room was almost completely taken up by large french windows which allowed plenty of light to glint off the silver candlesticks and rosebowl on the sideboard. On the walls hung attractive modern watercolours of cottage gardens. Lindsay took all this in and turned to the woman sitting at the table. Her pose was as stiff as the straight-backed chair she sat in. At her feet now lay the dog, who opened one eye from time to time to check that no one had moved significantly.

'Mrs Crabtree, this is Miss Lindsay Gordon. Miss Gordon's the writer I spoke to you about on the phone. She's to write a feature for *Newsday*. I give you my word, you can trust her. Don't be afraid to tell her about your husband,' Rigano said.

Emma Crabtree looked up and surveyed them both. She looked as if she didn't have enough trust to go round, but she'd hand over what she had in the full expectation that it would be returned to her diminished. Her hair was carefully cut and styled, but she had not been persuaded either by husband or hairdresser to get rid of the grey that heavily streaked the original blonde. Her face showed the remnants of a beauty that had not been sustained by a strong bone structure once the skin had begun to sag and wrinkle. But the eyes were still lovely. They were large, hazel and full of life. They didn't look as if they had shed too many tears. The grief was all being carried by the hands, which worked continuously in the lap of a tweed skirt.

She didn't try to smile a welcome. She simply said in a dry voice, 'Good afternoon, Miss Gordon.'

Rigano looked slightly uncomfortable and quickly said, 'I'll be on my way now. Thank you for your co-operation, Mrs Crabtree, I'll be in touch.' He nodded to them both and backed out of the room.

Emma Crabtree glanced at Lindsay briefly, then turned her head slightly to stare through the windows. 'I'm not altogether sure why I agreed to speak to you,' she said. 'But I suppose the superintendent knows best and if that's the only way to get rid of that rabble that's driving my neighbours to distraction, then so be it. At least you've not been hanging over my garden gate all day. Now, what do you want to know?'

Her words and her delivery cut the ground from under Lindsay's feet. All the standard approaches professing a spurious sympathy were rendered invalid by the widow's coolness. The journalist also sensed a degree of hostility that she would have to disarm before she could get much useful information. So she changed the tactics she had been working out in the car and settled on an equally cool approach. 'How long had you been married?' she asked.

'Almost twenty-six years. We celebrated our silver wedding last May.'

'You must have been looking forward to a lot more happy years, then?'

'If you say so.'

'And you have two children, is that right?'

'Hardly children. Rosamund is twenty-four now and Simon is twenty-one.'

'This must have come as an appalling shock to you all?' Lindsay felt clumsy and embarrassed, but the other woman's attitude was so negative that it was hard to find words that weren't leaden and awkward.

'In many ways, yes. When the police came to the door last night, I was shaken. Though the last thing that I would have expected was for Rupert to be bludgeoned to death taking Rex for his bedtime stroll.'

'Were you alone when the police arrived with the news?'

She shook her head. 'No. Simon was in. He'd been working earlier in the evening, he rents a friend's lock-up garage in Fordham. He's got all his computing equipment there. He's got his own computer software business, you know. He commutes on his motorbike so he can come and go as he pleases.'

At last she was opening up. Lindsay gave a small sigh of relief. 'So the first you knew anything was amiss was when the police came to the door?'

'Well, strictly speaking, it was just before they rang the bell. Rex started barking his head off. You see, the poor creature had obviously been frightened off by Rupert's attacker and he'd bolted and come home. He must have been sitting on the front doorstep. Of course, when he saw the police, he started barking. He's such a good watchdog.'

'Yes, I'd noticed,' Lindsay replied. 'Forgive me, Mrs Crabtree, but something you said earlier seems to me to beg a lot of questions.'

'Really? What was that?'

'It seemed to me that you implied that you're not entirely surprised that your husband was murdered. That someone should actively want him dead.'

Mrs Crabtree's head turned sharply towards Lindsay. She looked her up and down as if seeing her properly for the first time. Her appraisal seemed to find something in Lindsay worth confiding in.

'My husband was a man who enjoyed the exercise of power over people,' she said after a pause. 'He loved to be in control even in matters of small degree. There was nothing that appealed to Rupert so much as being able to dictate to people, whether over their plea on a motoring offence or how they should live their entire lives.

'Even when shrouded in personal charm of the sort my husband had, it's not an endearing characteristic. Miss Gordon, a lot of people had good cause to resent him. Perhaps Rupert finally pushed someone too far . . .'

'Can you think of anyone in particular?' Lindsay asked coolly, suppressing the astonishment she felt at Mrs Crabtree's open admission but determined to cash in on it.

'The women at the peace camp, of course. He was determined not to give up the battle against them till every last one was removed. He didn't just regard it as a political pressure campaign. He saw it as his personal mission to fight them as individuals and as a group and wear them down. He was especially vindictive towards the one who broke his nose. He said he'd not be satisfied till she was in prison.'

'How did you feel about that mission of your husband's? How did it affect you?' Lindsay probed.

Mrs Crabtree shrugged. 'I thought he was doing the right thing to oppose the camp. Those women have no morals. They even bring their children to live in those shocking conditions. No self-respecting mother would do that. No, Rupert was right. The missiles are there for our protection, after all. And that peace camp is such an eyesore.'

'Did it take up a lot of your husband's time?'

'A great deal. But it was a good cause, so I tried not to mind.' Mrs Crabtree looked away and added, 'He really cared about what he was doing.'

'Was there anyone else who might have had a motive?'

'Oh, I don't know. I've no idea who might hold a professional grievance. But you should probably talk to William Mallard. He's the treasurer of Ratepayers Against Brownlow's Destruction. He and Rupert were in the throes of some sort of row over the group's finances. And he'd be able to tell you more about Rupert's relations with other people in the group. There was one man that Rupert got thrown out a few weeks ago. I don't know any details, I'm afraid. Does any of this help?'

'Oh yes, I need to get as full a picture as possible. Your husband was obviously a man who was very active in the community.'

Emma Crabtree nodded. Lindsay thought she detected a certain cynicism in her smile. 'He was indeed,' she concurred. 'One could scarcely be unaware of that. And for all his faults, Rupert did a lot for this area. He was very good at getting things done. He brooked no opposition. He was a very determined man, my husband. Life will be a lot quieter without him.' For the first time, a note of regret had crept into her voice.

Lindsay brooded on what had been said. It seemed to her that it was now or never for the hard questions. 'And did his forcefulness extend to his family life?' she pursued.

Mrs Crabtree flashed a shrewd glance at her. 'In some ways,' she replied cautiously. 'He was determined the children shouldn't be spoilt, that they should prove themselves before getting any financial help from him. Rosamund had to spend three years slaving away in restaurants and hotel kitchens before he'd lend her enough to set up in business on her own. Then Simon wanted to set up this computer software company. But Rupert refused to lend him the capital he needed. Rupert insisted that he stay on at college and finish his accountancy qualifications. But Simon refused. Too like his father. He went ahead with his business idea, in spite of Rupert. But of course, without any capital, he hasn't got as far as he had hoped.

'Presumably, though, he'll inherit a share of his father's money now?' Lindsay pursued cautiously.

'More than enough for his business, yes. It'll soften the blow for him of losing his father. He's been very withdrawn since . . . since last night. He's struggling to pretend that life goes on, but I know that deep down he's in great pain.'

Her defence of her son was cut off by the opening of the dining-room door. Lindsay was taken aback. She failed to see how anyone could have entered the house without the dog barking as it had when she and Rigano arrived. She half turned to weigh up the new arrival.

'I'm back, mother,' he said brusquely. 'Who's this?'

Simon Crabtree was a very tall young man. He had his father's dark curling hair and strong build, but the impression of forcefulness was contradicted by a full, soft mouth. Lindsay suddenly understood just why Emma Crabtree was so swift to come to his defence.

'Hello, darling,' she said. 'This is Miss Gordon. She's a journalist. Superintendent Rigano brought her. We're hoping that now all the other journalists will leave us alone.'

He smiled, and Lindsay realised that he had also inherited his slice of Rupert's charm. 'That bunch? They'll go as soon as they've got another sensation to play with,' he said cynically. 'There was no need to invite one in, mother.' He turned to Lindsay and added, 'I hope you've not been hassling my mother. That's the last thing she needs after a shock like this.'

'I realise that. I wanted to know a bit about your father. I'm writing a magazine feature about the camp, and your father played an important role that should be recognised. I need to talk to everyone who's involved and your mother kindly agreed to give me some time. In return, I've promised to get rid of the mob at your gate. A few quotes should persuade them to leave,' Lindsay replied, conciliatory.

'You'd be better employed talking to those women at the peace camp. That way you'd get an interview with my father's murderer, since the police don't seem to be in any hurry to arrest her.'

'I'm not sure I understand what you mean,' Lindsay said.

'It's obvious, isn't it? One of those so-called peace women had already assaulted my father. It doesn't take much intelligence to work it out from there, does it?' Lindsay wondered if it was grief that made him appear so brusque.

'I can understand why you feel like that,' she sympathised. 'I'm sure your father's death has upset you. But at least now you'll be able to afford to set up your business properly. That will be a kind of tribute in a way, won't it?'

He shot a shrewd look at Lindsay. 'The business is already set up. It's going to be successful anyway. All this means is that I can do things a bit quicker. That's all. My father's death means more to me than a bloody business opportunity. Mother, I don't know why you brought this up.' Turning back to Lindsay he added. 'I'm going to have to ask you to leave now. My mother is too tired to deal with more questioning.' He looked expectantly at his mother.

The conditioned reflex built up over the years of marriage to Rupert Crabtree came into play. Simon had come into his inheritance in more ways than one. 'Yes,' she said, 'I think I've told you all I can, Miss Gordon. If you don't mind.'

Lindsay got to her feet. 'I'd like to have a few words with your daughter, Mrs Crabtree. When will she be home?'

'She doesn't live here any more. We're not expecting her till the funeral,' Simon interjected abruptly. 'I'll show you out now.' He opened the door and held it open. Lindsay took the hint and thanked the widow routinely.

In the hall, with the door closed behind them, Lindsay tried again. 'Your father's death has obviously upset you. You must have cared for him very deeply.'

His face remained impassive. 'Is that what you've been asking my mother about? Oh well, I suppose it's what the masses want to read with their cornflakes. You can tell your readers that anyone who knew my father will realise how deeply upset we all are and what a gap he has left in our lives. Okay?' He opened the front door and all but shoved her through it. 'I'm sure you've already got enough to fabricate a good story,' was his parting shot as he closed the door behind her.

She flipped open her bag, switched off the tape recorder and headed off down the drive to offer a couple of minor tit-bits to her rivals.

7

Bill Bryman had offered to drive Lindsay the mile back to the peace camp principally because he thought he might be able to prise more information from her than the bare quotes she had handed out to the pack. He was out of luck. Neither gratitude nor friendship would make Lindsay part with those pearls she had that were printable. But as she left the Crabtree's house, she noticed that the Special Branch man with the red Fiesta was back, which added indefinably to her eagerness to leave the scene. So she had frankly used Bill's car as a getaway vehicle to escape her colleagues and any watching eyes. As soon as he pulled up near the van, she was off. There was hardly a sign of life at the camp, and she realised a meeting must be in progress. Clever Cordelia, she thought.

She struggled through the mud in her high heels to Cordelia's car and retrieved her other clothes. Back at the van, she changed into jeans and a sweater then set off jogging down the road towards the phone box on the main road, in the opposite direction to Brownlow Common Cottages. She had deliberately chosen the further of the two boxes in the neighbourhood to avoid being overheard by any fellow journalists hanging around waiting to talk to their offices. To her relief the box was empty. She rang the police at Fordham to check that there were no new developments, then got through to the *Clarion*'s copy room. She dictated a heavily edited account of her interview with Emma and Simon Crabtree, coupled with an update on the case.

When she was transferred to the newsdesk, Duncan's voice reverberated in her ear. 'Hello, Lindsay. What've you got for me?'

'An exclusive chat with the grieving widow and son,' she replied. 'Nobody else got near them, but I had to give a couple of quotes to the pack in exchange for the exclusive. You'll see them from the agency wire services, probably. Nothing of any importance. Any queries on the feature copy I did earlier?'

'No queries, kid. Your copy has just come up on screen and it looks okay. Any progress on the exclusive chat with the bird who broke his nose?'

Lindsay fumed quietly. How much did the bastard want? 'Hey, Duncan, did you know that women get called birds because they keep picking up worms? I doubt if I'll get anything for tonight's paper on that. The woman concerned is still a bit twitchy, you know? First thing tomorrow, though. I'll file it before conference. And I've got another possible angle for tomorrow if the lawyers won't let us use the interview. Apparently there were one or two wee problems with Crabtree's rate-payers' association. Possible financial shenanigans. I'm going to take a look at that, okay?' Lindsay couldn't believe she was taking control of the conversation and the assignment, but it was actually happening.

'Fine,' Duncan acknowledged. 'You're the man on the spot, that sounds all right to me. Stick with it, kid. Speak to me in the morning.' The line went dead. Man on the spot, indeed. She made a face at the phone and set off at a leisurely pace to the camp.

As the benders came into sight, she saw that things were no longer quite so quiet. Outside the meeting tent were several figures. As she got closer, Lindsay could distinguish Cordelia, Jane, Deborah, Nicky and a couple of other women. There seemed to be an argument in progress, judging by the gestures and postures of the group. Lindsay quickened her pace.

'Lindsay!' Jane exclaimed. 'Thank goodness you're here. Maybe you can sort this mess out.'

Cordelia interrupted angrily. 'Look, Jane, I've said already, there's nothing *to* sort out. Just count me out in future.'

'Look, just calm down, all of you,' soothed Deborah. 'Everybody's taking this all so personally.

It's not any sort of personality thing. It's about the principle of trust and not reneging on the people you've entrusted something to. You know?'

'Are you saying I'm not to be trusted?' Cordelia flashed back.

'Personally, I don't think either of you are,' Nicky muttered.

'It's really nothing to do with you, Cordelia,' Jane replied in brisk tones. 'The women find it very hard to trust people they see as outsiders and they used up all their available goodwill on Lindsay.'

Exasperated, Lindsay demanded, 'Will someone please tell me what the hell is going on?'

The others looked at each other, uncertain. Cordelia snorted. 'Typical,' she muttered. 'Everything by committee. Look, Lindsay, it's pretty simple. You asked me to sort out the alibis for you and your pet policeman. I figured the quickest and most logical way to do it was get everyone together. So I got Jane to call a meeting. Which eventually got itself together only to decide that I wasn't right-on enough for them to co-operate with. So I upped and left, which is where you find us now.'

Lindsay sighed. Jane said with no trace of defensiveness, 'I think that's a bit loaded, Cordelia. The women didn't like someone they perceive as an outsider calling a meeting and making demands. We had enough difficulties getting agreement on asking Lindsay for help. Maybe you could have been a bit less heavy. I still think they'll be okay if you both explain to them why we need the information to protect ourselves and to protect Deborah. Right now, it's seen as being simply a case of us doing the police's job for them and exposing ourselves to groundless suspicion.'

Cordelia scowled. 'You can do all the explaining you want, but you can leave me out of the negotiations. I've had it. I'm going back to London,' she said, and stalked off towards her car.

'How childish can you get?' Nicky asked airily of no one in particular.

'Shut it,' Lindsay snarled. 'Why the hell did nobody help her? Debs, could you and Jane please go and talk them down in there? I want a word with Cordelia before she goes. I'll be back as soon as I can.' She ran off in Cordelia's wake and caught up with her before she could reach the car.

Lindsay grabbed her arm, but Cordelia wriggled free. Lindsay caught up again and shouted desperately, 'Wait a minute, will you?'

Cordelia stopped, head held high. 'What for?'

'Don't take off like this,' Lindsay pleaded. 'I don't want you to go. I need you here. I need your help. It's perfectly bloody trying to deal with this situation alone. I've got to have a foot in both camps. Nobody really trusts me either; you know I'm just the lesser of two evils, both for the women and for the police. Don't leave me isolated like this.'

Cordelia continued to stare at the ground. 'You're not isolated, Lindsay. If you go into that meeting, you won't be humiliated like I was. It's not enough with these women to have your heart in the right place. You've got to have the right credentials too. And my face just doesn't fit.'

'It's not like that, Cordelia. Don't leave because there was one hassle between you.' Lindsay reached out impulsively and pulled Cordelia close. 'Don't leave me. Not now. I feel . . . I don't know, I feel I'm not safe without you here.'

'That's absurd,' Cordelia replied, her voice muffled by Lindsay's jacket. 'Look, I'm going back to London to get stuck into some work. I'm not mad at you at all. I simply choose not to have to deal with these women solely on their terms. All right? Now don't forget, I want to know where you are and what you're doing, okay? I'm worried about you. This deal you've done with Rigano could get really dangerous. There are so many potential conflicts of interest – the women, the police, your paper. And you should know from experience that digging the dirt on murderers can be dangerous. Don't take any chances. Look, I think it will be easier for you to deal with the peace women if I'm not around. but if you really need me, give me a call and I'll come down and book myself into a hotel or something.'

Lindsay nodded and they hugged each other. Then Cordelia disengaged herself and climbed into the car. She revved the engine a couple of times and glided off down the road, leaving a spray of mud and a puff of white exhaust behind her. Lindsay watched till she was long gone, then turned to walk slowly back to the meeting tent.

She pushed aside the flap of polythene that served as a door and stood listening to Deborah doing for her what someone with a bit of sense and sensitivity should have done for Cordelia. Deborah finally wound up, saying, 'We've got nothing to hide here. We asked Lindsay to help us prove that. Well, she can't do it all by herself. When she asks us for help, or sends someone else for that help, we should forget maybe that we have some principles that can't be broken or suspicions we won't let go, or else we're as bad as the ones on the other side of that wire.'

Lindsay looked round. The area was crowded with women and several small children. The assortment of clothes and hairstyles was a bewildering assault on the senses. The warm steamy air smelled of bodies and tobacco smoke. The first woman to speak this time was an Irish woman; Lindsay thought her name was Nuala.

'I think Deborah's right,' she said in her soft voice. 'I think we were unfair the way we spoke before. Just because someone broke the conventions of the camp was no reason for us to be hostile and if we can't be flexible enough to let an outsider come in and work with us, then heaven help us when we get to the real fight about the missiles. Let's not forget why we're really here. I don't mind telling Lindsay everything I know about this murder. I was in my bender with Siobhan and Marieke from about ten o'clock onwards. We were all writing letters till about twelve, then we went to sleep.'

That opened the floodgates. Most of the women accepted the logic of Nuala's words, and those who didn't were shamed into a reluctant co-operation. For the next couple of hours, Lindsay was engaged in scribbling down the movements of the forty-seven women who had stayed at the camp the night before. Glancing through it superficially, it seemed that all but a handful were accounted for at the crucial time. One of that handful was Deborah who had gone on alone to the van while Lindsay talked to Jane. No one had seen her after she left the sing-song in Willow's bender.

Trying not to think too much about the implications of that, Lindsay made her way back to the van. She looked at her watch for the first time in hours and was shocked to see it was almost eight o'clock. She dumped the alibi information then went down to the phone box yet again. She checked in with the office only to find there were no problems. She phoned Cordelia to find she had gone out for dinner leaving only the answering machine to talk to Lindsay. She left a message, then she checked in with Rigano.

'How is our deal progressing?' he asked at once.

'Very well. I'll have the alibi information collated by morning and I should have a fairly interesting tape transcribed for you by then. Tomorrow, I'm going to see William Mallard. Do I need your help to get in there?'

'I shouldn't think so. He's been giving interviews all day. The standard hypocrisy – greatly admired, much missed, stalwart of the association.' She could picture the expression of distaste on his mouth and thought a small risk might be worth the taking.

'Any mention of the financial shenanigans?' she enquired.

'What financial shenanigans would they be, Miss Gordon?'

'Come, come, Superintendent. You live here, I'm just a visitor, after all. There must have been talk, surely.'

'I heard they had a disagreement but that it had all been cleared up. The person you want to talk to in the first instance is not Mallard but a local farmer called Carlton Stanhope. He was thoroughly disenchanted with the pair of them.'

'Do you think he'll play for an interview? That's just the sort of person I need to crack this,' Lindsay said.

'I don't know. He's not as much of a stick-in-the-mud as a lot of them round here. He's been helpful to me already. He might be persuaded to talk to you off the record. Being outside his circle, he might tell you a bit more than he was prepared to tell a policeman. And, of course, you could pass that on to me, unofficially, couldn't you?'

'Any chance of you helping me persuade him?' In for a penny, thought Lindsay.

There was a silence on the other end of the phone. Lindsay crossed her fingers and prayed. Finally, Rigano spoke. 'I'll ring him tonight and fix something up. I'm sure if I ask him, he'll give you all the help he can. Besides, he might even enjoy meeting a real journalist. How about half past ten tomorrow morning in the residents' lounge of the George Hotel in Fordham?'

'Superintendent Rigano, you could easily become a friend for life. That will do splendidly. I'll see you then.'

'Oh, there won't be any need for me to be there. But I'll see you at ten o'clock in my office with the information you've gathered for me so far. Goodnight, Miss Gordon.'

By the time she got back to the camp, Lindsay was exhausted and starving. She made her way to Jane's bender, where she found her deep in conversation with Nuala. Jane looked up, grinned at her and said, 'Cara's with Josy's kids. Deborah's in the van cooking you some food. You look as if you could do with it too. Go on, go and eat. And get a good night's sleep, for God's sake. Doctor's orders!'

Lindsay walked back to the van, realising that she was beginning to find it hard to remember life outside the peace camp with real houses and all their pleasures. But the thought was driven from her head as soon as she opened the van door. The smell that greeted her transported her back into the past. 'Bacon ribs and beans,' she breathed.

Deborah looked up with a smile. 'I got Judith to whizz me round Sainsbury's this morning. Cooking your favourite tea's about all I can do to thank you for all you've done.'

'Wonderful,' said Lindsay, 'I'm starving. Is it ready now?'

Deborah stirred the pot and tried a bean for tenderness. 'Not quite. About fifteen minutes.'

'Good, just long enough for you to tell me your version of events on the night of the murder during the crucial time for which you have no alibi. Care to tell me exactly what you did?'

Deborah left the stove and sat down at the table. She looked tired. Lindsay took pity, went to the fridge and took out a couple of coolish cans of lager. Both women opened their beer and silently toasted each other. Then Deborah said, 'I'm afraid you're not going to like this very much.

'After I left you, I came back to the van and made sure Cara was sleeping quietly. I was just about to brew up when I remembered I wanted to get hold of Robin. He's staying at my place just now. We did a deal. I said he could stay rent free if he did the plumbing for me. I've never been at my best with water. It's the only building job I always try to delegate. Anyway, I'd been thinking that I wanted him to plumb in a shower independent of the hot water system.

'So I thought I'd better let him know before he went any further and I decided to phone him.'

Lindsay broke in. 'But your house isn't on the phone.'

'No. But if I want to get hold of Robin, I ring the Lees. They've got the farm at the end of the lane. They send a message up with the milk in the morning telling Rob to phone me at a particular time and number. It works quite well. So I went to the phone.'

'Which box did you go to?'

'The wrong one from our point of view. The one nearer Brownlow Common Cottages.

'Will the Lees remember what time it was when you phoned?'

'Hardly. No one answered. They must have been out for the evening. So I just came straight back and made a brew.'

'Did you see anything? Hear anything?'

'Not really. It was dark over by the perimeter fence anyway. I thought I might have seen Crabtree walking his dog, but it was quite a bit away, so I wasn't sure.'

Lindsay sat musing. 'Any cars pass you at all?'

'I don't remember any, but I doubt if I would have noticed. It's not exactly an unusual sight. People use these back lanes late at night to avoid risking the breathalyser.'

Lindsay shrugged. 'Oh, Debs, I don't know. I

just can't seem to get a handle on this business.'

Deborah smiled wanly. 'You will, Lin, you will. For my sake, I hope you will.'

Later, fortified by a huge bowl of bacon and beans, Lindsay settled down to work. It took her over an hour to transcribe the tape, using her portable typewriter. Next came the even more tedious task of typing up her notes of the camp women's alibis. It was after midnight before she could put her typewriter into its case and concentrate again on Deborah, who was curled up in a corner devouring a new feminist novel.

'You look like a woman who needs a hug,' said Deborah, looking up with a sympathetic smile.

'I feel like a woman who needs more than a hug,' Lindsay replied, sitting down beside her. Deborah put her arms round Lindsay and gently massaged the taut muscles at the back of her neck.

'You need a massage,' she said. 'Would you like me to give you one?'

Lindsay nodded. 'Please. Nobody has ever given me backrubs like you used to.'

They made up the bed, then Lindsay stripped off and lay face down on the firm cushions. Deborah undressed and took a small bottle of massage oil from a cupboard. She rubbed the fragrant oil into her palms and started kneading Lindsay's stiff muscles.

Lindsay could feel warmth spreading through her body from head to foot as she relaxed.

'Better?' Deborah asked.

'Mmm,' Lindsay replied. She had become aware of Deborah's body against hers. She rolled over and lightly stroked Deborah's side. 'Thank you,' she said, moving into a half-sitting position where she could kiss Deborah.

Deborah slid down beside her and their two bodies interwined in an embrace that moved almost immediately from the platonic to the passionate, taking them both by surprise. 'Are you sure about this, Lin?' Deborah whispered.

For reply, Lindsay kissed her again.

8

The morning found Lindsay in good humour as she breezed into the police station at Fordham. She had dived into the local Marks and Spencer and bought a new pair of smart mushroom coloured trousers and a cream and brown striped shirt that matched her brown jacket. She felt she looked her best and was on top of things professionally. The events of the night before were fresh in her memory, and for as long as she could put Cordelia out of her mind, she felt good about what had happened with Deborah too.

Her benign mood lasted for as long as it took her to reach the reception counter. At a desk at the back of the office she spotted a now familiar blond man flicking through some papers. Lindsay frowned as the SB man glanced up at her. Pressing the bell for service, she turned her back to wait. By the time the duty constable responded, the man had disappeared.

Rigano didn't keep her waiting. As soon as she

sat down in his office, he attacked. 'We've turned up a witness who saw Deborah Patterson walking down the road towards the camp at approximately ten forty-five.

'In that case, Deborah's statement won't come as a surprise to you,' Lindsay retorted. 'It's all here, Superintendent. Where she went, when and why.' She put two files on the desk. 'This one: the peace women. That one: Emma and Simon Crabtree.'

He smiled coldly. 'Thank you. It might have made things a little simpler if Miss Patterson had chosen to make her statement when she was here, don't you think?' Lindsay shrugged. 'Anyway, I've spoken to Stanhope. He's expecting you in the George.'

Lindsay deliberately lit a cigarette, ignoring the implicit dismissal. 'Do you know where I can get hold of Rosamund Crabtree?' she enquired. 'I didn't have the chance to get that information from Mrs Crabtree.'

'Don't know why you want to see her,' Rigano grumbled. 'The way this case seems to be breaking, we're going to have to take another long hard look at Miss Patterson. But if you really feel it's necessary, you'll probably be able to catch up with her at work. She and a partner run this vegetarian restaurant in London. Camden Town. Rubyfruits, it's called.'

'Rubyfruits?' Lindsay exclaimed. 'Quick, ring Arthur Koestler.'

He looked at her uncomprehendingly. 'Funny sort of a name, eh?' he said.

'It isn't that, it's just the small-world syndrome striking again.'

'You know it?'

Lindsay nodded. 'Fairly well. We go there quite a lot.'

'You surprise me. I wouldn't have put you down as one of the nut cutlet brigade. Anyway, you're going to be late for Carlton Stanhope, and I wouldn't recommend that. I'd like to hear how you get on. If you're free at lunchtime, I'll be in the snug at the Frog and Bassett on the Brownlow road. Now run off and meet your man.'

Lindsay got to her feet. 'How will I recognise him?' she asked.

Rigano smiled. 'Use your initiative. There won't be that many people in the residents' lounge at half past ten on a Tuesday morning, for starters. Besides, I've described you to him so I don't imagine there will be too many problems of identification.'

Lindsay scowled. 'Thanks,' she muttered on her way to the door. 'I'll probably see you later in the pub. Oh, and by the way, do tell your Special Branch bloodhound to stop following me around. I'm not about to do a runner.' She congratulated herself on her smart response. She would remember that arrogance later.

Ripe for takeover by the big boys, thought Lindsay as she entered the George Hotel. The combination of the faded fifties decor and odd touches of contemporary tatt was an unhappy one. She could imagine the prawn cocktail and fillet steak menu. A neon sign that looked like a museum piece pointed up a flight of stairs to the residents' lounge. Lindsay pushed open the creaky swing door. The chairs looked cheap and uncomfortable. The only occupant of the room was pouring himself a cup of coffee. Lindsay's heart sank. So much for Rigano's assumption that they'd have the place to themselves, for the young man sprawled leggily in an armchair by the coffee table didn't look like a farmer called Carlton Stanhope.

He wore tight blue jeans, elastic-sided riding boots and an Aran sweater. His straight, dark blond hair was cut short at the sides, longer at the back, and had a floppy fringe that fell over his forehead from its side parting. He didn't look a day over twenty-five. He glanced over at Lindsay hesitating by the door and drawled, 'Miss Gordon, do sit down and have a cup of coffee before it gets cold.'

As he registered the surprise in her eyes, he smiled wickedly. 'Not what you expected, eh? You thought a Fordham farmer called Carlton Stanhope who was a sidekick of Rupert Crabtree was bound to be a tweedy old foxhunter with a red face and a glass of Scotch in the fist, admit it! Sorry to disappoint you. Jack Rigano really should have warned you.'

Lindsay's mouth wavered between a scowl and

a smile. She sat down while Stanhope poured her a cup of coffee. 'Do say something,' he mocked. 'Don't tell me I've taken your breath away?'

'I was surprised to see someone under fifty, I must say. Other than that, though, I can't say I'm greatly shocked and stunned. Don't all young gentlemen farmers dress like you these days?'

'*Touché*,' he replied. 'And since you're not what I expected of either a journalist or a peace woman, I'd say we're probably about quits. You see, Miss Gordon, we moderate men are just as much subject to stereotyping as you radical women.'

Lindsay felt a hint of dislike in her response to him. She reckoned he knew himself to be a highly eligible young man; but she gave him credit for trying to build on his physical charm with an entertaining line in conversation. His manner irritated rather than appealed to her, but that didn't stop her acknowledging that it would normally find its admirers. 'Superintendent Rigano seemed to think you might be able to fill me in on some background about Ratepayers Against Brownlow's Destruction.'

'Jack says you're doing the investigative crime reporter bit over Rupert's death. He seems to think you're a useful sort of sleuth to have on his side, so I suppose I'm the quid pro quo,' he observed.

'I appreciate the help,' she responded. 'I'm sure you've got more important things to be doing – drilling your barley or whatever it is farmers do in March.'

'Lambing, actually. My pleasure, I assure you. Now, what exactly is it you want to know?'

'I'm interested in RABD. How did you come to get involved with it?' Lindsay asked. She found her cigarettes and offered Stanhope the packet. He dismissed it with a wave of his hand as he began his story.

'Let's see now . . . I got involved shortly after it was formed. That must have been about six or seven months ago, I guess. I hadn't been back in the area long. My father decided he wanted to bow out of the day-to-day hassle of running the farm, so he dragged me back from my job with the Forestry Commission to take over what will one day be mine. That is, what the bank and the taxman don't get their hands on.

'Anyway, to cut a long story short, I was appalled when I arrived back home and found these women camped on the common. I mean, Brownlow Common was always a place where people could walk their dogs, take their sprogs. But who'd actually want to take their offspring for a walk past that eyesore? All that polythene and earth-mother cooking pots and lesbians hugging each other at the drop of a hat or any other garment. Grotesque, for those of us who remember what a walk on the common used to be like.

'Also, say what you will about the Yanks, their base has brought an extraordinary degree of prosperity to Fordham. It's cushioned the local people against the worst excesses of the recession. And that's not something to be sneezed at.'

He paused for breath, coffee and thought. Lindsay dived in. 'Was it actually Rupert Crabtree who recruited you, then?'

'I don't know if recruit is quite the word. You make him sound like some spymaster. I was having dinner with my parents at the Old Coach restaurant, and Rupert was there with Emma – Mrs Crabtree, you know? Anyhow, they joined us for coffee and Emma was complaining about how ghastly it was to have this bloody camp right on the doorstep and Rupert was informing anyone who'd care to listen that he was going to do something about it and that anyone with any civic pride left would join this new organisation to get rid of the women at the camp for good and all.'

Lindsay looked speculatively at the handsome, broad-shouldered young man. It would be nice to shake that self-assurance to its roots. But not today. 'That sounds a bit heavy duty,' she simply said.

'Oh no, nothing like that. No, RABD was all about operating within the law. We used the local press and poster and leaflet campaigns to mobilise public opinion against the camp. And of course, Rupert and a couple of other lawyers developed ways of harassing them through the courts using the by-laws and civil actions. And whenever they staged big demos, we'd aim to mount a token counter-demonstration, making sure the media knew.'

'In other words, peaceful protest within the law?'

'Absolutely.'

'Just like the peace women, in fact?' Avoiding Stanhope's glance Lindsay screwed out her cigarette in the ashtray. 'So, tell me about the in-fighting at RABD.'

He looked suddenly cautious. 'We don't want all this to become public knowledge.'

Lindsay shrugged. 'It already is. All sorts of rumours are flying round,' she exaggerated. 'It's better to be open about these things, especially when the world's press is nosing about, otherwise people start reading all sorts of things into relatively minor matters. You don't want people to think you've got something to hide, do you?'

Stanhope picked up the coffee jug and gestured towards Lindsay's cup 'More coffee?' He was buying time. When Lindsay declined the offer he poured coffee into his own cup. 'It's not quite that simple, though, is it?' he demanded. 'We're talking about a murder investigation. Something one would happily have gossiped about in a private sort of way last week can suddenly take on quite extraordinary connotations after a man has been murdered. I know I seem to take everything very lightly, but in fact I feel Rupert's death strongly. We didn't always see eye to eye – he could be bloody irritating, he was so arrogant at times – but he was basically an absolutely straight guy and that's something I find I have to respect. So I'm wary of pushing something he cared about into an area where it could become the subject of public scorn.'

Lindsay groaned inwardly. Scruples were the last thing she needed. She had to get something out of Stanhope to provide a fresh lead for the next day's paper, at the very least. And she needed to get it fast, before Duncan could start screaming for copy on Debs. She had foolishly thought that an interview set up by Rigano, with all the force of his authority, would be an easy answer. She set about overcoming Stanhope's objections. It took less persuasion than she anticipated and she suspected he had simply put her through the hoops in order to salve his conscience. And she managed to elicit the useful information that he had been alone in the lambing shed at the time of the murder.

'There were two things that might interest you,' he said. 'One, a lot of people knew about. The other, only a handful of people. So, while I don't mind what you do about the first matter, I want to be left well out of anything to do with the second. Okay?'

Lindsay nodded. 'Okay.'

'I really don't want to be brought into this as your source. I mean it,' he added.

'I said okay,' Lindsay replied. 'I'll cover your back.'

He sighed. 'The first concerns a man called Paul Warminster. He's local. He owns a couple of gents' outfitters in Fordham. He joined RABD shortly after I did and was always mouthing off against the women. He wasn't happy with the way our campaign was being run.

'He said we should take the fight into the enemy territory instead of simply reacting to them. He always speaks in that sort of jargon. I suspect he must have been in the Pay Corps or something like it in the war. He thought we should be actively banning them from shops, pubs, cinemas, the lot. He thought also that we should be harassing them in the town – insulting them, jostling them, generally making life hard for them.

'Rupert always managed to keep the lid on him till about a month or so ago. Paul stood against him in the election for chair and made the most scurrilous attack on him. He ended up by saying that Rupert was so wishy-washy that he was lucky the motorbike gangs weren't throwing pigs' blood on *his* house. That, I'm afraid, was his big mistake. Our group has always utterly repudiated the thugs who terrorise the women at the camp. But I'd certainly heard mutterings that perhaps Paul wasn't as quick to condemn as one would expect, if you catch my drift. As I said, this was all common knowledge.

'Well, Rupert was duly re-elected with a thumping majority and he announced that since

Paul's policies and attitudes had been so soundly defeated at the ballot box, it would seem there was no place for him within the group. It didn't actually leave Paul any option except resignation. So out he stormed, making sure we all knew he was right and Rupert was wrong. He didn't actually make any threats, but the inference was there to be taken.'

'Okay, Mr Stanhope. And the second incident?'

'Call me Carl, please. I'm not old enough yet for Mr Stanhope.' He radiated charm at her.

She felt like throwing up over his clean jeans. But she didn't even grind her teeth as she said, 'Okay, Carl. The second incident?'

'Look, I really meant what I said about keeping my name out of this. If I thought you'd drop me in it I'd shut up now . . .'

'No, no,' said Lindsay, 'I'll forget you told me. Just give me the details.'

'I was told this by someone I can't name. But I'm certain it's true, because it's referred to in the agenda for next week's meeting, though not in any detail that would make clear what it's about. William Mallard is the treasurer of RABD. He's a local estate agent. We're quite a wealthy organisation. We need to be because we try to fight civil court actions, which costs an arm and a leg. But we are a popular cause locally, and all our fundraising is well supported by the locals. And we've had some financial donations from outside the area too.'

'So at any given time, there's a few hundred in the kitty, is that what you're trying to say?' Lindsay interjected, frustrated.

'More like a few thousand,' he said. 'Rupert was a bit concerned that we weren't using our money properly – you know, that we should be keeping it in a high interest account instead of a current one. Mallard wouldn't agree. Now, being an awkward sort of bloke Rupert thought his reaction was decidedly iffy. So, armed with the latest treasurer's report, he zapped off to the bank and demanded a chat with the manager. The upshot was that instead of there being about seven thou. in the account, as the report stated, there was barely five hundred.

'Rupert blew a fuse. He hared off to see Mallard and confront him. They apparently had a real up and downer. Mallard claimed he'd simply been doing what he always did with large lumps of money in his care, to wit, dumping them in high interest, seven-day accounts. But he couldn't show Rupert the money then and there. Rupert accused him of speculating with the RABD's money and pocketing the profits – Mallard's known for having a taste for the stock market, you see.

'Anyway, Rupert went off breathing fire. Next thing is, the following day, Mallard came to see Rupert, with evidence that the missing six and a half grand was all present and correct. But this didn't satisfy Rupert once he'd slept on it; he was baying for blood. He'd had time to think things through and realised that at some point Mallard must have forged Rupert's signature to shift the cash, since a cheque required both signatures. He told Mallard he was going to raise the matter at the next meeting and let the association decide who was in the wrong. Mallard was apparently fizzing with rage and threatening Rupert with everything from libel actions to –' He broke off, then stumbled on, 'to you name it.'

'Murder perhaps? Cosy little bunch, aren't you?' Lindsay remarked. 'The wonder of it is that it's taken so long for someone to get murdered.'

He looked puzzled. 'I don't think that's quite fair,' he protested.

'Life isn't fair,' she retorted, getting to her feet. 'At least, not for most people. Who's got the files now, by the way? I'll need to see them.'

He shrugged. 'Mallard, I guess.'

'Could you call him and tell him Jack Rigano wants him to co-operate?' she asked.

'Look, I told you I didn't want to be connected with you on this,' he protested.

'So tell him the request came from Rigano. Otherwise you've wasted your breath talking to me, haven't you?'

He nodded reluctantly. 'Okay,' he said.

Lindsay was at the door when he spoke again. 'Jack says you'll be talking to a lot of people in Rupert's immediate circle?'

'That's right. It all helps to build up the picture.'

'Will you be seeing his daughter Ros?'

Lindsay nodded. 'I'm hoping to see her one evening this week,' she replied.

'Will you say hello from me? Tell her I hope the business is going well and any time she's down home, she should give me a call and we'll have a drink for old times' sake.'

'Sure, I didn't realise you knew Ros Crabtree.'

'Everyone knows everyone else around here, you know. Ask Judith Rowe. Ros and I were sort of pals in the school holidays when we were growing up. You know the routine – horses, tennis club.'

Lindsay grinned, remembering the summers of her youth fishing for prawns with her father in the thirty-foot boat that was his livelihood. 'Not quite my routine, Carl, but yes, I know what you mean. Was she your girlfriend, then?'

He actually blushed. 'Not really. We spent a lot of time together a few years ago, but it was never really serious. And then . . . well, Ros decided that, well, her interests lay in quite other directions, if you follow me?'

'I'm not entirely sure that I do.'

'Well, it rather turned out that she seems to prefer women to men. Shame, really. I think that's partly why she moved away from home.'

'You mean her parents were hostile about it?'

'Good God, no! They knew nothing about it. Rupert Crabtree would never have put up the money for her restaurant if he'd thought for one minute she was gay. He'd have killed her!'

9

'No, Duncan, I can't write anything about the RABD yet. I've only got one guy's word for it, and half of that's second-hand,' Lindsay said in exasperation. 'I should be able to harden up the ratepayers' routine by tomorrow lunchtime.'

'That'll have to do then, I suppose,' Duncan barked. 'But see if you can tie it up today, okay? And keep close to the cops. Any sign of an arrest, I want to be the first to know. And don't forget that interview with the suspect woman. Keep ahead of the game, Lindsay.'

The line went dead. Lindsay was grateful. The interview with Stanhope had produced more than she'd anticipated and she'd spent the rest of the morning trying to set up meetings with Mallard and Warminster. But neither could fit her in till the next day which left her with a hole in the news editor's schedule to fill and nothing to fill it with except for the one interview she didn't want to capitalise on. The fact that she was no stranger to living on her wits didn't mean she had to enjoy it. The one thing she wasn't prepared to admit to herself yet was that the job was increasingly turning into something she couldn't square either with her conscience or her principles. After all, once she had acknowledged the tackiness of the world she loved working in, how could she justify her continued determination to take the money and run?

It was half past one by the time she reached the Frog and Basset, a real ale pub about two miles out of the town in the opposite direction to Brownlow. She pushed her way through the crowd of lunchtime drinkers into the tiny snug, which had a hand-lettered sign saying 'Private Meeting' on the door. The only inhabitant was Rigano, sitting at a converted sewing-machine table with the remains of a pint in front of him. He looked up at her. 'Glad you could make it,' he said. 'I've got to be back at the station for two. Ring the bell on the bar if you want a drink. Mine's a pint of Basset Bitter.'

Lindsay's eyebrows rose, but nevertheless she did as he said. The barman who emerged in response to her ring scuttled off and returned moments later with two crystal-clear pints. Lindsay paid and brought the drinks over in silence. Rigano picked up his and took a deep swallow. 'So was Carlton Stanhope a help?'

Lindsay shrugged. 'Interesting. There seems to have been something going on between Crabtree and the treasurer, Mallard.'

Rigano shook his head. 'Don't get too excited about that. It's only in bad detective novels that people get bumped off to avoid financial scandal and ruin.'

Stung, Lindsay replied, 'I'm not so sure about that. There are plenty of cases that make the papers where people have been murdered for next to nothing. It all depends how much the murderer feels they can bear to lose.'

'And did Carlton Stanhope come up with anyone else that you think might have something to lose?'

Lindsay shrugged. 'He mentioned someone called Warminster.'

'A crank. Not really dangerous. All mouth and no action.'

'Thanks. And have you got anything for me? I could do with a bone to throw to my boss.'

Rigano took another deep swig of his beer. 'There's not much I can say. We're not about to make an arrest, and we're pursuing various lines of enquiry.'

'Oh come on, surely you can do better than that. What about CID? What are they doing? Who's in charge of that end of things?'

Rigano scowled, and Lindsay felt suddenly threatened. 'I'm in charge,' he answered grimly. 'I'll keep my end of the deal, don't worry. I've set you up with Stanhope, haven't I? I gave you the whereabouts of the daughter, didn't I? So don't push your luck.'

Frustrated, she drank her drink and smoked a cigarette in the silence between them. Then, abruptly, Rigano got to his feet, finishing his drink as he rose. 'I've got to get back,' he said. 'The sooner I do, the nearer we'll be to sorting this business out. Keep me informed about how you're getting on.' He slipped out of the snug. Lindsay left the remains of her drink, and drove back to the camp.

She parked the car and went to the van, which was empty. She put the kettle on, but before it boiled the driver's door opened and Deborah's head appeared. 'Busy?' she asked.

Lindsay shook her head. 'Not at all,' she replied. 'Actually, I was about to come looking for you. I need your help again.'

Deborah made herself comfortable. 'All you have to do is ask. Been on a shopping spree? I can't believe all these frightfully chic outfits came out of that little overnight bag.'

'I had to find something to wear that makes me look like an efficient journo. Your average punter isn't too impressed with decrepit Levis and sweatshirts. Anything doing that I've missed?'

'Judith is coming to see me at three o'clock.'

Lindsay poured out their coffee and said, 'Is it about the assault case?'

'That's right,' Deborah confirmed. 'She wants to explain exactly what the situation is. I think she's had some news today. Or an opinion or something. Now, what was it you wanted from me? Nothing too shocking, I hope.'

'I need you to have dinner with me tonight. In London.'

Deborah looked surprised. 'I thought Cordelia was in London? Doesn't she eat dinner any more?'

'For this particular dinner, I need you. We are going to a bijou vegetarian restaurant called Rubyfruits.'

'You're taking me to a dykey-sounding place like that? On your own patch? And you're not worried about who you might run into? Whatever happened to keeping it light between us?'

Lindsay grimaced. 'This is business, not pleasure. Rubyfruits is run by Ros Crabtree, our Rupert's daughter. The dyke that Daddy didn't know about, apparently. And I need you there to tell me if you saw anything of Ros or her partner around Brownlow recently. Okay?'

As Deborah agreed, Judith's car drew up outside.

She looked every inch the solicitor in a dark green tweed-mixture suit and a cream open-necked shirt. But behind the façade she was clearly bursting with a nugget of gossip that threatened to make her explode, and she was quite shrewd enough to realise that dumping it in Lindsay's lap was guaranteed to provide it with the most fertile ground possible.

'You look like the cat that's had the cream,' Lindsay remarked.

'Sorry, terribly unprofessional of me. We solicitors are not supposed to show any emotion about anything, you know. But this is such a wonderful tale of dirty linen washing itself in public, I can't be all cool and collected about it. A wonderful piece of gossip and the best of it is that it's twenty-four carat truth. Now Lindsay, if you're going to use this, you certainly didn't get it from me, all right?'

Lindsay nodded, bored with yet another demand for anonymity. When she was a young trainee reporter, it had always made the adrenalin surge when people required to be Deep Throats. But cynical experience of the insignificance of ninety per cent of people's revelations had ended that excitement years ago. Whatever Judith had to say might merit a few paragraphs. But she would wait and hear it before she let her pulse race.

'Rupert Crabtree's will is with one of the partners in the building next to ours. Anyway, the junior partner is by way of being a pal of mine and he's managed to cast an eye over the will. And you'll never guess who gets ten thousand pounds?'

Lindsay sighed. 'Ros Crabtree? Simon?'

Judith shook her head impatiently. 'No, no. They each get one third of the residue, about fifty thousand each. No, the ten thousand goes to Alexandra Phillips. Now isn't that extraordinary?' She was clearly disappointed by the blank stares from her audience. 'Oh Lindsay, you must know about Alexandra. You're supposed to be looking into Rupert Crabtree. Has no one told you about Alexandra? Lindsay, she was his mistress.'

That last word won Judith all the reaction she could have wished. Lindsay sat bolt upright and spilt the remains of her coffee over the table. 'His mistress?' she demanded. 'Why the hell did nobody tell me he had a mistress?'

Judith shrugged. 'I assumed you knew. It wasn't exactly common knowledge but I guess most of us lawyers had a notion it was going on. Anyway, I rather think it was cooling off, at least on Alexandra's side.'

Lindsay counted to ten in her head. Then she said slowly and clearly, 'Tell me everything you know about the affair, Judith. Tell me now.'

Judith looked surprised and hurt at the intensity of Lindsay's tone. 'Alexandra Phillips is about twenty-five. She's a solicitor with Hampson, Humphrey and Brundage in Fordham. She does all the dogsbody work, being the practice baby. She's a local girl, used to be friendly with Ros Crabtree, in fact. I know her through the job and also because she and Ros used to kick around with my younger sister Antonia. Anyway, Alexandra came back to Fordham about eighteen months ago and almost as soon as she got back, Rupert pounced. He asked her out to dinner at some intimate little *Good Food Guide* bistro that none of his cronies would be seen dead patronising. He spun the line that he wanted to give her the benefit of his experience and all that blah. And being more than a little impressionable, dear Alexandra fell for his line like an absolute mug. This much I know because she comfided in me right at the start. I warned her not to be a bloody fool and to see him off sharpish, which earned me the cold shoulder and no more confidences.

'But I saw his car outside her flat on a few occasions and the will obviously indicates an ongoing situation. However, there's been a whisper of a rumour going round Antonia's crowd that Alexandra was looking for a way out. There was a very definite suggestion that she rather fancied another fish to fry. Sorry, no names. I did ask Antonia, but she's pretty sure that Alexandra hasn't spilled that to anyone.'

'Great,' said Lindsay, getting to her feet and pulling on her jacket. 'Come on then, Judith.'

Judith looked bewildered. 'Where?'

'To wherever Alexandra hangs out. I want to talk to her, and the sooner the better before the rest of the world gets the same idea.'

'But we can't just barge in on her without an appointment. And besides, I came here to talk to Deborah about her pending court case.'

'Oh God,' said Lindsay in exasperation. 'Yes, of course. But after that we've just got to see Alexandra Phillips as soon as possible.'

Judith, looking startled and apprehensive,

rattled machine-gun sentences at Deborah. Following the demise of the sole prosecution witness, she told her, the police could offer no evidence against Deborah in the Crown Court and the case would therefore fall since she had made no admissions of guilt. It was unlikely that the police would be able to find an eye-witness at that late stage, particularly since they were pursuing that line of enquiry with something less than breathtaking vigour.

'Except in so far as it overlaps with the murder enquiry,' Lindsay muttered nonchalantly.

'Thanks for the reassurance,' Deborah remarked. 'Why don't you two run off now and prevent the police from making too many mistakes about me?'

Judith rose hesitantly. 'Are you sure this is a good idea? I mean, Alexandra is something of a friend, or at least a friend of the family. I can't imagine she's going to take too kindly to us barging in and demanding answers about Rupert . . .'

'Look at it this way.' said Lindsay. 'Events are conspiring to force Debs into Rigano's arms as the obvious and easy villain. Debs is your client. Therefore you'd be failing in your professional duty if you didn't explore every possible avenue to establish her innocence. Isn't that so?'

Judith nodded dubiously. 'I suppose so,' she conceded. 'But it doesn't mean I feel any better about going through with it.' Lindsay treated Judith to a hard stare. The solicitor pursed her lips and said, 'Oh, come on then. If we go now, we'll probably catch her at the office. I think it would be easier from every point of view if we saw her there.'

It took them nearly twenty minutes to reach Alexandra's office thanks to Judith's driving, rendered doubly appalling by her apprehensions about the approaching interview. Her nervousness grew in the fifteen minutes they spent in the waiting room of Hampson, Humphrey and Brundage while Alexandra dealt with her last client of the day. When they were eventually summoned by buzzer, Judith bolted into the office with Lindsay behind her. Barely bigger than a boxroom, Alexandra Phillips's office was dominated by filing cabinets and a standard-sized desk which looked enormous in the confined space.

Yet the surroundings did not diminish its occupant. Alexandra was stunning. Lindsay instantly envied Rupert Crabtree and despised herself for the reaction. The woman who rose to greet them, was, Lindsay estimated, about five foot nine tall. Her hair was a glossy blue-black, cut close to a fine-boned head dominated by almond-shaped luminous brown eyes. Her skin was a healthy glowing golden. Hardly the typical English rose, thought Lindsay. The clothes weren't what she expected either. Alexandra wore a black velvet dress, fitting across the bust, then flaring out to a full swirling skirt. She should have had all the assurance in the world, but it was painfully obvious that self-possession wasn't her long suit. There were black smudges under the eyes and she looked as if tears would be a relief. The exchange of greetings had been on the formal side, and Judith threw a pleading look at Lindsay, expecting her to take over from there.

Lindsay took pity and launched in on an explanation. 'Judith has a client called Deborah Patterson.' Alexandra's eyebrows flickered. 'I can see the name means something to you. Debs is one of my oldest and closest friends and the way things are going at the moment it looks as if she's likely to stand accused of Rupert Crabtree's murder, which I can assure you she did not do. Judith and I are determined to see that the charge won't stick, which is why I'm sticking my nose in where it's not wanted.'

Alexandra looked puzzled. 'I don't actually understand either your status or what you want with me.'

'I'm sorry,' said Lindsay, 'you do deserve a better explanation than that. I've no official status,' she went on. 'I'm a journalist. But as it happens my first concern with this business is not to get good stories but to make sure Debs stays free. I'm also co-operating to some degree with the police on behalf of the women at the peace camp. I find that people don't always want to tell things to the police in case too much emphasis gets placed on the wrong things and innocent people start to appear in a bad light. All I'm trying to do, if you like, is to act as a sort of filter. Anything you want kept within these four walls stays that way until I get the whole picture sorted out and I can be fairly sure of what's important and what isn't.'

'It's called withholding evidence from the police in the circles I move in,' Alexandra countered. 'I still don't understand what brings you to me.'

The last thing Lindsay wanted was to start putting pressure on the young solicitor, but it appeared that in spite of Alexandra's seeming vulnerability, that was what she was going to have to do. 'Rupert Crabtree's will is going to be public knowledge soon. If the police haven't already been here, they will be. And so will reporters from every paper in the land. You can bet your bottom dollar they aren't going to be as polite as me. Now, you can try to stall everyone with this disingenuous routine, but eventually you'll get so sick of it you'll feel like murder.

'Or you can short-circuit a lot of the hassle by talking to me. I'll write a story that doesn't make you look like the Scarlet Woman of Fordham. You can go away for a few days till the fuss dies down. You'll be yesterday's news by then, if you've already talked once. And by talking frankly to me, you can maybe prevent a miscarriage of justice. Now, I know you had been having an affair with Rupert Crabtree for over a year, and I know you were trying to get out of that situation. Suppose you tell me the rest?'

Alexandra buried her head in her hands. When she lifted her face her eyes were glistening. 'Nice to know who your friends are, Judith,' she said bitterly.

'Judith has done the best thing she could for you by bringing me. She could have thrown you to the wolves for the sake of her client, but she did it decently.' Lindsay said with a gentleness that was a sharp contrast to her previous aggression.

'You're not one of the wolves?'

'No way. I'm the pussy cat. Don't think Judith has betrayed you. There will be plenty of others happy to do that over the next few days.'

Alexandra gave a shuddering sigh. 'All right. Yes, I was Rupert's mistress. I'm not in the least ashamed of that.'

'Tell me about him,' Lindsay prompted.

Alexandra looked down at her desk top and spoke softly. 'He was wonderful company, very witty, very warm. He was also a very generous lover. I know you might find it hard to believe that he was a gentle man if all you've heard is the popular mythology. But he was very different when he was with me. I think he found it refreshing to be with a woman who understood the intricacies of the job.'

Lindsay prodded tentatively. 'But still you wanted to end it. Why was that?'

Alexanda shrugged. 'There seemed to be no future in it. He always made it clear that he would never leave his wife, that his domestic life was one he was not unhappy with. Well, I guess I felt that I wanted more from a long-term relationship than dinners in obscure restaurants and illicit meetings when he could fit them in. I loved him, no getting away from that, but I found I needed more from life. And just when I was at that low ebb, I fell in with someone I knew years ago, someone very different from Rupert, and I realised that with him I could have a relationship that held out a bit more hope for permanence.'

'And you told Rupert it was all over?'

Alexandra smiled wryly. 'It's easy to see you didn't know Rupert. He had a phenomenal temper. When he raged, he did it in style. No, I didn't tell him it was all over. What I did say was that I was going to have to start thinking about my long-term future. That one of these days I was going to want children, a full-time husband and father for them, and since Rupert wasn't able to fit the bill, we'd better face the fact that sooner or later I was going to need more.'

'And what was his reaction to that?' Lindsay asked gently.

'He seemed really devastated. I was taken aback. I hadn't realised how deep I went with him. He asked me – he didn't beg or plead, he'd never forget himself that much – he asked me to reconsider my options. He said that recently everything he had put his trust in seemed to have failed him and he didn't want that to happen to us. He said he wanted time to reconsider his future in the light of what I'd said. That was on Saturday. Time's the one thing he never expected not to have. You know how I found out he was dead? I read it in the papers. I'd been sitting watching television while he was being murdered.' Her voice cracked and she turned away from them.

Lindsay found it easy to summon up the set of emotions she'd feel if she read of Cordelia's death in her morning paper. She swallowed, then said, 'I'm sorry to go on pushing you. But I need to know some more. Do you know what he meant when he said everything he'd trusted had failed him? What was he referring to?'

Alexandra blew her nose and wiped her eyes before she turned back towards them. 'He said Simon had let him down. That he wasn't the son he wanted. He sounded very bitter, but wouldn't say what had provoked it. He seldom discussed family matters with me, though he did say a couple of weeks ago that he'd found something out about Ros that had upset him so much he was seriously considering taking his investment out of her restaurant. I asked him what it was because I've known Ros since we were kids, and I suspected he'd finally found out that she's a lesbian.'

'You knew about that?'

'Of course. I was one of the first people she told. I've not seen much of her since then, because

I felt really uncomfortable about it. But I'd never have uttered a word to Rupert about it. I knew what it would do to him. But I suspect that that was at the root of his anger against Ros.

'And he was terribly upset about the Ratepayers' Association. He'd discovered that the treasurer was up to something fishy with the money. Instead of there being a large amount, about seven thousand in the current account, there was barely five hundred pounds. Rupert confronted the treasurer with his discovery, and he couldn't account for the difference satisfactorily. Rupert was convinced he'd been using it to speculate in stocks and shares and line his own pockets. So he was bringing it up at the next meeting which I'm told would have been stormy, with Rupert baying for blood.'

Suddenly her words tripped a connection lurking at the back of Lindsay's brain. The combination of a repeated phrase and a coincidence of figures clicked into place. 'Carlton Stanhope,' she said.

Alexandra looked horrified. 'Who told you?' she demanded. 'No one knew. I made sure no one knew. I wouldn't hurt Rupert like that. Who told you?'

Lindsay smiled ruefully. 'You just did. You were unlucky, that's all. I had a talk with Carlton this morning. He told me the William Mallard story. The figures he gave me were identical to those you gave me, and figures are an area where people are notoriously inaccurate. Also, you used a couple of identical phrases. It had to be you who told him. And the only person you'd be likely to tell would be someone very close to you. By the way, I wouldn't bother trying to hide it from the police. I suspect they already know; it was they who pointed me in his direction as a source of good information on Rupert.'

'If they question me, I'll tell them the truth,' Alexandra said, in control of herself again. 'But I don't want to discuss it with you. I've said more than enough to someone who has no business interfering.'

Lindsay shrugged. 'That's your decision. But there's one more thing I have to ask. It's really important. Was Rupert in the habit of carrying a gun?'

Alexandra looked bewildered. 'A gun?' she demanded incredulously.

'I'm told, a high-standard double-nine point two two revolver, whatever that is. He was carrying it when he was killed.'

Alexandra looked stunned. 'But why? I don't understand. Do you mean he knew he was at risk?'

'It looks like it. Did you know he had a gun? I'm told it was registered to him. Perfectly in order.'

Alexandra shook her head slowly. 'I never saw him with a gun. My God, that's awful. He must have been so afraid. And yet he said nothing about it. Oh, poor, poor Rupert.'

'I'm sorry you had to know,' said Lindsay. 'Look, if you change your mind and want to talk a bit more, you can always reach me through Judith,' she added, moving towards the door.

'Oh, and by the way,' she added as Judith rose to follow her, 'when did you tell Carlton what Rupert had said about rethinking the future? Was it on Saturday night? Or was it Sunday morning?' She didn't wait for the answer she suspected would be a lie. The look of fear in Alexandra's eyes was answer enough.

10

Lindsay drove down the motorway at a speed that would have seemed tame in a modern high-performance car. In the soft-top sports car it was terrifying. Deborah was relieved that Lindsay's lecture on the current state of play was absorbing enough to occupy her brain. 'So you see,' Lindsay complained, 'Alexandra has opened a completely new vista of possibilities. But the more I find out, the less I know. I don't think I'm really cut out for this sort of thing. I can't seem to make sense of any of it.'

'That doesn't sound like you, Lin,' Deborah said with a smile. 'Just be logical about it. We now know there were a fair few people less than fond of Rupert. Let's run through them. Think out loud.'

'Okay,' Lindsay replied. 'One: his son Simon. For reasons unknown, he was in bad odour. It sounds like more than his assertion of the right to independence by opening up his computer firm. But how much more, we don't know. Yet.

'Two: his daughter Ros. For some unspecified reason, Rupert was seriously considering disinvestment. Now that may or may not be an effective weapon in the war against apartheid, but it sure as hell must be a serious threat to a small restaurant just finding its feet. Hopefully tonight will answer our questions about Ros. But the middle classes being what they are, five will get you ten that Daddy's disenchantment with daughter was deviance of the dykey variety.

'Three: Emma Crabtree. Our Rupert marched off on Saturday to think about his future. What we don't know is whether he told Emma about Alexandra; whether he'd decided he wanted a divorce and whether that prospect would have delighted or dismayed a woman who isn't the most obviously grieving widow I've ever encountered. A lot of questions there.

'Four: Alexandra. She's scared of his temper, she's afraid that he's not going to let her go without a very unpleasant fight. And she's had enough of him, she wants Stanhope. Personally, I'm disinclined to suspect her, though she seems to have no alibi. She did genuinely seem too taken aback by the gun to be a real candidate.' She paused to gather her thoughts.

'Go on,' Deborah prompted.

'Five: Carlton Stanhope. Alexandra undoubtedly told him of Crabtree's reaction. He may have figured that making an enemy of as powerful a bastard as Crabtree was not a good move and that murder might even have been preferable. Or it may have been that he felt the one sure way of keeping Alexandra was to get rid of the opposition. Depends how badly he wants Alexandra. I have to say that the bias I feel in her favour operates in the opposite direction as far as he's concerned. I took a real dislike to him, and he's got no alibi either.

'And finally, our two prize beauties from RABD. Mallard might have thought, knowing what a fair man Crabtree was, that his peculations would die with his chairman. And Warminster sounds dotty enough to opt for violence as a means of securing his takeover of RABD. What do you think, Debs?'

Deborah thought for a moment. 'You realise you haven't established opportunity for any of them?'

'That is a bit of a problem. I know the police have been pursuing their own enquiries. Maybe I can persuade Rigano that it's in the best interests of his investigation to swap that info for what I've got. Such as it is. Mind you, by the time I've flammed it up a bit, maybe he'll buy it as a fair exchange.'

'You also left me off the list of suspects. I should be on it.'

Lindsay laughed. 'Even though you didn't do it?'

'You don't know that because of facts. You only

know it because of history and because we're lovers again. Don't discount the theory that I might have seduced you in order to allay your suspicions and get you on the side of my defence. So I should be on that list till you prove I didn't do it.'

Lindsay looked horrified. 'You wouldn't!'

'I might have. If I were a different person.'

'Okay,' Lindsay conceded with a smile. 'But I don't reckon that you had put Rupert Crabtree into such a state of fear that he was carrying a gun to protect himself. He must have been armed because he feared a murderous attack.'

'Or because he intended to kill the person he was meeting.'

Lindsay threw a quick glance at Deborah, caught off guard by this flash of bright logic. She forced herself to examine Deborah's fresh insight.

Eventually, she countered it, tentatively at first and then more assuredly as she reached the end of the motorway and followed the route to Camden Town. 'You see,' she concluded, 'he didn't need to kill you. He was going to get all the revenge he needed in court.'

Deborah pondered, then blew Lindsay's hypothesis into smithereens as they approached Rubyfruits. 'Not necessarily,' she said thoughtfully. 'Everyone says he was a fair man. He also had a degree of respect for the law, being a solicitor. Now, supposing in the aftermath of the shock of the accident, he genuinely thought I had attacked him, and on the basis of that genuine belief he gave the statement to the police that triggered the whole thing off. In the interim, however, as time has passed, his recollection has become clearer and he's realised that he actually tripped over the dog's lead and I had nothing to do with it. Now, what are his options? He either withdraws his evidence and becomes a laughing-stock as well as exposing himself to all sorts of reprisals from a libel suit –'

'Slander,' Lindsay interrupted absently.

'Okay, okay, slander suit, to being accused of wasting police time, all thanks to me. Or he perjures himself, probably an equally unthinkable option for a man like him. His self-esteem is so wounded by this dilemma that he becomes unhinged and decides to kill me in such a way that he can claim self-defence. So he starts carrying the gun, biding his time till he gets me.alone. Think on that one, Lin. Now, we're here. Let's go eat.' And so saying, she jumped out of the car.

Lindsay caught up with her on the cobbled road outside the restaurant which occupied the ground floor of a narrow, three-storey brick building in a dimly lit side street near the trendy Camden Lock complex of boutiques, restaurants and market stalls. It stood between a typesetting company and a warehouse. A red Ford Fiesta turned into the street and they both stepped back to avoid it as it cruised past the restaurant. Lindsay grabbed Deborah's arm. 'As a theory, it's brilliant,' she blurted out. 'But in human terms, it stinks. You didn't do it, Debs.'

Deborah smiled broadly and said, 'Just testing.' She pushed open the door and moved quickly into the restaurant to avoid Lindsay's grasp. They were greeted by a young woman with short blonde hair cut in a spiky crest.

'Hello, Lindsay,' she said cheerfully. 'I kept you a nice table over in the corner.'

'Thanks, Meg.' They followed her, Lindsay saying, 'This is Debs, Meg. She's an old friend of mine.'

'Hi Debs. Nice to meet you. Okay. Here's the menu, wine list. Today's specials are on the blackboard, okay?' And she was gone, moving swiftly from table to table, clearing and chatting all the way to the swing doors leading into the kitchen.

Deborah looked around, taking in the stripped pine, the moss green walls and ceiling and the huge photographs ranging predictably from Virginia Woolf to Virginia Wade. She noticed that the cutlery and crockery on each table was different and appeared to have come from junk shops and flea markets. The background music was Rickie Lee Jones turned low. The other tables were also occupied by women. 'I can just see you and Cordelia here,' Deborah commented. 'Very designer dyke.'

'Cut the crap and choose your grub,' Lindsay ordered.

'Get you,' muttered Deborah. They studied the

menus and settled for Avocado Rubyfruits. ('Slices of ripe avocado interleaved with slices of succulent Sharon fruit, garnished with watercress, bathed in a raspberry vinaigrette') followed by Butter Beanfeast ('Butter beans braised with organically grown onions, green peppers and chives, smothered in a rich cheese sauce, topped with a *gratinée* of stoneground wholemeal breadcrumbs and traditional farm cheddar cheese') with choose-your-own salads from a wide range of the homely and the exotic colourfully displayed on a long narrow table at the rear of the room. To drink Lindsay selected a bottle of gooseberry champagne.

'My God,' Deborah exploded quietly when Meg departed with the order, 'I hadn't realised how far pretentiousness had penetrated the world of healthy eating. This is so over the top, Lin. Are there really enough right-on vegetarian women around to make this place a going concern?'

'Don't be too ready to slag it off. The food is actually terrific. Just relax and enjoy it,' Lindsay pleaded.

Deborah shook her head in affectionate acceptance and sat back in her chair. 'Now tell me,' she demanded, 'Since you hang out so much in this bijou dinette, how come you don't have the same intimate relationship with Ros Crabtree that you have with Meg?'

'It's very simple. Meg runs around serving at table. Meg answers the phone when you book.

Meg stands and natters over your coffee. Ros, on the other hand, must be grafting away in the kitchen five nights a week. She's too busy cooking to socialise, even with people she knows. And by the end of the evening, I'd guess she's too exhausted to be bothered making polite social chit-chat with the customers. It's hard work cooking for vegetarians. There's so much more preparation in Butter Beanfeast than in Steak au Poivre.'

Before Deborah could reply, their avocados appeared. Deborah tried her food suspiciously, then her face lit up. 'Hey this is really good,' she exclaimed.

When Meg returned to clear their plates and serve the champagne, Lindsay made her move.

'That was terrific, Meg. Listen, we'd like to have a word with Ros. Not right now, obviously, but when she's through in the kitchen. Do you think that'll be okay?'

Meg looked surprised. 'I suppose so. But . . . what's it all about, Lindsay? Oh, wait a minute . . . You're a reporter, aren't you?' Her voice had developed a hostile edge. 'It's about her father, isn't it?'

'It's not what you think,' Deborah protested. 'She's not some cheap hack out to do a hatchet job on you and Ros. You know her, for God's sake, she's one of us.'

'So what *is* it all about then?' The anger in her voice transmitted itself to nearby tables, where a few faces looked up and studied them curiously.

Deborah took a deep breath. 'I'm their number one suspect. I've already had one night in the police cells and I don't fancy another. Lindsay's trying her damnedest to get me off the hook and that means discovering the real killer. I'd have thought you and Ros would be interested in finding out who killed her father.'

'Him? The only reason I'd want to know who killed him is so that I could shake them by the hand. Look, I'm not too impressed with what you've got to say for yourselves, but I will go ask Ros if she'll talk to you.' She marched off and returned a few minutes later with their main courses, which she placed meticulously before them without a word.

They ate in virtual silence, their enjoyment dulled. Meg silently removed their plates and took their order for biscuits, cheese and coffee.

By half past ten and the third cup of coffee, Lindsay was beginning to despair of any further communication from the kitchen. The tension had dried up conversation between her and Deborah. The evening she'd been looking forward to had somehow become awkward and difficult. Then, a tall, broad woman emerged from the kitchen and exchanged a few words with Meg, who nodded in their direction. The woman crossed the room towards them. She was bulky, but she looked strong and sturdy rather than flabby. Her hair was short and curly, her face pink from the heat of the kitchen. Like her brother, Ros Crabtree strongly resembled their father. She wore a pair of chef's trousers and a navy blue polo shirt. In her hand was a brandy bowl with a large slug of spirit sobbing up the sides of the glass.

She pulled a chair up and said without preamble, 'So this is the sleuth. The famous Cordelia Brown's girlfriend. Accompanied, unless I am mistaken, by the brutal peace woman who goes around beating up helpless men.' She smiled generously. 'Enjoy your dinner?'

'As always,' Lindsay answered, stung by being defined as an adjunct to Cordelia.

'But tonight you came for more than three courses and a bottle of country wine.'

'We hoped you would help us,' Deborah stated baldly. 'Lindsay's trying to clear my name. I'm afraid that if there isn't an arrest soon, I'll be charged, just so they can be seen to be achieving something.'

'We also thought you would have an interest in seeing your father's killer arrested,' Lindsay added.

Ros laughed. 'Look, I have no feelings about my father one way or the other. I neither loved him nor hated him but I'm sorry about the way he died. I was glad to be out of his house but frankly, the notion of getting some atavistic revenge on the person who killed him leaves me unmoved. You're wasting your time here.'

Lindsay shrugged. 'So if it matters that little to you, why not talk to me, answer my questions? It could make a lot of difference to Debs.'

'I can't think of anything I could tell you that would be of the slightest use. But I suppose I owe something to the woman who cost my father his precious dignity and a broken nose. Oh, the hell with it, ask what you want. If I feel like answering, I will.' She swallowed a generous mouthful of brandy, seemingly relaxed.

'I'll ask the obvious question first. Where were you on Sunday night between ten p.m. and midnight?' Lindsay asked.

'Oh dear, oh dear, we have been reading all the snobbery with violence detective novels, haven't we?' The mockery in Ros's voice was still good-natured, but it was obvious that the veneer was wearing thin. 'I was here on Sunday night. We have a flat above the restaurant. I think I was reading till about eleven. Then I went to bed and I was woken up just after midnight when my mother phoned to tell me about my father's death.'

'I suppose Meg can back you up?'

'As it happens, no. Meg was on her way back from Southampton. She'd been visiting her parents. She didn't get home till about half past midnight. So I don't have much of an alibi, do I? No one phoned till mother, I phoned no one. You'll just have to take my word for it.' She grinned broadly.

'I'm surprised you didn't go down to Brownlow as soon as you heard the news. I mean, with your mother to comfort and all that . . . ?' Lindsay sounded offhand.

'Acting nonchalant cuts no ice with me, darling. I can spot the heavy questions without you signposting them. Why didn't I dash off home to Mummy? For one thing, I have a business to run. On Mondays, I go to the market and see what's looking good. On that basis I plan the special dishes for the week. We also do all the book-keeping and paperwork on Mondays. I simply couldn't just vanish for the day. It'll be hard enough fitting the funeral in. That's not as callous as it sounds. My father cared about this business too. But more importantly than all of that, I'm not at all sure I'd be the person to comfort my mother.'

'Why's that?'

'Because I'm not the weepy, sentimental sort. I'm far too bloody brisk to be much of a shoulder to cry on. I'm afraid I'd be more inclined to tell her to pull herself together than to provide tea and sympathy.

'So it's nothing to do with her attitudes to you being a lesbian? Oh, but of course, they didn't know, did they? Or so Carlton Stanhope reckons. Mind you, I always figure that parents know a lot more than they let on,' said Lindsay, her eyes on a distant corner of the room.

'You've talked to Carl?' Suddenly Ros had become guarded.

'He sends his best wishes. He's seeing Alexandra Phillips these days, you know,' Lindsay replied.

'How nice for him. She used to be a lovely girl when I knew her. I hope she treats him better than I did. Poor Carl,' she said ruefully. 'But to go back to what he said to you. He was right, as far as he was aware. They really didn't know. I'd kept it well under wraps. Let me explain the history. After I'd decided my career lay in the catering trade, my father was always keen that I should set up in business on my own when I'd done the training and got the experience. Meg and I did a proper business plan based on the costings for this place and I presented it to him as a good investment. He lent me twenty thousand pounds at a nominal rate of interest so we could get the project off the ground. He'd never have done that much if he'd even suspected. I suppose my cover was never blown because I'd spent so much time studying and working away from home, and when I was home, there were always old friends like Carl around to provide protective colouring. It was really funny when we launched Rubyfruits – we had to have two opening nights. One with lots of straight friends that we could invite the parents to and another with the real clientele.'

Lindsay lit a cigarette. 'It sounds like you had a lot to be grateful to him for?'

Ros shrugged. 'In some ways. But we were

never really close. He was always at arm's length, somehow. With all of us. As if his real life happened somewhere else. The office, I suppose. Or one of his causes.' The edge of bitterness in her voice was apparent even to Ros herself. She softened her tone and added, 'But I guess I owe this place to him. I'm sorry he's dead.'

'Then he didn't carry out his threat to take his money back?' Lindsay's casual words dropped into a sudden well of silence. Ros's face wouldn't have looked out of place on Easter Island.

'I have no idea what you're talking about,' she declared. 'No idea at all.'

'I'm told that he'd recently become disillusioned with you, that he was minded to take his money out of this business as a token of his disappointment. You really should tell me about it in case I go away with the wrong idea. And you not having much of an alibi. My news editor would like that story a lot.'

Ros stared hard at Lindsay. 'Well, well,' she muttered bitterly, 'So much for lesbian solidarity. You're not the pushover I took you for, are you? Fancy me thinking that anyone who tagged along on Cordelia's coat-tails could be toothless. All right. Since you obviously know enough to make a bloody nuisance of yourself, I'd better tell you the rest.

'Ten days ago I had a phone call from my father. He informed me that he was instructing his bankers to recover the twenty thousand he'd loaned me. He refused to say why, or even to say anything else. So I rang my mother to see if she knew what the hell was going on. And she wouldn't say either.

'So I jumped on the bike and bombed down to the old homestead where I squeezed out of Mamma what it was all about. To cut a long story short, it was all down to my perfectly bloody little brother. You know he's got this business in computer software? Well, he had to start it on a shoestring, against my father's advice. Father wanted different things for Simon, and that was the end of the story as far as he was concerned. He wouldn't even listen when one of Simon's teachers came to see him and told us that Simon was the best computer programmer he'd ever encountered. Apparently, he was hacking into other people's systems by the time he was in the third form. Anyway, Simon got off the ground somehow and he's at the stage now where it's make or break, expand or fold, and he needs an injection of cash. God knows where he got the money to get this far, but he was determined that the next chunk of capital should come from Father, on the basis that he'd lent me money for the business and it was only right that he should do the same for Simon.

'Dad refused absolutely. He said I'd proved myself, which Simon still had to do before he could come chasing around for hard-earned handouts. Mum said they were going at it hammer and tongs then Simon blew a fuse and said something along the lines of how appalling it was that Father was prepared to finance a pair of lesbians running a restaurant for queers and he wouldn't finance his only son in a legitimate business. Mum says there was a ghastly silence then Simon walked out. Father apparently wouldn't say a thing, just went off in the car. She thinks he came up here to see for himself. And the next day – bombshell.'

'I thought it must have been something like that,' Lindsay said. 'So I suppose that put you right in the cart.'

'Until the death of my father, that's what you're getting at, isn't it? Not quite that easy, I'm afraid. You see, we've been doing better than we projected. It knocked some of our personal plans on the head, like new furniture for the flat, but we've simply transferred to a bank loan. We can just afford the extra interest. Any money from my father's will, unless he's cut me out of that too, will be an absolute godsend, there's no getting away from that. But we could have managed without it. I had no need to kill him. Now, you've got what you came for. Is there anything else before I get you the bill?'

'Just one thing. Any idea why your father was carrying a gun?'

'Carrying a gun? I knew nothing about that. No one said anything to me about a gun!'

'The police are trying to keep it fairly quiet. A point two two revolver.'

'I can't begin to think why he had his gun with him. He used to be a member of a small-arms shooting club at Middle Walberley. But he hadn't been for . . . oh God, it must be eight years. He gave it up because he didn't have time enough for practising and he could never bear to do anything unless he did it to perfection. I didn't even know he'd kept his gun. I can't believe he had enemies – I mean, not the sort you'd have to arm yourself against. Wow, that really is weird.' For the first time, she looked upset. 'Somebody must have really got to him. That's horrible.' She swallowed the remains of her brandy and got to her feet. 'I'll get Meg to bring your bill.' She vanished through the swing door at the back of the restaurant followed by Meg, whose eyes had never left them during the interview.

Lindsay rubbed her forehead with her fingertips. Deborah reached out and took her hand. Before they could speak, Meg re-emerged from the kitchen and strode over to them. By now, they were the centre of attention for the few diners remaining. 'Have this meal on me,' Meg said angrily. 'Just so long as you don't come back here again. Now go. I mean it, Lindsay. Just get out!'

11

The head office of Mallard and Martin, Estate Agents, Auctioneers and Valuers, was at the far end of the main street in Fordham. The retail developers who have turned every British high street into undistinguished and indistinguishable shopping malls had not yet penetrated that far down the street, and the double-fronted office looked old-fashioned enough to appeal to the most conservative in the district. Lindsay, dressed to match the office in her new outfit, studied the properties in the window with curiosity. She noticed several houses in the vicinity of Brownlow Common were up for sale. But their prices didn't seem to be significantly lower than comparable houses in other areas. She pushed open the door and as she entered, a sleek young woman in a fashionably sharp suit rose and came over to the high wooden counter.

'Can I help you?' she enquired.

'I'm due to see Mr Mallard,' Lindsay explained. 'My name's Lindsay Gordon.'

'Oh yes, he's expecting you. Do come through.' The woman raised a flap in the counter and showed Lindsay through into Mallard's own office. He got up as Lindsay was ushered in and genially indicated a chair. Mallard was a short, chubby man in his fifties, almost completely bald. He wore large, gold-rimmed spectacles and tufts of grey hair stuck out above his ears, making him look like a rather cherubic owl. He smiled winningly at Lindsay. 'Now, young lady,' he said cheerfully, 'you're a reporter, I think you said?'

'That's right. But I'm not just looking for stories. I believe Carlton Stanhope rang to pass on Superintendent Rigano's request?'

'He did indeed.' He smiled. 'Always delighted to help an attractive young lady like yourself. Mr Stanhope tells me you've been able to give the police some assistance concerning dear Rupert's death? A dreadful tragedy, quite, quite dreadful.'

Lindsay decided she did not care for this bouncing chauvinist piglet. But his seeming garrulity might be something she could turn to her advantage. She smiled at him. 'Absolutely. I have been able to come up with some quite useful information so far. And of course, not all of it is passed directly to the police. I mean, a lot emerges in these affairs that has no bearing on the main issue. It would be a pity to cloud matters with irrelevant information, wouldn't it? So if people are open with me, I can often get to the bottom of things that would otherwise cause a lot of wasted police time. If you see what I mean?' She let the question hang in the air.

'So you want to find out how well I knew Rupert, who his friends were, if he made enemies through RABD, that sort of thing? That's what Mr Stanhope said,' Mallard replied hastily.

'Not exactly,' Lindsay replied. 'Though I would like to look through the RABD records. I think Mr Stanhope arranged that with you?'

Mallard nodded vigorously. 'They're all upstairs in a little office I put at the disposal of the organisation. You can take as long as you want, you'll have the place to yourself. We've got nothing to hide, you know, though obviously we don't want our future plans made public. That would put an end to our strategies against those . . . those harpies down there,' he said, his geniality slipping as he referred to the peace women.

'I rather thought there were one or two matters you'd prefer to keep to yourself, Mr Mallard,' Lindsay remarked idly.

'No, no, we're not at all secretive. We're perfectly open, no conspiracies here.'

An odd thing to say, Lindsay thought. 'No conspiracies, perhaps, but one or two disagreements.'

'Disagreements?' He looked apprehensive.

'Paul Warminster?'

'Oh, that,' he muttered, looking uncomfortable.

'Yes, that was a little unfortunate. But then, it only supports what I was saying to you about being open. We're not extremists in RABD, just people concerned about our local community and the environment our families live in. We don't want to be involved in anything at all violent. That's what Paul Warminster felt we should be doing. He wanted us to be some kind of vigilante band, driving these awful women away by force. We were glad Rupert had the strength to stand up to him. That sort of woman isn't going to go away because you throw them out physically. If we'd gone ahead and taken violent action, the next day there would have been twice as many of them. No, Rupert was right.'

'And do you think Paul Warminster resented what he did?'

'No question about that, young lady. He was furious.'

'Furious enough for murder?'

Mallard's smile this time was sickly. 'I'm sure nobody in our circle, not even someone with Paul Warminster's views, would resort to murder.' He made it sound like a social solecism.

'But someone in Rupert Crabtree's circle did just that.'

Mallard shook his head. 'No. Those women are to blame. It certainly wasn't Paul Warminster. He had nothing to gain. Even with Rupert out of the way, he'll never win control of RABD and its membership. He must know that. He's not a fool.'

'I'm happy to take your word for it,' Lindsay flattered. 'Now, if I might see those papers?' She got to her feet.

'Of course, of course,' he said, rising and bustling her out of the room. They climbed two flights of stairs, Mallard chatting continuously about the property market and the deplorable effect the peace camp was having on house prices in the neighbourhood of the common.

'But houses at Brownlow seem about the same price as similar houses near by,' Lindsay commented.

'Oh yes, but they used to be the most highly sought after in the area, and the most expensive. Now it takes a lot of persuasion to shift them. Well, here we are.'

They entered a small office containing a battered desk, several upright chairs and a filing cabinet. 'Here you are, m'dear,' Mallard waved vaguely around him. He unlocked the filing cabinet. 'Chairman's files and my files in the top drawers. Minutes in the second. Correspondence in the third and stationery in the bottom drawer. Look at anything you please, we've no guilty secrets.'

'Will you be in your office for a while? I might come across some things I want to clarify.'

'Of course, of course. I shall be there till half past twelve. I'm sure you'll be finished by then. I'm at your disposal.' He twinkled another seemingly sincere smile at her and vanished downstairs.

Lindsay sighed deeply and extracted two bulging manila folders from the top drawer of the filing cabinet. They were both labelled 'Ratepayers Against Brownlow's Destruction. Chairman's File'. In red pen, the same hand had written '1' and '2' on them. She sat down at the desk and opened her briefcase. She took out a large notepad, pen and her Walkman. She slotted in a Django Reinhardt tape and started to plough through the papers.

The first file yielded nothing that Lindsay could see. She stuffed the papers back into it and opened the second file. As she pulled the documents out, a cassette tape clattered on to the desk. Curious, she picked it up. The handwritten label, not in Crabtree's by now familiar script, said, 'Sting: *The Dream of The Blue Turtles*'. Surprised, Lindsay put it to one side and carried on working. When her own tape reached the end, she decided to have a change and inserted the Sting tape. But instead of the familiar opening chords she heard an alien sequence of hisses, bleeps and sounds like radio interference. Lindsay knew very little about information technology. But she knew enough to realise that although this tape was mislabelled, it was actually a computer programme on tape. And fed into the right computer, it might explain precisely what it was doing in Rupert Crabtree's RABD file. She remembered the computers she had seen downstairs and wondered if that was where

Mallard stored the real information about RABD's finances.

She worked her way quickly through the financial records, making a few notes as she went. It seemed to be in order, though the book-keeping system seemed unnecessarily complex. Finally she skimmed through the minutes and correspondence. 'Waste of bloody time,' she muttered to herself as she neatly replaced everything. The cassette tape caught her eye, and she wondered again if it might hold the key to the questions Crabtree had been asking about money. She threw the computer tape into her briefcase along with her own bits and pieces and headed downstairs for the confrontation she'd been geared up to since breakfast. As she rounded the corner of the stairs, she noticed a man coming out of Mallard's office. From above, she could see little except the top of his head of greying, gingery hair and the shoulders of his tweed jacket. By the time she reached the bottom of the stairs, he had gone.

Mallard's office door was ajar and she stuck her head round. 'Can I come in?' she asked.

'Of course, of course, m'dear,' he answered her, beaming. 'I expect you've had a very boring morning with our papers.'

'It has been hard work,' Lindsay admitted. 'I'm surprised you haven't got the lot on computer, with Simon Crabtree being in that line of business.'

Mallard nodded. 'Couldn't agree more, m'dear.

But Rupert wouldn't hear of it. Lawyers, you see. Very conservative in their methods. Not like us. Our front office may look very traditional. But all the work gets done in the big office at the back – where our computers are. The latest thing – IBM-compatible hard-disk drives. I actually bought them on Simon's advice. But Rupert didn't trust them. He said you could lose all your work at the touch of a button and he felt happier with bits of paper that didn't vanish into thin air. Typical lawyer – wanted everything in black and white.'

'There was one other thing I wanted to ask you about.'

'Ask away, m'dear, ask away.'

'Why was Rupert Crabtree going to raise your handling of RABD funds at the next meeting?'

Mallard flushed, but managed to freeze his smile in place as he replied, 'Was he?'

'You know he was. The two of you had a row about it, and he said the association should decide.'

'I don't know where you've got your information from, young lady, but I can assure you nothing of the sort took place.' Mallard attempted to stand on his dignity. 'We had a very harmonious relationship.'

'Not according to my sources. Two separate people have told me the whole story, and I believe the police are aware of it. I already have enough to write a story. It's obviously doing the rounds locally. Hadn't you better put the record straight, give me your version of events before your reputation gets shredded beyond repair?'

He dropped the geniality and looked shrewdly at Lindsay. 'Young lady, even if *you* seem blissfully unaware, I'm sure your newspaper has lawyers who understand all about libel. If you are thinking of printing any sort of story about me, you had better be extremely careful.'

'We don't have to print a story about you for your reputation to be destroyed. Local gossip will see to that. All I have to write is that police are investigating alleged misappropriation of funds by one of the officials of a local organisation in connection with Rupert Crabtree's death,' Lindsay replied.

Mallard paused, sizing her up. Then, after a long enough pause to render himself unconvincing, he smiled again and said, 'Really, there's no need for all of this. I've told you that we've got nothing to hide in RABD. That goes for me personally too. Now, you've obviously heard some grossly distorted version of a conversation between Rupert and me. There's no reason on earth why I should attempt to explain to you, but because I'm concerned there should be no misunderstanding, I'll tell you all about it.

'We hold a substantial amount of money on behalf of our members. Most of it is for legal expenses and printing costs. As treasurer, I'm responsible for the money, and I know how important it is these days to make money work. Obviously, the more money we have, the better able we are to fight the good fight. Now, Rupert was checking something on the bank statements and he realised there was far less in the account than he thought there should be. He was always prone to jump to conclusions, so he came round here in a great taking-on, demanding to know where the money was. I explained that I had moved it into the currency markets, an area I know rather a lot about. I was simply maximising our returns. Rupert was perfectly satisfied with my explanation. And so he should have been since I had succeeded in making a substantial profit.'

'Then why was he raising the matter at the next meeting?'

'Why? So that I could pass on the good news to the membership, of course. Rupert felt it was a matter for congratulation, m'dear.'

His glibness lowered his credibility still further in Lindsay's eyes. She was determined to get him on the run, and she racked her brains to find some leverage in what Stanhope or Alexandra had said. 'But how did you move the money without Crabtree's knowledge? Surely that needed his signature?'

A momentary gleam of hatred flashed at Lindsay. 'Of course, of course, my dear girl. But Rupert had actually signed it among a pile of other papers for his signature and had simply not registered what it was. Easy to do that when you're signing several bits of paper.'

'I wouldn't have thought that was the action of a conscientious lawyer. But you seem to have an answer for everything, Mr Mallard.'

His smile was genuine this time. 'That's because I have nothing to hide, m'dear. Now, if that is all, I do have work to do . . .'

'One more thing. Since you've nothing to hide, perhaps you could tell me where you were on Sunday night from about ten?'

This time, Mallard couldn't keep the smile in place. 'That's none of your business,' he snapped.

'You're right. But I expect you've told the police already? No? Oh well, I'm sure they'll be round soon to ask. Superintendent Rigano's very interested in who I've been talking to . . .'

Lindsay felt she was doing battle. Mallard gave in. 'I was at home all evening.'

'Which is where, exactly?'

He shifted in his seat. 'Brownlow Common Cottages. Four doors away from the Crabtrees actually.'

Lindsay smiled. 'Convenient. Alone, were you?'

He shook his head. 'My wife was in. She . . . she almost always *is* in. She has MS, you see, confined to a wheelchair.'

Nothing's ever simple, thought Lindsay. Poor woman, stuck in a wheelchair with him. She waited, then he went on. He was clearly a man who felt uncomfortable with silence.

'I put her to bed about ten. So her evidence after that could only be negative – that she didn't hear me go out or come in, that she didn't hear my car. I have no idea why I'm telling you all this,' he added petulantly.

'Haven't you, Mr Mallard?' Lindsay enquired. 'Thanks very much for your time.' She abruptly rose and walked out. The woman in the front office looked up in surprise as she swept through. Lindsay marched down the main street to the car park where she'd left the MG, irritated that she hadn't broken Mallard's self-possession. She hadn't even thought to ask him who he thought the murderer was. But she knew deep down that the only answer she would have received was the utterly predictable one: 'those peace women'. And that would have made no difference to her own gut reaction to Mallard, namely that of all the people she'd spoken to so far, he was her favourite suspect. He had opportunity, she'd established that. He looked sturdy enough to cope with the means. And he had motive aplenty. A rumour with Rupert Crabtree behind it would be enough to terminate a man's career in a small town like Fordham when that career depended on trust. And Mallard clearly couldn't afford that, especially not with a wife whose disability gave him another pressing reason for maintaining a comfortable lifestyle.

She drove off, checking her mirrors for Rigano's blond SB man. There was no sign of the red Fiesta.

She pulled into the traffic to keep the appointment she'd made with Paul Warminster and following his directions, left Fordham in the opposite direction to Brownlow. Surburban streets gave way to more rural surroundings. Chocolate-box countryside, thought Lindsay, struck as she was occasionally with a sharp pang of longing for the sea lochs and mountains of her native landscape. A couple of miles out of the town, she pulled off the main road into a narrow country lane. Soon she came to a thatched cottage attached to a converted cruck barn. The garden was a mass of daffodils and crocuses with occasional patches of bright blue scilla. A powerful motorbike was parked incongrously by the side of the barn. Lindsay got out of the car and walked up a path made of old weathered brick.

The door was opened by a tall spare man in his late forties. His gingery hair was lank and greying, his face weather-beaten to an unattractive turkey red and a network of fine lines radiated from the corners of his lively blue eyes. In his tweed jacket with the leather patches he looked more like a gamekeeper than a shopkeeper. With a sudden shock, Lindsay realised this was the man she had seen leaving Mallard's office a short time earlier. Covering her confusion, she quickly introduced herself and established her bona fides with her Press card. Warminster ushered her into a chintzy, low-ceilinged living room with bowls of sweet-smelling freesias scattered around.

'So, you're writing about what local people are doing to put a stop to that so-called peace camp,' he said, settling himself in a large armchair.

Lindsay nodded. 'I understand you've been quite actively involved in the opposition.'

Warminster lit a small cigar as he replied. 'Used to be. Probably will be again soon.' 'Why is that?' Lindsay asked. 'Had a bit of a run-in with that chap Crabtree, the fellow who was murdered at the weekend, so I hadn't been doing too much lately. Blighter thought he ran Fordham. Perhaps now we'll really get to grips with those left-wing lesbians,' he said.

'You weren't happy with the policies of Ratepayers Against Brownlow's Destruction, then?' Lindsay probed.

He snorted. 'Could say that. Policies? Appeasement, that's what they were about. And look where that got us in the thirties. We should have been taking the war into their territory, getting them out of their entrenched positions instead of pussyfooting around being nicey-nicey to those bloody communist harridans.' Warminster was off and running in what were clearly not fresh fields. As she listened to the tirade, trying to control her feelings of disgust and anger, Lindsay gradually began to understand why violence so often seems a solution.

She pretended to take extensive notes of his speech. There was no need to interrogate Warminster. The only difficulty was getting him to stop. Eventually, he ended up with a rabble-rousing peroration. 'Very stirring, sir,' Lindsay muttered.

'You think so? That's exactly what I told them on Sunday night in Berksbury. I was speaking there, you know, at the instigation of the local Conservative Party. They staged one of those debates about the issues. Had some woolly vicar in a woolly pullover from CND, the local candidate and me. Well worth the trip, I can tell you.'

Lindsay's mind had leapt to attention as soon as Sunday was mentioned. 'That was Sunday night just past?' she asked. 'The night Crabtree was killed, you mean?'

'That's right. Round about when he bought it, we were having a celebratory drink in the Conservative Club. An excellent night. Didn't get home till the small hours. I must say the hospitality was excellent. Good job I'd taken my wife along to drive me home or I'd never have made it. Sorry she's not in, by the way, gone to visit her sister in Fordham. Now, anything else you want to know.'

It all seemed so innocent. And the alibi appeared sound. But Lindsay didn't like what her instincts told her about Paul Warminster. 'I see you've got a motorbike outside. Have you ever come across any of those yobs that have been attacking the peace camp?'

He looked startled. 'Of course not,' he said. 'Why should I have?'

Lindsay shrugged. 'I just wondered. I thought since you were into direct action they might have made contact with you.'

Warminster shook his head violently. 'Absolutely not. Ill-disciplined rabble.'

'How do you know that?' Lindsay demanded, pouncing on the inconsistency.

'How do I know what?'

'That they're ill disciplined. If you've got nothing to do with them, how do you know that?'

He looked angry and flustered. 'Heard about it, didn't I? Small place, Fordham, you hear things. Absurd of you to think I'd have anything to do with them. Nearly as incompetent as the RABD softies.'

'But you obviously maintain contact with some of your friends in RABD,' Lindsay probed.

'What d'you mean by that?' he was now deeply suspicious. His hostility was tipping him over the borderline of rudeness.

'I thought I saw you this morning coming out of William Mallard's office,' she said.

'So? The man runs a business. I do business in Fordham. Hardly surprising that we do business together, is it? I can't turn my back on every liberal I meet just because I don't agree with their way of going about things.'

Lindsay shook her head. 'There's no need to get so het up, Mr Warminster. I just wondered if the business you were doing with Mr Mallard was anything to do with the funding of your direct action group.'

Her barb hit home. Warminster, leaving high spots of colour in his cheeks. 'Rubbish,' he blustered, 'absolute rubbish. Now, if you've nothing more to ask me, I'd be obliged if you'd let me get on. I'm a very busy man.' He got to his feet, leaving Lindsay little choice but to follow suit. Standing in the doorway he watched her into her car then turned back into the house as she drove away.

An interesting encounter, thought Lindsay. Warminster might have a rock-solid alibi for Sunday night but a tie-in between himself, Mallard and the bikers looked suspiciously probable. It seemed likely to Lindsay that someone had put those bikers up to their attacks on the camp. If it had been only a single incident, it could have been written off as drunken hooliganism. But the concerted attacks of firebombing, blood-throwing and damage to the benders looked like something more sinister. And youths like that wouldn't take those chances without some kind of incentive. Money was the obvious choice. The destination of Mallard's funny money now seemed clear too. Driving thoughtfully back to Brownlow Common, Lindsay wondered just how much it would cost to persuade a bloodthirsty biker to make the escalation from fire-bombing to murder.

12

As Lindsay joined the tight group round the smoky fire, the conversation faltered. Nicky glowered at her and turned away, but Willow moved to one side of the crate she was sitting on and offered Lindsay a place. 'We were just sorting out an action for tonight,' Deborah said rather too brightly.

'So you'd better rush off and tell your tame policeman,' Nicky muttered loudly.

Lindsay ignored the hostility with difficulty, since it triggered her own qualms of conscience about dealing with Rigano, and asked what was planned. Willow explained. 'A few of the women were in court yesterday for non-payment of fines and they've been sent to Holloway as per usual. So we're having a candle-lit procession and silent vigil round the wire tonight. There's a couple of coachloads coming down from London. It might be quite a big action – we've tipped off the TV and radio news so we'll get some publicity.'

'And with all you journalists kicking round

looking for titbits about that creep Crabtree we might even get some decent newspaper publicity for a change,' added Nicky bitterly.

'I shouldn't think so,' Lindsay replied acidly. 'Why should a candle-lit procession alter all our preconceived notions? You don't still believe in Santa Claus, do you, Nicky?'

'Oh, stop it, you two,' protested Deborah. 'You're like a pair of kids. If you've nothing constructive to say to each other, then don't waste your breath and our time.'

Lindsay got to her feet. 'I've got to do some work now, but I'll be back for the demo. What time's it all starting?'

'About seven,' Deborah answered. 'meet me at Gate Six, near Brownlow Common Cottages. Will you pass the word on to the other reporters if you see them?'

'Sure,' Lindsay said. 'If that's not too much like consorting with the enemy.'

Deborah gave her a warning look and she grinned back at her as she set off for the van. Lindsay dumped her notebook on the table that dropped down and slotted into the long L-shaped bench at night to form the base of the bed. She opened the tiny fridge set next to the two-ring gas cooker and grill, and took out a pint of milk. She swigged a couple of mouthfuls, then sat down to work. She felt comfortable in the van, a big Ford Transit conversion with enough room to stand up and move around in.

She started to scribble down the outline of her story about the in-fighting in RABD with a sneaking feeling that she'd be lucky to get it into the paper. At the end of the day, it was just a rather silly story about a bunch of grown men behaving like schoolboys, and she suspected that Duncan's sharp news sense would come to the same conclusion. Her growing suspicion that William Mallard was somehow implicated in the murder of Rupert Crabtree was not something she could commit to paper yet. Till then, the RABD story was all she had. At least it was exclusive.

She set off for Fordham, in the MG, on a search for a phone box from which to file her copy. As she drove she remembered the computer tape she'd thrust into her briefcase. It occurred to her that she'd have to find out what computer system Simon Crabtree worked with so she could unravel the contents of the tape, since he'd sorted out Mallard's computers in the first place. The obvious way to find out was to pay a visit to his lockup garage. But that meant another fencing session with Rigano first.

Finding an empty phone box on the outskirts of the town she read over her copy laboriously, silently wishing for the next phase in computer technology that would reduce the transmission of stories to a few seconds of telephone time, thanks to portable remote terminals. The copy transmitted, she spoke to Duncan, telling him about the evening's procession at the base and squeezing from him agreement that she should file copy on it later.

She rang Rigano. After a long delay that involved explaining her identity to the switchboard, the duty officer and Rigano's sergeant, she was finally connected to her contact. He was abrupt to the point of rudeness. 'What is it?' he demanded.

'I need some help,' Lindsay replied.

'So what's new? What do you need?'

'Just an address. Simon Crabtree's computer workshop. I want to talk to him on his own territory.'

'Try the phone book. I thought you were supposed to be full of initiative.'

'I can't try the phone book if I don't know what the company's called, can I?'

There was a brief pause. 'Okay. I'll leave a note for you at the front counter. I want to talk to you about what you've been up to. I suspect there's a lot you could tell me that you haven't been passing on. Ring me tomorrow morning before ten,' he said and put the phone down.

Puzzled and irritated at having to make a detour to the police station, Lindsay set off. Why didn't Rigano just give her the address over the phone? Why go to all the bother of leaving a note for her to pick up? It surely couldn't be an excuse to get her into the station so he could interview her or he wouldn't have made the arrangement for the next day's phone call. Unless that was a red herring . . . There seemed to be no easy answer.

The envelope she collected from the reception desk in Fordham police station fifteen minutes later, contained the address neatly hand written: Megamenu Software, Unit 23, Harrison Mews, Fordham. Lindsay checked the index on the street map she'd bought. No Harrison Mews, but a Harrison Street on the seedier side of town, near the industrial estate. The mews would probably be an alley round the back, she speculated.

She put the car into gear and routinely checked her rear mirror. What she saw nearly caused an accident. The red Ford Fiesta, driven by the man whom she had labelled Special Branch and who seemed a semi-permanent feature of her landscape was right behind. Lindsay shot into the traffic without signalling and cursed her lack of familiarity with the terrain. While she concentrated on finding her route across the town centre, she was aware of the Fiesta two cars behind her, and an explanation for Rigano's perplexing telephone manner dawned on her. The man now on her tail might have been with Rigano when she called, which begged the more disturbing question: had Rigano lured her into the station just so that the Special Branch man could follow her? And if so, why was the SB interested in a routine murder? And more importantly, why the hell were they so interested in her?

The heaviness of the traffic and the search for

her destination forced her to shelve the question. But as she pulled into a back alley with a roughly painted signboard saying 'Harrison Mews: Megamenu Software this way', she noticed the red hatchback drive slowly past the narrow entrance. She parked the car up against the wall opposite Unit 23 and pondered. If the blond man was SB, then it went a long way towards explaining why a uniformed copper like Rigano had been left in charge of a major murder investigation instead of a plainclothes CID officer. But since the powers that be were so firmly convinced that Brownlow Common women's peace camp was a nest of subversives with sufficient resources to undermine the whole of western democracy, Lindsay supposed it wasn't really so amazing that the SB were taking such a keen interest in a murder that seemed to have some of its origins in the camp.

Lindsay got out of the car and surveyed Megamenu Software's premises. They scarcely inspired confidence. The double doors had been given a cheap and cheerful coat of pale green paint which was already beginning to flake off. There was a large sign in the same style as the one at the mouth of the alley, proclaiming 'Megamenu Software: we turn your needs into realities'. Plenty of scope for a good PR officer, thought Lindsay cynically, when the budget eventually ran to it. But as she rang the bell beside the small door set in one of the larger pair, she noted with some surprise that no expense had been spared on security. The several locks all looked substantial and in spite of the peeling paint, the doors were solid. She didn't have time to speculate further, for the door was opened abruptly by Simon Crabtree.

He frowned and demanded, 'What do you want?'

'A few words,' Lindsay replied. 'Won't take long, I promise.'

'I've got nothing to say to the press,' he retorted angrily. 'You've had enough mileage out of my mother. Bloody vultures.'

Lindsay smiled wryly. 'Fair enough. But I'm not really here in my role as bloody vulture. Think of me as a seeker after truth. Your father has been murdered and the police seem keen to put one of my oldest friends in the frame for it. I know she didn't do it, and I'm trying to prove that. All I want is a bit of information.'

'Why should I help you? You and your bloody friends are no business of mine.' He started to close the door, but Lindsay leaned gently against it.

'You don't owe me anything; but I'd have thought you owe your sister,' she replied.

He was clearly taken aback. 'Ros? What's she got to do with it?'

'I spent yesterday evening at Rubyfruits. She understood the importance of what I'm trying to do. If you rang her, I'm sure she'd tell you to help. And from what I hear, you've got a few debts to pay in that area.

His frowned deepened. 'You'd better come in, I suppose.'

She followed him inside. It was her turn to be taken aback. Inside the shabby lock-up was a complete high-tech environment. The walls were painted matt grey. There was sound-absorbent carpet tile on the floor and the ceiling was covered with acoustic tiling, relieved only by discreet, low-level lighting. One wall was lined with filing drawers. There were four desks, each with a different type of computer terminal on it, including a small portable one, and two expensive-looking, ergonomically designed desk chairs. Several other pieces of equipment, including a standard cassette player and three printers, were sitting on the desks. In the background, baroque music played softly. Simon stood looking truculently at her as she walked round, desperately trying to memorise the names on the computers.

'Quite a set-up you've got here,' she said admiringly. 'You must be doing well to afford all this.'

'I'm good with computers,' he said.

'What sort of software do you produce, then?'

'Mainly programmes for managers. So they can interpret what's going on in the business. Now, what did you mean about my sister?'

'People like me and Ros live our lives on the edges of society. That makes it that little bit harder to achieve things. Ros has managed to get something together. And you blew it out of the water for her by telling your father what the score was. In my book, that means you owe her. And because she perceives herself as being part of a group, that means you owe the women she identifies with. Like my friend Deborah. If you don't agree with that analysis, ring up Ros and ask her yourself.' Lindsay stopped abruptly, challenging him to make the phone call she knew would have her thrown out instantly.

Her gamble on his sense of guilt paid off. His scowl didn't lift, but he said grudgingly, 'And what would you want to know?'

Lindsay hastily searched for a question that would justify her presence. 'I wanted to know about his routine with the dog – was it something he always did at around the same time? Would someone have been able to rely on him being on the common with the dog at that time?'

Simon shrugged. 'Not really. Rex always gets a walk any time between ten and midnight, depending on all sorts of things like the weather, what's on the box, who's at home. It wasn't always my father who took him out. I did sometimes too. So if someone had been lying in wait, they might have had to hang around for hours on more than one occasion. If I'd been home earlier on Sunday, it could just as well have been me that walked him.'

'So you think it's more likely that he met someone by arrangement?'

'Not necessarily. It might have been a chance meeting that turned nasty.'

Lindsay recalled Crabtree's distinctive figure. 'Your father would have been easy to recognise at a distance and chase after if you were looking for a chance encounter. After all, Deborah thought she spotted him from quite a way off on the night he died, when he was walking the dog,' she added. 'And she wasn't even on the common. She was walking back from the phone box.' Simon shrugged. 'But he was carrying a gun, Simon,' Lindsay continued. 'Surely that suggests he was expecting trouble?'

Simon paused to think. 'Yes, but maybe he was just expecting trouble in a general way and had started carrying the gun when he took Rex out last thing.'

Lindsay shook her head in disbelief. 'This is rural England, not the New York subway. People don't wander round with guns just because they think someone might give them a hard time. If he was genuinely afraid of being attacked, if he'd been threatened in any serious way, surely he'd have gone to the police?'

Simon shrugged. 'Don't ask me. It would probably have given him a buzz to confront someone with his gun and then turn them over to the cops. And I think he was genuinely frightened by those peace women. Especially after that one attacked him.'

Lindsay shook her head. 'I can't believe he

thought the peace women were coming after him,' she said. 'It must have been something else. He said nothing?'

'No. And if you've no more questions, I'd appreciate the chance to get back to work,' he replied.

'Okay. Thanks for the time. I'm sure Ros will appreciate your solidarity,' she threw over her shoulder as she left.

Back in the car, she scribbled down the names of the computers she had seen and drove off, keeping an eye out for the red Fiesta. But her rear-view mirror was clear, so she stopped at the first phone box she came to. Typically, it was prepared to allow 999 calls only. Three boxes later, she found one that would accept her money, and she dialled an Oxford number. She was quickly connected with a friend from her student days, Annie Norton, a whizz-kid in computer research.

After an exhaustive exchange of gossipy updates while she pumped coins into the box, Lindsay wound her way round to the point of the call. 'Annie, I need your help on an investigation I've got tangled up with,' she tossed into a gap in the conversation.

'If it's anything to do with Caroline Redfern's much publicised love-life, my lips are sealed,' Annie replied.

'No, this is serious, not chit-chat. It's about computers. I've acquired a cassette tape that I think is a computer programme. It could have been made on any one of four computers, and I need to know what it says. Can you help?'

'A cassette tape? How extraordinary. We're talking real computers here, are we, not video games?'

'I think so, yes.'

'Hmm. No indication of what language it's in?' Annie asked.

'English, I suppose.'

'No, no, what computer language – BASIC, FORTRAN, ALGOL, etc., etc.'

'Oh,' said Lindsay, bewildered. 'No, nothing at all, unless there's a computer language called "Sting: *The Dream Of The Blue Turtles*".'

'You what? Are you serious?'

Lindsay laughed. 'No, that's what's written on the cassette, that's all.'

'And what computers are we talking about?'

'An Apple Macintosh, an IBM, an Apricot, an Amstrad and a Tandy.'

'A Tandy? Little lap-top job, would fit in a brief-case? With a flip-up screen?'

'Yes, that's right.'

Annie sighed in relief. 'That explains the tape. It's probably been transferred from one of the other machines,' she mused. 'It should be fairly simple to run it through our Univac and read it for you. When can you get it to me?'

'I could drop it off in an hour or so – I'm only down the road in Fordham.'

'Tremendous. We could have dinner together if you fancy it.'

Lindsay was tempted. She had reached the point where she wanted more than anything to walk away from the conflict of interests with the peace camp, the police and the job. She felt guilty about two-timing Cordelia, and was unsure how she felt about Debs. But she had promised to be at the vigil and she had to keep that promise. She could just fit in the round trip to Oxford if she didn't hang about too long with Annie. 'Sorry,' she said. 'But I'm working tonight. Maybe when I pick it up again, yeah? How long will it take you?'

'Hard to say. A day? Two, maybe, if it's not something obvious. If the person who's made it is a real computer buff, which he or she presumably is, if they really use those four systems to their full potential, then it could be a bit subtle. Still, a nice bit of hacking makes a pleasant change. I'll see you again in about an hour, then. You know where to find me?'

'Sure, I remember. I'll be with you soon as possible.' Lindsay rang off and was about to leave the box when she realised she hadn't spoken to Cordelia since her angry departure on Monday. Her mind had been too occupied with Crabtree and Debs for her to pay attention to her lover's needs. It wouldn't be an easy call, for Lindsay knew she'd have to lie about what had happened with Debs. The phone wasn't the place for confessions. And Cordelia would be quite justifiably hurt that Lindsay hadn't made time for her. Especially with Deborah Patterson back on the scene. The stab of guilt made her rake through her pockets for more change and she hastily dialled their number. On the fourth ring, the answering machine picked up the call. 'Oh shit,' she muttered as she listened to her own voice instructing her to leave a message. After the tone, she forced a smile into her voice and said, feeling foolish as she always did on their own machine, 'Hello, darling, it's me. Wednesday afternoon. Just a check call to let you know I'm okay. Duncan's leaving me here on the murder story because of my peace camp contacts, so God knows when I'll be home. Probably not till after the funeral, or an arrest, whichever comes first, I'll try to ring tonight. Love you. Bye.' She put the phone down with relief and set off for Oxford.

13

Deborah was waiting impatiently by the Gate Six encampment for Lindsay. Already, most of the women taking part in the vigil were in place. The traffic on the main road back from Oxford and the need to change into more suitable clothes had delayed Lindsay enough for her to have missed the procession, but she could see that there were not sufficient numbers there to encircle the base holding hands, so they had spread out along as much of the perimeter as they could cover, with gaps of about fifty yards between them. The flicker of candles, feeble against the cloudy winter night, was gradually spreading.

Deborah hustled Lindsay along the muddy clearing by the fence for half a mile till they reached their agreed station, a corner of the fence near a deep drainage ditch. They kissed goodbye, then Lindsay walked on round the corner to her position.

She turned towards the base, where the buildings

and bunkers were floodlit against the enemy – not the red menace, but the monstrous regiment, she thought. She turned back and peered towards the nearest flame. She could just make out the silhouette of the next woman in the vigil and in the distance she could hear the faint sound of singing. She knew from experience that it would soon work its way round to her like Chinese whispers. She had been pleasantly surprised to see that for once the police and military presence were fairly low key. She hadn't seen any journalists, but assumed they would all be down by the main gates, reluctant to stagger through the mud unless it became absolutely necessary. She smiled wryly. At least her story would have the unmistakable air of verisimilitude.

She took her Zippo lighter from her jacket pocket and flicked the flame into life. She hadn't remembered to ask Debs for a candle, so the lighter would have to do. She stamped her feet to keep the circulation going and started mentally planning her story.

Her thoughts were interrupted by a short scream, which was cut off by a squelching thud and the sound of crashing in the undergrowth. It came from Deborah's direction. Before she had time to think, she was charging back round the corner in the fence towards her lover. In her panic, she forgot about the drainage ditch and plunged headlong into it, twisting her ankle in an explosion of pain as she fell. But instead of landing in muddy water, she fell on something soft and yielding. Lindsay pushed herself away and fumbled with the lighter which she'd somehow managed to hang on to. The little flare of light was enough to show her a sight that made her heart lurch.

Deborah lay face down in the ditch, blood flowing from a gaping wound in the left side of her head. 'Oh my God,' moaned Lindsay, as she struggled upright. 'Debs, Debs,' she cried, fighting back tears of panic as she grabbed her by the shoulders. She remembered all the rules of first aid that instruct not to move victims with head wounds. But Deborah would drown if left lying face down in the mud. So she pulled at her left shoulder till she managed to turn her on her side. Lindsay pulled her scarf off and gently wiped the mud from Deborah's face. She gritted her teeth and cleared the silt from her nose and mouth and checked if she was still breathing by putting her ear to Deborah's mouth. She could feel nothing. 'Debs, Debs, breathe, you bastard, breathe,' she muttered desperately, pummelling Deborah's chest. After a few moments that felt like an eternity, she was rewarded by a spluttering cough as Deborah retched. Lindsay, herself facing nausea, checked her lover was still able to breathe in spite of her unconsciousness, then stood upright, yelling for help at the top of her voice.

It seemed hours before another couple of women appeared with a torch, looking bewildered.

'Get help, get help!' Lindsay almost screamed. 'Debs has been attacked. Get the bloody police. We need an ambulance.'

The next half hour was a blur of action as first police and then ambulancemen arrived and rushed Deborah to hospital. Lindsay realised how serious the situation was when a young constable helped her into the ambulance and she found herself racing through the lanes with flashing lights and siren.

At Fordham General, the stretcher on which Deborah's immobile body lay was immediately hurried away on a trolley with the policeman still in attendance. Lindsay sat, exhausted, wet and filthy on the steps of the casualty unit, smoking a battered cigarette. She was numb with fear for Deborah. One of the ambulancemen stopped to speak to her on the way back to his vehicle. 'You did well, back there,' he said. 'Your friend might have died if you hadn't got her head out of the mud. Just as well you kept your head.'

Lindsay shook her head. 'I didn't keep my head. I panicked. I just acted on pure instinct. I was so afraid I'd lost her. How is she? Do you know?'

He shrugged. 'Not out of the woods yet. But they're good in there. You should go inside in the warm, you'll get a chill out here. Get yourself a cuppa.'

Lindsay nodded wearily. 'Yeah.' She got to her feet as he climbed back into the ambulance. As she turned to go a heavy hand clapped her on the shoulder. It belonged to a reporter she recognised by sight.

'What's the score?' he demanded. 'We heard someone had been attacked, but the cops are saying nothing.' Lindsay stared at him uncomprehendingly. 'Come on, Lindsay,' he pressed. 'Don't be selfish. I've only got half an hour to close copy time on the next edition. You've had every bloody other exclusive on this job. Give us a break.'

She wanted more than anything to put a fist in his face. Instead, she simply said, 'Fuck off,' and turned on her heel, shaking his hand loose. But the incident had reminded her that there was something she could do to put a bit of distance between the attack and her emotions. She walked like a zombie into the hospital, asked a passing nurse where the nearest phone was and transferred the charges to the *Clarion* newsdesk. Luckily, Cliff Gilbert took the call himself.

'Lindsay here, Cliff,' she said, speaking very slowly. 'Listen. I'm in no fit state to write copy, but there's a very good story going on here and I've got chapter and verse on it. If I give you all the facts, can someone knock it into shape?'

'What?' he exclaimed. 'What the hell's the matter with you? Are you pissed?'

'Look, someone's just tried to kill one of my best friends. I'm exhausted, I'm wet, I'm probably in shock and I'm at the end of my rope. I need help.'

He realised from her voice as much as her words that Lindsay was serious. 'Okay, Lindsay,' he said. 'I'm sorry. I'll put you on to Tony and you tell him what he needs for the story. No problem. Do you need back-up? I can get someone down there in an hour. Or a local freelance –'

'I don't want anyone else, Cliff. Maybe you should get some more cover down here, though. I'm through for tonight. Now give me Tony.' A series of clicks followed, and Lindsay found herself talking to Tony Martin, one of her reporting colleagues. Cliff had obviously warned him what to expect, for his voice was quiet and coaxing. Lindsay forced the lid on her emotions and stumbled through the events of the evening. At the end of her recital, he asked for the number of the police station and the hospital. Her mind was a blank.

'Never mind,' he said. 'Listen, I'll make sure they put your by-line on this. It's a helluva story. I hope your mate pulls through. But you go and get yourself a stiff drink. You sound as if you need one. Okay?'

'Yeah, okay,' she sighed, and put the phone down. Through the door of the booth, she could see other reporters arriving. She knew she couldn't cope with them now, so she turned back to the call box and dialled home. Cordelia picked up the phone on the third ring. Lindsay's voice shook as she said, 'It's me. Can you come down?'

'What?' Cordelia demanded. 'Now? Whatever's

the matter? You sound terrible. What's going on?'

'It's Debs. She's . . . she's been attacked. Someone tried to kill her. I'm at the hospital now. I found her. I really could do with you being here.'

There was incredulity in Cordelia's voice. 'Someone tried to kill Deborah? How? What happened?'

'There was a candle-lit vigil. We were by the fence, about fifty yards from each other. Someone hit her on the head and left her drowning in a ditch,' Lindsay said, on the verge of tears.

'That's awful! Are you okay?'

'Physically, yes. But I'm absolutely drained. I thought she was dead, Cordelia,' Lindsay wailed, tears finally coursing down her face. She sobbed helplessly, oblivious to Cordelia's words.

When she managed to control herself again, she could hear her lover's voice soothing her, saying, 'Calm down it'll be okay. Why don't you come home now? There's nothing more you can do there tonight. I'd come down and get you, but I've had too much wine.'

'I can't,' Lindsay said numbly.

'Why ever not?' Cordelia asked. 'Look, you'd be better off here. You can have a nice hot bath and a drink and try to get a decent night's sleep. Come home, Lindsay. I'll only worry about you otherwise.'

'I just can't,' Lindsay replied. 'There's too much going on here for me to walk away from it all.

I'm sorry. I'll ring you in the morning, okay. Thanks for listening. Goodnight, love.'

'I'll come down first thing, how's that?'

'No, it's okay, leave it. I'm not sure what I'll be doing or where I'll be. I'll speak to you soon.'

'Be careful, Lindsay, please. Ring me in the morning.'

Bleakness descended on Lindsay. She stared across the busy casualty department in time to see Rigano shoulder his way through the flapping celluloid doors and head for the desk. He was immediately surrounded by reporters. She became aware that the phone was squawking.

'Lindsay? Are you there?'

'Yes, I'm here. Bye.'

She put the phone down, feeling utterly defeated. She left the phone booth but could not face the mêlée round the information desk. She leaned against the wall, shivering slightly in spite of the airless warmth of the hospital. Rigano, whose eyes had been sweeping the room for her, picked her up almost immediately.

'That's it for now,' he said brusquely to the crowd of reporters and strode over to her, followed at a few paces by her colleagues. He took her by the elbow and piloted her into a corridor. He stopped briefly and said firmly to their followers. 'Go away. Now. Or I'll have the lot of you removed from the hospital altogether.' Reluctantly, they backed off and he steered

Lindsay into an alcove with a couple of chairs. They sat down.

'She's going to be all right,' he said. 'There's a hairline fracture of the skull and a big superficial wound. She's lost quite a bit of blood and had stitches, but they say there's no brain damage.'

The relief was like a physical glow that spread through Lindsay. 'When can I see her?' she asked.

'Tomorrow morning. Come round about nine and they'll let you in. She'll still be heavily sedated, so they tell me, but she should be awake. It'll be a while before we can get any sense out of her, though, so I need to know anything you can tell me about the attack.'

Lindsay shrugged. 'I don't know anything. I don't even know what she was hit with. What was it?'

'A brick,' he replied. 'There's any number of them lying around. You use them to pin down the corners of your benders.'

'That's ironic,' said Lindsay, stifling the hysterical giggle she felt bubbling inside her. 'I really can't tell you anything. I heard a short scream – not a long-drawn-out one, quite brief – and a squelch that must have been Debs falling into the ditch. Then I heard what sounded like someone trying to run off through the woodland.'

'Can you say in what direction?'

'Not really. It seemed to be more or less dead ahead of me as I ran towards the ditch, but that's the vaguest of impressions and I wouldn't swear to it. I wish I could tell you that I'd seen someone, but even if he'd still been there, I doubt if I would have seen him. There was really no light to speak of.'

'Him?'

'Well, it wouldn't have been one of us, would it?'

It was Jane who woke Lindsay at eight the next morning with a pot of hot coffee. Settling herself down on the end of the bunk, she waited patiently for Lindsay to surface. Brought back to the camp by one of Rigano's men, Lindsay had needed several large whiskies before sleep had even seemed a possibility. Now she was reaping the whirlwind.

Jane smiled at her efforts to shake off the stupor and said, 'I thought I'd better make sure you were up in time to get to the hospital. I've already rung them – Deborah is out of danger and responding well, they said. Translation – she's been sedated to sleep but her vital signs are looking good. They say it's okay for you to go in, but they don't think Cara should visit yet.'

'How is Cara?' asked Lindsay, who felt as if her limbs were wooden and her head filled with cotton wool.

'A bit edgy, but she's with Josy and the other kids so she'll be more or less all right,' Jane replied. 'She wants her mummy, but at least she's old enough to understand when you say that

Deborah's in the hospital but she's going to be all right.'

'Do you think we can keep her here and look after her okay, or are we going to have to get something else sorted out?' Lindsay asked anxiously.

Jane smiled. 'Don't worry about Cara. She's used to the routine here now. It's better that she's somewhere she can see Deborah as much as possible.'

'I'm just worried in case social services find out about her and take her into care,' Lindsay said.

'If anyone comes looking for her from the council, we'll deny all knowledge of her and say she's with her father. By the time they sort that little one out, Deborah will be convalescent,' Jane reassured her. 'Now, drink this coffee and get yourself over to the hospital.'

'Five minutes,' warned the nurse as she showed Lindsay into a small side room.

Deborah lay still, her head swathed in bandages. There was a tube in her nose and another in her arm. Her face was chalky white and dark bruises surrounded her closed eyelids. Lindsay was choked with a mixture of pity, love and anger. As she moved towards the bed, she sensed another presence in the room and half turned. Behind the door, a uniformed constable sat, notebook poised. He smiled tentatively at her and said, 'Morning, miss.'

Lindsay nodded at him and sat down by the bed. Reaching out cautiously she took hold of Deborah's hand. Her eyelids flickered momentarily then opened. The pupils were so dilated that her eyes no longer appeared blue. Frowning slightly, as she tried to focus, she registered Lindsay's presence and her face cleared.

'Lin,' she said in a voice that lacked all resonance. 'It's really you?'

'Yes, love, it's me.'

'Cara?'

'She's okay. Josy's in charge, everything's under control.'

'Good. I'm so tired, Lin. I can't think. What happened?'

'Somebody hit you. Did you see anyone, Debs?'

'I'm so glad it's really you, Lin. I think I'm seeing ghosts. I think Rupert Crabtree's haunting me.'

'I'm no ghost, Debs. And he can't hurt you. He's out of your life for good.'

'I know, but listen, Lin. It's crazy, I know, but I have this weird impression that it was Rupert Crabtree who attacked me. I must be going mad.'

'You're not mad, you're just concussed and sedated up to the eyeballs. It'll all be clear soon, I promise.'

'Yes, but I'm sure it was him that I saw. But it couldn't be, could it? Just like it couldn't have been him I saw walking his dog on Sunday night. Because he was already dead by then, wasn't he?'

'What?' Lindsay suddenly stiffened. 'You saw him after he was dead?'

'I told you before that I saw him. But he was walking towards his house. And he'd already been killed up by the fence. It's his ghost, Lin, it's haunting me.' Her voice was becoming agitated.

Lindsay stroked her arm. 'It's okay, Debs. There's no ghost, I promise you. You've got to go to sleep now, and when you wake up, I swear you'll be much clearer. Now close your eyes, go back to sleep. I'll be back tonight, I promise. No ghosts, just good old Lindsay.'

Her soothing voice lulled the panic from Deborah's face and soon she was sleeping again. Lindsay rose to go and the policeman followed her. Outside he said, 'Could you make head or tail of that, miss? All that stuff about being attacked by a ghost?'

Lindsay shook her head. 'She's delirious, at a guess. It made no sense to me, officer,' she said.

But she knew as she walked away from the ward that she had lied. The echo of her words seemed to pursue her. Deborah's words had triggered off a chain of thought in Lindsay, making a strange kind of sense. At last, vague suspicions were crystallising into certainties. Lindsay felt a growing conviction that Oxford was where the answers lay.

14

Lindsay cursed the one-way system that had turned a city she knew like the back of her hand into a convoluted maze. Wryly she remembered the April Fool's Day joke that had been played by a bunch of maths students when she'd been an undergraduate. They'd worked out that if they reversed just one sign in the traffic system, vehicles would be able to enter but not to leave it. The city had ground to an infuriated, hooting halt by eight in the morning, a problem it had taken the traffic experts till noon to solve. The memory kept Lindsay mildly amused until she finally pulled into the car park at the Computer Sciences Laboratory at eleven. She had stopped only to plead with Duncan for a day off, a request he reluctantly granted after she had delivered a short, first-person piece about her visit to the hospital. Since the *Clarion* had changed the front page to accommodate her story from the night before, the pugnacious news editor was determined to milk their exclusive line for all it was worth. Lindsay had deliberately left out all references to ghosts and stressed Deborah's ignorance of her attacker's identity. Then, with great satisfaction, she switched off her radio pager for the day.

'Lindsay!' exclaimed Annie as she emerged into the reception area looking more like an earth mother than a computer scientist, dressed as she was in a Laura Ashley print. 'I thought you were going to phone.' She escorted Lindsay through the security doors and down an air-conditioned corridor.

'Sorry,' said Lindsay. 'It's just that . . . well, I needed to be doing something and I can't get any further till I know what's on that tape.

Annie stopped in her tracks and studied her friend carefully. 'What's happened, Lindsay? You look completely out of it. Getting involved with murders doesn't seem to agree with you.'

Lindsay sighed. 'Can we sit down somewhere? I don't even know where to begin.' Annie ushered Lindsay into her office, a tiny cubby hole with a remote terminal dominating it. Lindsay slumped into a low easy chair while Annie sat at her desk. Lindsay lit a cigarette then stubbed it out almost immediately, remembering that it was forbidden in the computer areas.

'Last night, somebody tried to kill her and nearly succeeded. It was me who found her. I thought . . . I thought she was going to die. It was terrible, Annie. Made me realise . . . I don't know . . . how dangerous all of this is. Unless someone equally screwy is out to avenge Crabtree's death it's got to be Crabtree's murderer. But it's too much of a coincidence to believe there are two different killers on the loose. And that means as far as I'm concerned that it's a race against time to prove who really did it before he has another go and succeeds.' Annie nodded encouragingly.

'I thought I could rely on the police to get their fingers out,' Lindsay went on. 'But I don't know, it all seems very strange to me. For some reason it's a uniformed copper who's running the show, not the CID, and there's some guy who's always around who's either Special Branch or something odd. And somehow there doesn't seem to be any urgency about what's going on. This cop, Rigano, *seems* dead straight but even he's not getting the action going. To begin with, he was keen enough to enlist my help and stay abreast of what I was up to. But now it's almost as if he doesn't want me to get any closer to the truth.

'I think I'm beginning to have just an inkling of an idea about who did it but I haven't a clue why and I think the answer, or part of it, is that tape.'

Annie grimaced. 'Well, add that to the murderer's assumption that Debs will have told you all she knows and you could be the next target. And knowing you, I suppose all this is upfront in the *Daily Clarion?*'

'Sort of. I mean, I've done a couple of exclusives.'

Annie thought for a moment. 'And?' she prompted.

'And what? Isn't that enough? That I could be next on a killer's hit list?'

'I know you. There's something else. Something personal.'

Lindsay gave a tired smile. 'I'd forgotten how sharp you can be,' she said. 'Yes, there is something more. But it seems hellish trivial beside the real problems of people getting hurt and killed. I'm having a difficult time with Cordelia just now. She seems jealous of the time I spend at the camp, especially now Debs is there.

'Hmm,' Annie murmured. 'She does have a point, though, doesn't she?'

Lindsay looked astonished. 'I didn't –'

'You didn't have to, lovey. It's not what you say, Lindsay, it's how you say it. 'Twas ever thus with you. And if it's that obvious to me who hasn't seen you for months, then it must stick out like a sore thumb to Cordelia. She must be feeling very threatened. If I were you, I'd make a point of going home tonight, no matter what other calls you think there are on your time.'

Lindsay smiled. 'I'd love to do just that. But a lot depends on what you've got to tell me about that tape. I'm convinced that that's where the answers lie.'

Annie frowned. 'I hope not,' she said. She

unlocked her desk and took out a pile of print-out paper and the tape. 'I'm sorry to disappoint you,' she said. 'I don't think you'll find many answers here.'

'You mean you haven't been able to crack it?' Lindsay asked, her voice full of disappointment.

'Oh no, it's not that,' said Annie cheerfully. 'I won't bore you with the details, but I must thank you for a really challenging task. It took me a lot longer than I thought. I didn't get to bed till three, you know, I was so caught up in this. Whoever constructed that programme knew exactly what he was doing. But it was one of those thorny problems that I can't bear to give up till I've solved it.

'So I stuck with it. And this is what I came up with.' She handed Lindsay a sheaf of print-out. It consisted of pages of letters and numbers in groups.

'Is this it?' asked Lindsay. 'I'm sorry, it's completely meaningless to me. What does it represent?'

'That's what I don't know for sure,' Annie admitted. 'It may be some encoded information, or that in itself could be the information. But unless you know what it is you're looking for it doesn't take you any further forward in itself. I've never seen anything quite like it, if that's any help.'

Lindsay shook her head. 'I hoped that this would solve everything. I think I was looking for a motive for murder. But I seem to have ended up with yet another complication. Annie, do you know anybody who might be able to explain this print-out?'

Annie picked up her own copy of the printed message and studied it again. 'It's not my field and I'm not sure whose it is until I know what it is, if you see what I mean.' She sighed. 'The only thing that occurs to me, and it's the vaguest echo from a seminar I went to months ago, is that it might possibly be some kind of signals traffic. I don't know for sure, and I can't even put my finger on why I believe that. But that's all I can go on. And I can't put you in touch with anyone who might help because if it is signals intelligence, then the ninety-nine per cent probability is that it's Official Secrets Act stuff. I'm bound by that and so is anyone else who might help. And if I put you in touch, they'll have to report the contact in both directions. Just what have you got yourself into this time, Lindsay?'

Lindsay sighed again. 'Deep waters, Annie.'

'You should be talking to the police about this.'

'I can't, not yet. I don't trust what's going on, I told you.'

'Where did this come from, Lindsay? For my own protection, I think you need to tell me a bit more about the provenance of this tape. It all looks extremely dodgy to me.'

'I found it in a collection of papers belonging to Rupert Crabtree, the man who was murdered.

His son owns a small software house in Fordham. It was in such a strange place, I figured it might be significant. And now, from what you tell me, it could be more than just a clue in a murder mystery. Have you made a copy of the tape?'

Annie nodded. 'I always do, as a precaution.'

'Then I'd suggest you disguise it as Beethoven string quartets or something and hide it in your tape collection. I'd like there to be a spare in case anything happens to my copy. Or to me.'

Annie's eyebrows rose. 'A little over the top, surely?'

Lindsay smiled. 'I hope so.'

'You can make a copy yourself on a decent tape-to-tape hi-fi, you know,' Annie remarked in an offhand way. 'And you will be going home tonight, won't you?'

Lindsay grinned. 'Yes, Annie. I'll be going home. But I've got a couple of things to do first.' She stood up. 'Thanks for all your work. Soon as all of this is over, we'll have a night out on me, I promise.'

'Let's hope those aren't famous last words. Be careful, Lindsay, if this is what I think it might be, it's not kid's stuff you're into.' Suddenly she stood up and embraced Lindsay. 'Watch your back,' she cautioned, as the journalist detached herself and made for the door.

Lindsay turned and winked solemnly at Annie. 'Just you watch me,' she said.

As she wrestled with the twin horrors of the

one-way system and the pay phones of Oxford, Lindsay decided that she was going to invest in a mobile phone whatever the cost. In frustration, she headed out towards the motorway and finally found a working box in Headington. Once installed, she flipped through her contacts book until she found the number of *Socialism Today*, a small radical monthly magazine where Dick McAndrew worked.

She dialled the number and waited to be connected. Dick was a crony from the Glasgow Labour Party who had made his name as a radical journalist a few years earlier with an exposé of the genetic damage sustained by the descendants of British Army veterans of the 1950s atom bomb tests. He was a tenacious Glaswegian whose image as a bewildered ex-boxer hid a sharp brain and a dogged appetite for the truth. Lindsay knew he'd recently become deeply interested in the intelligence community and GCHQ at Cheltenham. If this was a record of signals traffic, he'd know.

Her luck was still with her. Dick was at his desk, and she arranged to meet him for lunch in a little pub in Clerkenwell. That gave her just enough time to go home and swap her bag of dirty washing for a selection of clean clothes. She made good time on the motorway, which compensated for the time she lost in the heavy West London traffic. Being behind the wheel of her MG relaxed her, and in spite of the congested streets she was almost sorry when she turned off by Highbury Fields and parked outside the house.

She checked her watch as she walked through the front door and decided to make time for herself for a change. She stripped off and dived into a blessedly hot shower. Emerging, she carefully chose a crisp cotton shirt and a pair of lined woollen trousers still in the dry cleaners' bag. She dressed quickly, finishing the outfit off with an elderly Harris Tweed jacket she'd liberated from her father's wardrobe. In the kitchen, Lindsay scrawled a note on the memo board: '12.45. Thurs. I intend to be back by eight tonight. If emergency crops up, I'll leave a message on the machine. Love you.'

She pulled on a pair of soft grey moccasins, light relief after her boots, and ran downstairs to the street. There she picked up a passing cab which deposited her outside the pub. She shouldered her way through the lunchtime crowds till she found Dick sitting in a corner staring morosely at a pint of Guinness. 'You're late,' he accused her.

'Only ten minutes, for Chrissake,' she protested.

'It's the job,' he replied testily. 'You get paranoid. What you drinking?' In spite of Lindsay's attempts to buy the drinks, he was adamant that he should pay, and equally adamant that she had to have a pint. 'I'm no' buying bloody half pints for an operator as sharp as you,' he explained. 'If I'm on pints, so are you. That way I'm less likely to get conned.'

He returned with the drinks and immediately scrounged a cigarette from Lindsay. 'So,' he said, 'how's tricks? You look dog rough.'

'Flattery will get you nowhere, McAndrew. If you must know, I'm in the middle of a murder investigation, my ex-girlfriend is recovering from a homicidal attack, Cordelia's in a huff and Duncan Morris expects the moon yesterday. Apart from that, life's the berries. Howsabout you?' she snarled.

'Oh well, you know?' He sighed expansively.

'That good, eh?'

'So what have you got for me, Lindsay? What's behind this meet? Must be good or you'd have given me some clue on the phone and chanced the phone-tap guy not being sharp enough to pick it up. Hell mend them.'

'It's not so much what I've got for you as what you can do for me.'

'I've told you before, Lindsay, I'm not that kind of boy.'

'You should be so lucky, McAndrew. Listen, this is serious. Forget the Simon Dupree of the gay repartee routine. I've got a computer print-out that I'm told might be coded signals traffic. Could you identify it if it was?'

Dick looked alert and intent. 'Where d'you get this from, Lindsay?'

'I can't tell you yet, Dick, but I promise you

that as soon as it's all sorted, I'll give you chapter and verse.'

He shook his head. 'You're asking a lot, Lindsay.'

'That's why I came to you,' she said. 'Want to see it?' He nodded and she handed him the print-out. He helped himself to another cigarette and studied the paper. Ten minutes later, he carefully folded it up and stuffed it back in her handbag. 'Well?' she asked cautiously.

'I'm not an expert,' he said warily, 'but I've been looking at intelligence communication leaks for a wee while now. As you well know. And that looks to me like a typical pattern for a US military base. Somewhere like Upper Heyford, Mildenhall.'

'Or Brownlow Common?'

'Or Brownlow Common.'

'And what does it mean?'

'Oh Christ, Lindsay. I don't know. I'm not a bloody expert in codes. I've got a source who might be able to unscramble it if you want to know that badly. But I'd have thought it was enough for you to know that you're walking around with a print-out of top secret intelligence material in your handbag. Just possessing that would be enough for them to put you away for a long time.'

'It's that sensitive?'

'Lindsay, the eastern bloc spend hundreds of thousands of roubles trying to get their hands on material like that. Quite honestly, I don't even want to know where you got that stuff. I want to forget I've ever seen it.'

'But if you know what it is, you must have seen other stuff like it.'

Dick nodded and took a long draught of his pint. 'I've seen similar stuff, yes. But nothing approaching that level of security. There's a system of security codes at the top of each set of groups. And I've never encountered anything with a code rated that high before. It's the difference between Hansard and what the PM tells herself in the mirror in the morning. You are playing with the big boys, Lindsay.' He rose abruptly and went to the bar, returning with two large whiskies.

'I don't drink spirits at lunchtime,' she protested.

'You do today,' he said. 'You want my advice? Go home, burn that print-out, go to bed with Cordelia, forget you ever saw it. That's trouble, Lindsay.'

'I thought you were a tough-shit investigative journo, the sort that isn't happy unless you're taking the lid off the Establishment and kicking the Official Secrets Act into touch?'

'It's not like pulling the wings off flies, Lindsay. You don't just do it for the hell of it. You do it when you think there's something nasty in the woodpile. I'm not one of those knee-jerk lefties who publishes every bit of secret material that comes my way, like Little Jack Horner saying "See what a good boy am I." Some things should stay secret; it's when that's abused to protect crime and pettiness and sloppiness and injustice and self-seeking that people like me get stuck in,' he replied passionately.

'Okay,' she said mildly. 'Cut the lecture. But take it from me, Dick, something very nasty has been going on, and I've got to get to the bottom of it before it costs any more lives. If I have to use my terrifying bit of paper to get there, I'll do it. There's nothing wrong with my bottle.'

'I never said there was. That's the trouble with you, Lindsay – you don't know when it's sensible to get scared.'

By silent consent they changed the subject and spent half an hour gossiping about mutual friends in the business. Then Lindsay felt she could reasonably make her excuses and leave. She got back to the three-storey house in Highbury at half past two, with no recollection of the journey through the North London streets. The answering machine was flashing, but she ignored it and went through to the kitchen to brew a pot of coffee. She had the frustrating feeling that she had all the pieces of the jigsaw but couldn't quite arrange them in a way that made sense. While the coffee dripped through the filter, she decided to call Rigano.

For once, she was put straight through. As soon as she identified herself, he demanded, 'Where are you? And what have you been up to?'

Puzzled, she said, 'Nothing. I'm at home in London. I visited Deborah this morning and since then I've seen a couple of friends. Why?'

'I want to know what you make of your friend's remark when you saw her in the hospital. My constable thought it might be significant.'

'I told him then that I didn't understand it,' she replied cautiously.

'I know what you told him. I don't believe you,' he retorted.

'That's not my problem,' she replied huffily.

'It could be,' he threatened. 'I thought we were co-operating, Lindsay?'

'If I had any proof of who attacked Deborah, do you think I'd be stupid enough to sit on it? I don't want to be the next one with a remodelled skull, Jack.'

There was a heavy silence. Then he said in a tired voice, 'Got anything for me at all?'

'These bikers who have been terrorising the camp – I think Warminster and Mallard are paying them.'

'Have you any evidence of that?'

Briefly, Lindsay outlined what she had learned the day before. 'It's worth taking a look at, don't you think? I mean, Warminster and Mallard both wanted Crabtree out of the way. Maybe they used the yobs they'd already primed for the vandalism.'

'It's a bit far-fetched, Lindsay,' he complained. 'But I'll get one of my lads to take a look at it.'

Having got that off her chest, Lindsay got to

the point of the call. 'Has it occurred to you that there might be a political dimension to this situation?'

His voice became cautious in its turn. 'You mean that RABD is only a front for something else? That's nonsense.'

'I mean real politics, Jack. Superpowers and spies. The person you're looking for didn't really kill for personal reasons; I think we're looking at a wider motive altogether. Somebody doesn't want us to do that. And that's why I think this investigation has got bogged down in trivial details about peace women's alibis.'

'That's an interesting point of view, but that sort of thing is all out of my hands. I'm just a simple policeman, Lindsay. Conspiracy theories don't do much for me. I leave all that to the experts. And you'd be well advised to do the same.'

Simple policeman, my foot, thought Lindsay. 'Is that a warning, Jack?' she asked innocently.

'Not at all, Lindsay. I'm just telling you as simply as I know how that this case isn't about James Bond, it's about savage responses to petty situations. It's about people carrying offensive weapons for mistaken notions of self-defence. Anything else is out of my hands. Do I make myself clear?'

'So who is that blond man who keeps following me? Special branch? MI5?'

'If you mean Mr Stone, he's not Special Branch. There's no SB man around here, Lindsay. And no one is following you. I'd know about it if they were. If anyone's being followed, it's not you. You should stop being so paranoid.'

Lindsay almost smiled. 'Haven't you heard, Jack? Just because you stop being paranoid doesn't mean they're not out to get you.'

15

Lindsay raked around in her desk drawer until she found a blank cassette. Going through to the large L-shaped living room where the stereo system with the twin tape decks occupied a corner she set it up to make a copy of the computer tape and sprawled on one of the elegant grey leather chesterfields while she waited for the recording to finish. It was wonderful to lie back on the comfortable sofa surrounded by the restful atmosphere created by Cordelia's unerring talent for interior design, though she felt a pang of guilt when she remembered the squalid conditions back at Brownlow. Lindsay ruefully recalled her feelings when she had first entered Cordelia's domain two years before. She had been overwhelmed with the luxurious interior of the tall house by the park, and it had been months before she got out of the habit of pricing everything around her with a sense of puritanical outrage. Now, it was her home, far more than her Glasgow flat which she rented out to students at a rent that covered her overheads.

She turned over again what Rigano had said. As far as the blond man was concerned, it seemed plain to Lindsay that he was something to do with intelligence, since Rigano had denied so vehemently that he was SB while pointedly ignoring her MI5 allegation. And if Stone wasn't following *her*, that didn't leave many options for the focus of his interests. And that in turn meant she wasn't barking up the wrong tree as far as the existence of wider political implications was concerned. What she couldn't understand was why Rigano was just sitting back and letting it happen without pursuing the same person that she was interested in.

Unless, of course, she was completely wrong and the two strands were unrelated, leaving the murder as a purely personal matter. That would leave the ball firmly in the court of Warminster, Mallard and the putative biker or Alexandra/Carlton. The interest of the security forces could then be explained away as concern about police action jeopardising some operation of theirs. Since Lindsay was still far from clear about the point of killing Rupert Crabtree, either option seemed possible. However, the attempt on Deborah's life seemed logical only if one assumed that it had been made to silence her. And if that was the case, Lindsay argued to herself, how did the murderer know that Debs hadn't already spilled whatever beans she possessed; and if she hadn't, then was she likely to do so now, especially since her silence must have come not from fear but from a failure to recognise what she knew or its importance? Lindsay shook her head vigorously. She was going round in circles.

She mentally replayed her conversation with Rigano again. Something he had said as a throw-away line came back into sharp focus. 'It's about people carrying offensive weapons for mistaken notions of self-defence,' he had remarked bitterly. Suddenly the jigsaw fell into place. Lindsay jumped to her feet and went to the phone. If Cordelia had been accessible, she would have outlined her theory then and there and waited for the holes to be picked in it. Failing that, she punched in the number of Fordham police station and drummed her fingers impatiently till the connection was made.

'Hello . . . Can I speak to Superintendent Rigano,' she demanded. The usual sequence of clicks and hollow silences followed. Then the switchboard operator came back to her and reported that Rigano was out of the building. But Lindsay was not to be deflected.

'Can you get a message to him, please? Will you tell him that Lindsay Gordon rang and needs to talk to him urgently? I'm just setting off to drive to Fordham now, and I'll be at the police station in about an hour and a half; say five o'clock. If he's not back by then, I'll hang on. Got that?'

The woman on the switchboard seemed slightly bemused by Lindsay's bulldozer tactics, but she dutifully repeated the message and promised it would be passed on over the radio. Taking the original cassette tape out of the machine and stuffing it in her pocket, Lindsay left the house, completely forgetting the flashing answering machine and her promise to Cordelia.

She walked round to the mews garage where she kept the car and was soon weaving through the traffic, seeing every gap in the cars ahead as a potential opportunity for queue jumping. Excited as she was by the new shape her thoughts had taken, she forced herself not to think about murder and its motives while she negotiated the busy roads leading to the M4.

She arrived at Fordham police station ten minutes ahead of schedule. The elderly constable on reception desk duty told her Rigano was due back within the next half hour and that he was expecting her. She was taken through to a small anteroom near his office and a matronly policewoman brought her a cup of tea, freshly brewed but strong. Lindsay found it hard to sit still and chain-smoked through the twenty minutes she was kept waiting. She looked at one cigarette ruefully as she blew smoke at the ceiling. No matter how hard she tried to give up or cut down, at the first crisis she leapt for the nicotine with the desperate fixation of the alcoholic for the bottle.

Rigano himself came to escort her to his room. More cheerful now, there was no sign that he resented her demand to see him. But he seemed determined to keep a distance between them. In his office, there was no sign of his sergeant or any of the other officers to take notes of the interview. Lindsay was disconcerted by that, but nevertheless relieved. What she had to say didn't need a big audience. And if some hard things were going to be said on both sides, it was probably just as well that they should go unrecorded.

'Well,' he said, indicating a chair to her as he walked round his desk to sit down. 'You seem in a big rush to talk to me now, when you could barely spare me a sentence earlier on. What's caused the big thaw? Surely not my overwhelming charm.'

'Partly it's fear,' she replied. 'I said to you earlier that I'd be a fool if I knew who had killed Crabtree and tried to kill Deborah and persisted in keeping my mouth shut. Well, I think that now I know, and I'm ready to talk.'

If she expected him to show signs of amazement or shock, she was disappointed. His eyebrows twitched slightly and he simply said, 'That's assuming the two incidents are directly related.'

Lindsay was puzzled. 'But of course they are. You can't seriously expect anyone to believe that there are two homicidal maniacs running around out there? Deborah was connected to Crabtree while he was alive; in my book, that makes a strong case for a connection when they're both involved in murderous attacks in the same place within days of each other.'

'The attack on Deborah Patterson could have been a random attack on one of the peace women by someone who's got a grudge against the camp,' he argued mildly.

Lindsay shook her head. 'No way. If anyone was going to do that, they'd pick a spot much nearer the road, where they could make a quick getaway. The woods are really dense around where Debs was attacked. That was someone watching and waiting and biding his time, someone who knows enough about the way things work round here to know where to keep his eyes open.'

Rigano smiled. He almost seemed to be enjoying their sparring. 'All right,' he conceded. 'I'll grant you the assumption for now that the incidents were connected. Where do we go from there?'

'Do you want the hypothesis or the evidence?'

'I'll have the evidence, then you can give me the theory.'

'Item one. A cassette tape. It was among Rupert Crabtree's papers in the RABD files. It's not what it says on the label – it's a recording of signals traffic on computer that would be of interest both to this country's allies and our enemies.' She put the tape on his desk. He picked it up, studied it and put it down again. He nodded encouragingly.

'Item two. Debs thinks she's being haunted by the ghost of Rupert Crabtree. She thinks she saw him walking the dog after he was dead, and she's convinced it was Crabtree who attacked her.

'Item three. There is someone around, the guy you called Mr Stone, who is taking an interest in what's going on. He's not CID. You tell me he's not SB. That means, given the contents of this tape, that he's MI5 or 6. I imagine from what little I know about intelligence that he's MI6 K Branch. They're the ones who keep track of Soviet and satellite state agents, aren't they?'

A trace of the lighter side of his personality flickered across Rigano's face as he smiled and said, 'You seem to know what you're talking about.'

Lindsay immediately bristled. She was determined not to grant him any rights where she was concerned. 'Please don't patronise me. I'm not a little woman who needs patting on the head because she can play the big boys' game.'

The shutters came down over his eyes again. 'That wasn't my intention,' he replied coolly. 'Is that the extent of your evidence?'

'There's one more thing. But that's conjecture rather than hard fact. What if Rupert Crabtree's gun was being carried not for defence but for attack?'

For the first time, Rigano looked truly alert, as if she was telling him something he did not know; or something he did not want her to know. 'Why should he?' he demanded.

'If I can explain my idea about what really happened, you'll see why he should,' Lindsay replied. 'Are you prepared to hear me out?'

He glanced at his watch. It was almost half past five. 'I've got half an hour,' he said. 'Will it take longer than that?'

Lindsay shook her head. 'It's not a long story. It's not a very edifying one either. Treachery and greed, that's what we're into here, Jack.' He nodded and sat back attentive.

'Simon Crabtree is a computer prodigy. He's one of those people who reads a programme like you or I read a page in the newspaper. And he's a hacker. Even when he was at school, they commented on his rare skill at busting into other people's private programmes. No one had any doubt that he should be looking at a future in computers; no one, that is, except his father, who was conservative enough to be determined that his only son should be properly qualified in something. So he refused to help Simon set up his software business.

'I've seen inside that lock-up and while I don't know too much about computers, I'd say that the equipment in there must run into several thousands of pounds, easily. Maybe even five figures. Now, he wouldn't have got that kind of money from a bank, so where did it come from?

'It's my belief that it came from a foreign power. Almost inevitably the Soviets or an East European Soviet satellite. That cassette you've got there contains a recording of signals traffic from a US military base. I don't know enough about these things to swear that it comes from Brownlow, but the chances are that it does, given that I found it among Rupert Crabtree's papers. What I think happened was this. I think that either Simon was scouted by the Soviets, who learned about his hacking skills and his need for capital; or he approached them with the revelation that he had the key to hack into the base's signals computer. I don't think it's been going on too long, if that's any consolation, because he's only had the business up and running for a few months.

'I'm a bit hazy about what happened to put Rupert Crabtree on to the trail; I'd guess that maybe he saw his son behaving suspiciously, or saw him with someone he shouldn't have been with. Either way, he got hold of this tape. I'm still guessing here, but I think he probably did what I did – took it to someone who knows how to crack computer codes and discovered just what I did – that it's top-secret signals traffic. Only, for him, the discovery must have been utterly devastating. Here he is, a pillar of the community, a man in the vanguard of an anti-left-wing campaign, and his son's spying for the Ruskies. Also, to be fair, I think from what I've learned about him that it wouldn't just have been the personal disgrace that would have upset him.

'I think he was a patriotic man who genuinely

loved his country. I could never have agreed with his politics, but I don't think he was your stereotype fascist on a power trip. I believe that the discovery of what Simon was doing must have shattered him. And something had really got to him, according to Alexandra Phillips. Are you with me so far?'

Rigano said seriously, 'It's a very interesting hypothesis. I think your analysis of Crabtree's character is pretty much on the ball. But do go on. I'm fascinated. You've obviously done a lot of digging that you haven't told me about.'

Lindsay smiled. 'Isn't that what journalists are supposed to do?'

He frowned. 'In theory. But not when they've struck deals with me. Anyway, carry on.'

'Crabtree's options once he had discovered Simon's treason were fairly limited. He'd realise at once he couldn't ignore it and carry on as if nothing had changed. He couldn't come to you lot because that would completely destroy his life. It would bring his world crashing down about him, and once the press started digging, it would expose all sorts, like his relationship with Alexandra, like RABD's connections with the violent right. It would make it almost impossible for him to go on practising locally. The shame for him and his wife would have been too much and he was too old to think about starting elsewhere.

'He could have confronted Simon with his knowledge and ordered him to stop, with the blackmail that if he didn't he would go to the authorities. But there's no way that could have been done effectively – Rupert had no way of checking that Simon had really stopped. And Simon probably knew his father well enough to realise that he wouldn't have carried through his bluff. So there would have been a stalemate. And it wouldn't have taken much imagination on Crabtree's part to work out what his fate would probably be once Simon reported back to his control that his father knew he was spying.

'The only other option was to dispose of the son whose treachery was putting his family and his country at risk.'

Rigano picked up a pencil and started doodling on a sheet of paper by his phone. He looked up. 'Tell me more,' he said.

'Not much more to tell, is there? Crabtree had a gun. He was licensed for it. He knew how to shoot. But I'd guess that he probably didn't intend to use it unless he had to. He'd have tried to divert suspicion to the peace women so he'd likely have used the gun as a threat and then killed Simon some other way. He arranged to meet Simon on the common to have a private talk. When he pulled the gun, Simon panicked and overpowered him. Then, realising there was nothing else for it, he killed him.

'Then that cool young man went home, bringing the bemused and terrified family dog, which of course explains why the dog was on the doorstep and not howling over the corpse of his master as one would expect. Then Simon stripped off his muddy bike leathers, and put up a good show for when the police arrived. That, by the way is when Deborah saw him. You must have noticed that he's physically, if not facially, very like his father. Deborah knew Crabtree but not Simon, and she thought it was the father and not the son she saw outlined against the night sky. It was only much later that she realised he must already have been dead by then.

'And appallingly, it was I who tipped Simon off that Deborah had seen him; I said she'd seen his father, but he was quicker to the point than me and immediately knew who Deborah had really got a glimpse of. He understood the significance, and decided Deborah was too high a risk to leave unattended. Hence the attack on her, and hence her conviction that Rupert Crabtree was haunting her. She must have caught a brief, peripheral glimpse of Simon, and subconsciously identified him wrongly. I hope you've still got a guard on her.'

Rigano put his pencil down and sighed. 'Very plausible,' he muttered. 'Fits all the facts in your possession.'

'It's the only theory that does,' Lindsay replied sharply. 'Anything else relies on a string of completely implausible coincidences.'

'I tend to agree with you,' he replied in an offhand way.

'So what are you going to do about it? You've got the evidence there,' Lindsay said, pointing at the tape. 'You can get your forensic people to examine the clothes Simon was wearing that night. There must be traces.'

'I'm going to do precisely nothing about it, except to say, well done, Lindsay. Now forget it,' he said coldly.

Lindsay looked at him in stunned amazement. 'What?' she demanded, outraged. 'How can you ignore what I've just told you? How can you ignore the evidence I've given you? You've got to bring him in for questioning, at least!'

He shook his head. 'No,' he said. 'Don't you understand?'

'No, I bloody don't,' she protested bitterly. 'You're a policeman. You're supposed to solve crimes, arrest the culprits, bring them to trial. You're quick enough to do people for speeding – suddenly murder is a no-go area?'

'This murder is,' he replied. 'Why else do you think a uniform is in charge instead of the CID? Why else am I working with two men, a dog and a national newspaper hack? I am supposed to fail.'

Lindsay was dumbstruck. It didn't make any sense to her. 'I . . . I don't get it,' she stuttered.

Rigano sighed deeply. He spoke quietly but firmly. 'I shouldn't tell you this, but I feel I owe it to you after the way you've worked through this. Simon Crabtree is part of a much bigger operation that's out of my hands and way over my head. I am not allowed to touch him. If he ran amok in Fordham High Street with a Kalashnikov, I'd have a job arresting him. Now do you understand?'

Lindsay's fury suddenly erupted. 'Oh yes, I bloody understand all right. Some bunch of adolscent spymasters think they can get to some tuppenny-ha'penny KGB thug via Simon Crabtree. So it's hands off Simon. And that means it's open season on Deborah. She can't be kept under police guard for ever. Simon doesn't know he's sacrosanct, he'll have another go. And next time Deborah might not be so lucky. You expect me to stand by while an innocent woman is put at risk from that homicidal traitor? Forget it!'

'So what are you going to do about it?'

'I'm a journalist, Jack,' she replied angrily. 'I'm going to write the story. The whole bloody, dirty story.' She got to her feet and made for the door. As she opened it, she said, 'But first of all, I'm going to talk to Simon Crabtree.'

16

The roar of the MG's engine was magnified by the high walls of Harrison Mews as Lindsay drew up for her showdown with Simon Crabtree. It was a cold, clear night with an edge of frost in the air and she wound down the car window to take a few deep breaths. The alleyway was gloomy, lit only by a few dim bulbs outside some of the lock-ups. The immediacy of her anger had subsided far enough for her to be apprehensive about what she intended to do. She cursed her lack of foresight in failing to bring along her pocket tape recorder. Although she was desperate for the confrontation, she was enough of a professional to realise that the difficulties she would encounter in getting this story into the paper would only be compounded by an unwitnessed, unrecorded interview with Simon. She could try to find the *Clarion*'s back-up team and enlist their help, but she knew she could only expect the most reluctant co-operation from them unless specifically ordered by Duncan. After her string of exclusives, the poor bastard who'd been sent down as back-up was not going to be too inclined to help her out.

She lit a cigarette and contemplated her options. Behind her apprehension lay the deep conviction of all journalists, that somehow they were immune from the risks faced by the rest of the world. It was that same conviction that had made her face a killer alone once before. She could dive in now, feet first; the chances were that Simon would deny everything. Even if he admitted it, she'd have no proof. Then he'd tip off his masters, she'd be in the firing line, and as sure as the sun rises in the morning, Duncan would send her back anyway with a photographer to get pictures and a witnessed interview. It wouldn't matter so much then if he denied it; the office lawyer would be satisfied that he'd been given a fair crack of the whip. The other alternative was to leave it for now, go and visit Debs in hospital, go home and talk it over with Cordelia, and discuss the best approach with Duncan in the morning. Then everyone would be happy. Everyone except Lindsay herself, in whom patience had never been a highly developed character trait.

Sighing, she decided to be sensible. She wound up the window but before she could start the engine, she saw a Transit van turn into the alleyway and drive towards her. Only its sidelights were on, and it was being driven up the middle of the roadway, making it impossible for Lindsay to pass. Instinctively, she glanced in the rear-view mirror. In the dim glow of her tail lights, she saw a red Fiesta, parked diagonally across her rear, preventing any escape by that route. The Transit stopped a few feet from her shiny front bumper and both doors opened. There was nothing accidental about this, she thought.

Two men emerged. One was around the six foot mark, with the broad shoulders and narrow hips of a body builder. He had thinning dark hair cut close to his head, and his sharp features with their five o'clock shadow were exaggerated by the limited lighting. He looked like a tough Mephistopheles. The other was smaller and more wiry, with a mop of dark hair contorted into a curly perm. Both wore leather bomber jackets and training shoes. All this Lindsay absorbed as they moved towards her, understanding at once that something unpleasant was going to happen to her. She discovered that she couldn't swallow. Her stomach felt as if she'd been punched in the middle of a period pain. Almost without thinking, Lindsay locked the driver's door as Curly Perm tried the passenger door and Mephistopheles reached her side of the car. He tried the handle, then said clearly and coldly, 'Open it.'

Lindsay shook her head. 'No way,' she croaked through dry lips. She was too scared even to demand to be told what was going on.

She saw him sigh. His breath was a white puff in the night air. 'Look,' he said reasonably. 'Open it now. Or else it's a brick through the window. Or, since you've done us the favour of bringing the soft-top, the Stanley knife across this very expensive hood. You choose.'

He looked completely capable of carrying out his threat without turning a hair. Unlocking the door, Lindsay suddenly ached for a life with such certainties, without qualms. Immediately, he wrenched the door open and gestured with his thumb for her to get out. Numbly, she shook her head. Then, behind her, another voice chimed in.

'I should do as he asks if I were you.' Lindsay twisted in her seat and saw Stone leaning against the car. Somehow it came as no surprise. She even felt a slight sense of relief. At least she could be sure which side had her. You bastard, Jack Rigano, she thought.

Stone smiled encouragingly. 'I assure you, you'll be out of that car one way or another within the next few minutes. It's up to you how painless the experience will be. And don't get carried away with the notion of extracting a price in pain from us. I promise you that your suffering will be immeasurably greater. Now, why don't you just get out of the car?' His voice was all the more chilling for having a warm West Country drawl.

Lindsay turned back to Mephistopheles. If he'd stripped naked in the interval, she wouldn't have noticed. What grabbed her attention was the short-barrelled pistol which was pointing unwaveringly at her right leg. The last flickering of defiance penetrated her fear and she said abruptly, 'Because I don't want to get out of the bloody car.'

Curly Perm marched round the back of the car, past Stone. He took something from his pocket and suddenly a gleaming blade leapt forward from his fist. He leaned into the car as Lindsay flinched away from him. He looked like a malevolent monkey. He waved the knife in front of her, then, in one swift movement, he sliced her seat belt through the middle, leaving the ends dangling uselessly over her. He moved back, looking speculatively at the soft black vinyl roof.

'The first cut is the deepest,' said Stone conversationally. 'He's very good with the knife. He knows how to cause serious scars without endangering your life. I wonder if Deborah Patterson would be quite so keen then? Or indeed, that foxy lady you live with. Don't be a hero, Lindsay. Get out of the car.'

His matter-of-fact air and the use of her first name were far more frightening than the flick-knife or the gun. The quiet menace Stone gave off was another matter. Lindsay knew enough about herself to realise that he was the one whose threats had the power to invest her life with paranoid nightmares. Co-operation seemed the best way to fight her fear now. So she got out of the car. 'Leave the keys,' said Mephistopheles as she reached automatically for them on the way out.

As she stood up, Stone moved forward and grasped her right arm above the elbow. Swiftly, he fastened one end of a pair of handcuffs round her wrist. 'Am I under arrest, or what?' she demanded. He ignored the question.

'Over to the van, please,' he said politely, betraying his words by twisting her arm up her back. Stone steered her round to the back of the Transit. Curly Perm opened the doors and illuminated the interior with a small torch. Lindsay glimpsed two benches fixed to the van's sides then she was bundled inside and the other shackle of the cuffs was fixed to one of the solid steel struts that formed the interior ribs of the van. The doors were hastily slammed behind her, casting her into complete darkness, as she asked again, 'What's going on? Eh?' There were no windows. If she stretched out her leg as far as she could reach, she could just touch the doors. She could stand almost upright, but couldn't quite reach the opposite side of the van with her arm. It was clear that any escape attempt would be futile. She felt thankful that she'd never suffered from claustrophobia.

Lindsay heard the sound of her MG's engine starting, familiar enough to be recognisable even inside the Transit. Then it was drowned as the van's engine revved up and she was driven off. She had to hold on to the bench to keep her balance as the van lurched. At first, she tried to memorise turnings, but realised very quickly that it was impossible; the darkness was disorientating. With her one free hand she checked through the contents of her pockets to see if she had anything that might conceivably be useful. A handkerchief, some money (she guessed at £30.57), a packet of cigarettes and her Zippo. Not exactly the Count of Monte Cristo escape kit, she thought bitterly. Why did reality never provide the fillips of fiction? Where was her Swiss army knife and her portable office with the scissors, stapler, adhesive tape and flexible metal tape measure? In her handbag, she remembered, on the floor of the MG. Oh well, if she'd tried to bring it, they would have taken it from her, she decided.

The journey lasted for over an hour and a half. Debs would be wondering why she hadn't appeared, thought Lindsay worriedly. And Cordelia would soon start getting cross that she wasn't home when she said she'd be. They'd probably each assume she was with the other and feel betrayed rather than anxious; no hope of either of them giving the alarm. She was beginning to wonder exactly where she was being taken. If it was central London, they should have been there by now, given the traffic at that time of night. But there were none of the stops and starts of city traffic, just the uninterrupted run of a motorway or major road. If it wasn't London, it must be the other direction. Bristol? Bath? Then it dawned. Cheltenham. General Communications Headquarters. It made a kind of sense.

The van was behaving more erratically now, turning and slowing down at frequent intervals. At 8.12 p.m., according to Lindsay's watch, it stopped and the engine was turned off. She could hear indeterminate, muffled sounds outside, then the doors opened. Her eyes adjusted to the surge of light and she saw they were in an underground car park. The MG was parked opposite them, the red Fiesta next to it. Stone climbed into the van and unlocked the handcuff linking Lindsay to the van. He snapped it round his left wrist and led her out into the car park.

The four of them moved in ill-assorted convoy to a bank of lifts. Stone took a credit-card-sized piece of black plastic from his pocket and inserted it in a slot, which swallowed it. Above the slot was a grey rubber pad. He pressed his right thumb to the pad, then punched a number into a console. The slot spat the black plastic oblong out and the lift doors opened for them. Curly Perm hit the button marked 5 and they shot upwards silently. They emerged in an empty corridor, brightly lit with fluorescent tubes. Lindsay could see half a dozen closed doors. Stone opened one marked K57 and ushered Lindsay in. The other two remained outside.

The room was almost exactly what Lindsay expected. The walls were painted white. The floor was covered with grey vinyl tiles, pitted with cigarette burns. A couple of bare fluorescent strips illuminated a large metal table in the middle of the room. The table held a telephone and a couple of adjustable study lamps clamped to it. Behind the table stood three comfortable-looking office chairs. Facing it, a metal-framed chair with a vinyl-padded seat and back was fixed to the floor. 'My God, what a cliché this room is,' said Lindsay.

'What makes you think you deserve anything else?' Stone asked mildly. 'Sit in the chair facing the table,' he instructed. There seemed no point in argument, so she did as she was told. He unlocked the cuffs again and this time fastened her to the solid-looking arm of the chair.

A couple of hours had passed since she had been really frightened, and she was beginning to feel a little confidence seeping back into her bones. 'Look,' she said. 'Who are you, Stone? What's going on? What am I here for?'

He smiled and shook his head. 'Too late for those questions, Lindsay. Those are the first things an innocent person would have asked back in that alley in Fordham. You knew too much. So why ask questions now when you know the answers already?'

'Jesus Christ,' she muttered. 'You people have got minds so devious you think everyone's part of some plot. When you hemmed me in that alleyway, I was too bloody stunned to come up with the questions that would have made you happy.

Why have I been brought here? What's going to happen to me?'

'That rather depends on you,' he replied grimly. 'Don't go away, now,' he added as he left the room.

She was left alone for nearly half an hour, by which time, all her determined efforts to be brave had gone up in the smoke of her third cigarette. She was scared and she had to acknowledge the fact, although her fear was tempered with relief that it was Rigano's masters rather than Simon Crabtree's who were holding her. She wouldn't give much for her chances if it had been the other way round.

Lindsay had just lit her fourth cigarette when the door opened. She forced herself not to look round. Stone walked in front of her and sat down at one corner of the desk, facing her. He was followed by a woman, all shoulders and sharp haircut, who stood behind the desk scrutinising Lindsay before she too sat down. The woman was severely elegant, in looks as well as dress. Her beautifully groomed pepper-and-salt hair was cut close at the sides, then swept upwards in an extravagant swirl of waves. Extra strong hold mousse, thought Lindsay inconsequentially; if I saw her in a bar, I'd fancy her until I thought about running my fingers through that. The woman had almost transparently pale skin, her eyes glittered greenish blue in her fine-boned face. She looked about forty. She wore a fashionably cut trouser suit in natural linen over a chocolate brown silk shirt with mother-of-pearl buttons. As she studied Lindsay, she took out a packet of Gitanes and lit one.

The pungent blue smoke played its usual trick on Lindsay, flashing into her mind's eye a night in a café in southern France with Cordelia, playing pinball, smoking and drinking coffee, and listening to Elton John on the jukebox. The contrast was enough to bring back her fear so strongly she could almost taste it.

Perhaps the woman sensed the change in Lindsay, for she spoke then. 'Mr Stone tells me you are a problem,' she said. 'If that's the case, we have to find a solution.' Her voice had a cool edge, with traces of a northern accent. Lindsay suspected that anger or disappointment would make it gratingly plaintive.

'As far as I'm concerned, the problems are all on your side. I've been abducted at gunpoint, threatened with a knife, the victim of an act of criminal damage and nobody has bothered to tell me by whom or why. Don't you think it's a little unreasonable to expect me to bend over backwards to solve anything you might be considering a problem?' Lindsay demanded through clenched teeth, trying to hide her fear behind a show of righteous aggression.

The woman's eyebrows rose. 'Come, come, Miss Gordon. Let's not play games. You know perfectly well who we are and why you're here.'

'I know he's MI6 K division, or at least I've been assuming he is. But I don't know why the hell I've been brought here like a criminal, or who you are. And until I do, all you get from me is my name.'

The woman crushed out her half-smoked cigarette and smiled humourlessly at Lindsay. 'Your bravado does you credit. If it helps matters any, my name is Barber. Harriet Barber. The reason you've been brought here, in your words like a criminal, is that, according to the laws of the land, that's just what you are.

'You are, or have been in unauthorised possession of classified information. That on its own would be enough to ensure a lengthy prison sentence, believe me, particularly given your contacts on the left. You were apprehended while in the process of jeopardising an operation of Her Majesty's security forces, another matter on which the courts take an understandably strong line. Superintendent Rigano really should have arrested you as soon as you tossed that tape on his desk.'

Thanks a million, Jack, Lindsay thought bitterly. But she recognised that she had begun marginally to relax. This authoritarian routine was one she felt better able to handle. 'So am I under arrest now?' she asked.

Again came the cold smile. 'Oh no,' said Harriet Barber. 'If you'd been arrested, there would have had to be a record of it, wouldn't there?'

The fear was back. But the moment's respite had given Lindsay fresh strength. 'So if I'm not under arrest, I must be free to go, surely?' she demanded.

'In due course,' said Stone.

'Don't be too optimistic, Mr Stone,' said Barber. 'That depends on how sensible Miss Gordon is. People who can't behave sensibly often suffer unfortunate accidents due to their carelessness. And someone who drives an elderly sports car like Miss Gordon's clearly has moments when impulse overcomes good sense. Let's hope we don't have too many moments like that tonight.'

There was a silence. Lindsay's nerve was the first to go and she said, struggling to sound nonchalant, 'Let's take the posturing as read and come to the deal. What's the score?'

'There's that unfortunate bravado again,' sighed Barber. 'We are not offering any deal, Miss Gordon. That's not the way we do things here. You will sign the Official Secrets Act and will be bound by its provisions. You will also sign a transcript of your conversation with Superintendent Rigano this evening, as an insurance policy. You will hand over any copies of that tape still in your possession. And then you will leave here. You will not refer to the events of this evening or to your theories about the murder of Rupert Crabtree to anyone. On pain of prosecution. Or worse.'

'And if I don't?'

'The answer to that question is not one that will appeal, believe me. What have you to lose by co-operating with what are, after all, your own country's national interests?'

Lindsay shook her head. 'If we started to debate where the national interest really lies, we'd be here a long time, Ms Barber. I've got a more immediate concern than that. I understand that you're not going to let Simon Crabtree be charged with the murder of his father?'

'Superintendent Rigano's indiscretions were quite accurate.'

'So that means he stays free until you're ready?'

The woman nodded. 'You have a good grasp of the realities, Miss Gordon.'

'Then what?'

'Then he will be dealt with, believe me. By one side or the other.'

'But not immediately?'

'That seems unlikely. He has – certain uses, shall we say?'

Lindsay lit another cigarette. 'That's my problem, you see, Ms Barber. Simon Crabtree is a murderer and I want him out of circulation.'

'I'm surprised that the Protestant ethic is still so firmly rooted in you, given how the rest of your lifestyle has rejected it. I didn't expect a radical lesbian feminist to be so adamant for justice,' Barber replied sarcastically.

'It's not some abstract notion of justice that

bothers me,' Lindsay retorted. 'It's life and death. The life and death of someone I care about. You see, no one's told Simon Crabtree that he's immune from prosecution. And he thinks that Deborah Patterson has information that will tie him to his father's murder and put him away. For as long as he's on the streets, Deborah Patterson is at risk, and I can't go along with any deal that means there's a chance that she's going to die. So I'm sorry, it's no deal. I've got to tell my story. I've got to put a stop to Simon Crabtree.'

'That's a very short-sighted view,' Barber responded quietly. 'If you don't accept the deal, Deborah will be in exactly the same position of risk that you have outlined.'

Lindsay shook her head. 'No. Even if I can't get the paper to use the story, I can get her out of the firing line. I can take her away somewhere he'll never find us.'

Harriet Barber laughed softly. 'I don't think you quite understand, Miss Gordon. If you don't accept our offer, you'll be in no position to take Deborah anywhere. Because you won't be going anywhere. Accidents, Miss Gordon, can happen to anyone.'

17

The phone was ringing when Cordelia let herself in, but before she could reach the nearest extension, the answering machine picked up the call. No hurry, she thought, climbing the stairs. She took off her sheepskin, went into their bedroom and swapped her boots for a pair of slippers. She carried her briefcase through to her study, then headed for the kitchen. She put on some coffee to brew, and with a degree of anticipation went to read the note from Lindsay she'd spotted on her way past the memo board. She wished she'd been able to dash down to Brownlow to be with Lindsay when she'd needed her and was gratified when she found that her presumed errant lover was due home within the half hour. Only then did she play back the messages stored on the machine.

All were for Lindsay, and all were from Duncan, increasingly angry as one succeeded another. There were four, the earliest timed at noon, the latest the one she'd nearly picked up when she came in. It was all to do with some urgent query from the office lawyer about her copy, and Duncan was clearly furious at Lindsay's failure to keep in touch. Cordelia sighed. It was really none of her business, but she toyed with the idea of calling Duncan and making soothing noises while explaining that Lindsay was due back at any minute. She got as far as dialling the number of the newsdesk, but thought better of it at the last minute and replaced the receiver. Lindsay wouldn't thank her if she had the effect of irritating Duncan still further, which, knowing him, was entirely possible.

Cordelia poured herself a mug of coffee, picked up the morning paper and ambled through to the living room. She sat down to read the paper, but decided she needed some soothing music and went over to the record and tape collection to select her current favourite, a tape Lindsay had compiled of Renata Tebaldi singing Mozart and Puccini arias. She slotted the tape into the stereo, noting with annoyance that the power was still switched on and that there was an unidentified tape in the other deck. It aroused her curiosity, so she rewound the tape and played it back. The series of hisses and whines puzzled her, but she shrugged and put it down to some bizarre exercise of Lindsay's. She stopped the tape and went back to her coffee and paper to the strains of 'Un Bel Di Vedremo'.

She was immersed in the book reviews when the phone rang again. She picked it up, checking her watch, surprised to see it was already ten past eight. 'Cordelia Brown here,' she said.

'Thank Christ somebody answers this phone occasionally!' It was Duncan, sufficiently self-confident not to bother announcing his identity. 'Where the hell is she, Cordelia? I've been trying to get hold of her all bloody day. She's got her bloody radio pager switched off too, the silly bitch. I mean, I told her she could have the day off, but she knows better than to do a body-swerve when she's got a story on the go. Where is she, then?'

'I really don't know, Duncan,' Cordelia replied. 'But I'm expecting her back any minute. She left a note saying she'd be back by eight and she's usually very good about punctuality. I'll get her to call as soon as she gets in, okay?'

'No, it's not okay,' he retorted with ill-grace. 'But it'll have to do. I'll have her on the dog watch for a month for this. Makes me look a bloody idiot, you know?'

'I'm sorry, Duncan. You know it's not like her to let you down.'

'She's got some bloody bee in her bonnet about this peace camp. It was the same over that bloody murder in Derbyshire but at least she was freelance then. She owes me some loyalty for giving her a job. I'll get no proper work out of her till this is cleared up,' he complained.

'You don't have to tell me, Duncan,' Cordelia sympathised. 'I'll get her to call you, okay?'

Cordelia sat for a moment, the first stirrings of worry beginning. Lindsay was pathologically punctual. If her note said 'home by eight,' then home by eight she'd be, or else she'd have phoned a message through. She always managed it; in the past she'd bribed passing motorists or British Rail porters to make the phone calls on her behalf. Presumably, Lindsay was visiting Deborah, since she'd been so worried about her condition. And there was no point in fretting about that. She was only twenty-five minutes late, after all.

On an impulse, Cordelia went through to Lindsay's desk and checked her card-index file to see if there was any contact number for the peace camp. The only number that seemed to suit her purpose was that of the pub the women used regularly. She keyed in the nine digits and when a man answered, she asked if Jane was in. She was told to hang on and after a few minutes a cautious woman's voice said, 'Hello? Who is this?'

'Is that Jane?' asked Cordelia. 'This is Cordelia.'

'No, it's not Jane. She's not here. Do you need to get a message to her?'

'Yes, I do. It's really urgent. Would you ask her to call Lindsay Gordon's home number as soon as possible, please?'

'No problem. Lindsay Gordon's home number,' the voice said. 'A couple of the women are going back in five minutes, so they can tell Jane then.

She'll get your message in about quarter of an hour.'

Fifteen minutes stretched into twenty for Cordelia. She poured herself a glass of wine, though what she craved was a large Scotch. But she wasn't taking the chance of being over the limit if she had to drive anywhere to rescue Lindsay from some mess or other. After twenty-five minutes, she raked around the house till she found a packet with a couple of Lindsay's cigarettes left in it, and lit one.

The phone had barely rung when Cordelia snatched it up, praying for Lindsay's familiar voice. She was unreasonably disappointed to find Jane on the other end of the line.

'Hi, Cordelia. I got this urgent message to phone Lindsay. Is she there?'

'No,' Cordelia sighed. 'The message was from me. I'm trying to track her down. She seems to have dropped out of sight, and given the events of the last few days, I'm a bit worried. I don't suppose you know where she's got to?'

'I'm sorry, love, I was hoping this message was from her, to be honest. She was supposed to come to the hospital to see Deborah tonight, but she hasn't shown up. I took Cara in for five minutes to see her mum, and I deliberately left it till towards the end of visiting time to give Lindsay a chance to spend a bit of time with Deborah if she was up to it, but the policeman on duty said Lindsay hadn't been at all. I was pretty amazed because the last thing she said this morning was that she'd see me there tonight,' Jane said.

'So when was the last time you saw Lindsay?' Cordelia asked.

'This morning. Not long after nine. She'd been in to see Deborah and I went along for moral support. She came out from seeing Deborah and asked if I could make my own way back to the camp because she'd got to go to Oxford urgently. Look, Cordelia, I wouldn't worry about her. She's probably been held up on something to do with work,' Jane reassured her.

'No,' Cordelia replied. 'Her office are going nutso because she hasn't been in touch with them either. It's odd – she's been back here and left a note since then. God knows where she's gone now. She didn't say why she was going to Oxford, did she? Or who she was going to see?'

'She didn't mention any names, but she did say it was something to do with a computer,' said Jane. 'I'm sorry I can't be more help.'

'No, you've been great,' said Cordelia. 'Look, if by any remote chance she turns up, will you tell her to phone the office as soon as possible, on pain of death? And me too?'

'Of course I will,' said Jane. 'I hope you get hold of her soon. She'll probably be chasing some story that's the most important thing in the world to her right now. I'm sure she's okay, Cordelia.'

'Yeah, thanks. See you.' Cordelia put the phone down. Oxford and computers. That could only mean Annie Norton. She trailed back to Lindsay's desk to try and find a number for Annie. There was nothing in the card-index, and Lindsay's address book listed Annie without a phone number. Cordelia tried directory enquiries, but wasn't surprised, given the way her luck was running, to find that Annie was ex-directory. A trawl through Lindsay's address book produced three other mutual friends who might be able to supply a number for Annie. Predictably, it took her three attempts to get what she wanted.

Annie's phone rang nearly a dozen times before she answered. Her voice was irritable as she gave her number.

'Annie? I'm sorry to interrupt you. It's Cordelia Brown here,' she apologised. 'I was wondering if by any chance you know where Lindsay is? Did she come to see you this morning by any chance? The thing is she's disappeared, and her office are desperate to contact her.'

'I'm sorry, Cordelia, I really have no idea where she might be. Yes, she was here, but she left my office about half past ten, I guess. She gave me no indication of where she was heading then.' Annie sounded reluctant to continue the conversation.

'I'm sorry if this is an awkward time . . .' Cordelia trailed off.

'I have some people for dinner, that's all,' said Annie.

'I'm just really worried about her, Annie. She never goes walkabout like this. Not when she's got work on. She's far too conscientious. Do you mind me asking, what was it she wanted to know about?'

Annie relented, touched by the concern in Cordelia's voice. 'She had left a computer tape with me for analysis, and she came round to collect the results. She did say that she intended to get back to London tonight. This attack on Deborah has taken a lot out of her. I think it frightened her badly.'

'I know that,' Cordelia replied, 'but what was this tape all about? What kind of tape was it?'

'It was an ordinary cassette tape.' That made sense, thought Cordelia, remembering the tape in the stereo. 'But I think you'd better ask Lindsay what it was about. I'm not in a position to discuss it, Cordelia. I'm sorry, I'm not being obstructive, just cautious. I think there are too many people involved already.'

'What do you mean, Annie? You can't leave it at that!'

'I'm sorry. I shouldn't have said as much as I have. Lindsay's mixed up in something that could cause a lot of hassle. I told her she should be talking to the police about it, not me. Maybe she took my advice.'

'Jesus, Annie, what the hell's going on? Are you saying she's in danger?'

'Don't worry, Cordelia. I don't imagine for one minute that she's in any danger. She'll be in touch. She could be trying to phone now, for all we know. Take it easy and don't worry. Lindsay's a born survivor. Look, I'd better go now. Tell her to give me a call in the morning, okay?' Annie's tone was final.

'Okay,' said Cordelia coldly. 'Goodbye.' Her anger at Annie's nonchalance had the salutory effect of making her do something to fight her own growing anxiety. She collected the mystery tape, pulled on her boots and sheepskin and ran downstairs. She climbed into the BMW and joined the night traffic. When she reached the motorway, she put her foot down and blasted down the fast lane. 'Please God,' she said aloud as she drove. 'Please let her be all right.' But the appalling fantasy of Lindsay's death would not be kept at bay by words. Cordelia was near to tears when she pulled up in the car park of Fordham police station just before ten o'clock. She marched inside, determined to find out what had happened to Lindsay.

She marched up to the duty officer. 'I need to see Superintendent Rigano,' she said. 'It's a matter of great urgency.'

The officer looked sceptical. 'I don't know if he's still here, miss,' he stalled. 'Perhaps if you could tell me what it's all about we'll see if we can sort it out.'

'Why don't you check and see if he is here? You can tell him that I need to speak to him about the Deborah Patterson attack,' she responded crisply.

He compressed his lips in irritation and vanished behind a frosted-glass partition. Five minutes later he reappeared to say grudgingly, 'If you follow me, I'll take you to the Super.'

She found Rigano sitting alone at his desk going through a stack of files. The lines on his face seemed to be etched more deeply and there were dark shadows under his eyes. 'So what is it now, Miss Brown? Can't Miss Gordon run her own errands? Or is she just keeping out of my way?'

'I was hoping you might be able to tell me where she is,' Cordelia enunciated carefully. 'She appears to have vanished, and I rather thought that was police business.'

'Vanished? If she's vanished, she's done it very recently. She was here till about six o'clock. And that's only four hours ago.'

Suddenly, Cordelia felt foolish. 'She was due home at eight o'clock. She hadn't phoned by nine. I know that probably sounds nothing to you, but Lindsay's got a real fetish about punctuality. She never fails to let me know if she's not going to make it at a time she's prearranged. Especially when we've not seen each other for a day or two.' Don't dismiss me as a hysterical female, she pleaded mentally.

'You don't think that you might be over-reacting?'

'No. I believe she had some information concerning Rupert Crabtree's death and the attack on Deborah that might have put her in danger. I'm scared, Superintendent. I've got a right to be.'

A spasm of emotion crossed his face. But his voice was cool. 'Do you know what that information was?'

'Not in detail. But something to do with a computer tape, I believe.' He nodded. 'Okay. I think we may be a little premature here, but let's make a few enquiries anyway.'

She expected him to dismiss her or summon a subordinate, but he picked up his phone and dialled an outside number. 'Mrs Crabtree?' he said. 'Superintendent Rigano here. I'm sorry to trouble you. Is Simon there by any chance? . . . In London? When did he go, do you know? . . . Yesterday? I see. And you expect him back Saturday. Yes, a computer exhibition. I see. Do you know the number of his stand? You don't? Never mind. No, it's not urgent. Has anyone else been trying to contact him? . . . No? Fine, thanks very much. Sorry to have disturbed you. Good night.'

He clicked a pen against his teeth. Then he dialled an internal number. 'Davis? Get in here, lad,' he demanded. A moment later the door opened and a plain clothes officer in shirtsleeves entered. 'Where's Stone?' Rigano asked him abruptly.

'I don't know, sir. He rushed off about six, just before you went out. He's not been back since.'

'What do you mean, he rushed off?'

'He came out of his room like a bat out of hell, sir, and ran out to the car park. He took off in that souped-up Fiesta of his.'

'Jesus,' Rigano swore softly. 'I don't believe this. Is his room locked, Davis?'

'I suppose so, sir. He always locks up after himself.'

'Okay. Get me the master key from the duty officer. I'm bloody tired of not knowing what's going on in my own station.' The young officer looked startled. 'Go on, lad, get it.' He departed on the double.

'What's going on?' Cordelia asked.

'Sorry, can't say,' he replied with an air of such finality that Cordelia couldn't find the energy to challenge him. There was silence till Davis returned. Then the two men left the room together. Five interminable minutes passed before Rigano stormed back into the room. His fury was frightening, his face flushed a dark crimson. Ignoring Cordelia he grabbed the phone, dialled a number and exploded into the phone, 'Rigano here. I'm letting you know that I intend to lodge a formal complaint about Stone. Do you know he's been bugging my office? Not only has he destroyed this force's credibility over this whole investigation but now he's taking the law into his own hands.

'Listen, I have good reason to believe that someone could be in a situation of extreme prejudice thanks to this, and I'm not going to lie down and die any longer. You'll be hearing from me formally in the morning.' He slammed the receiver down. His hands were trembling with the force of his rage.

The storm had done nothing to ease Cordelia's growing fear. Rigano turned to face her and said carefully, 'I'm sorry about that. I think I know where Lindsay is, and I'm not happy about it.' He sighed. 'I wish to hell she'd listened to me. Is she always so damned headstrong?'

'Never mind the bloody character analysis. Where is she? Who is she with? She's in some kind of trouble, isn't she? What's going on?' Cordelia almost shouted.

'Yes, she's in trouble. Deep trouble.'

'Well, why are we sitting here? Why aren't we doing something about it?'

'I'm going to get her,' he said decisively. 'It's going to cause all sorts of bloody aggravation. But I can't leave her to stew. I can't walk away from it. Miss Brown . . . I suggest you go home and try not to worry. She should be home by morning. If not, I'll let you know.'

Cordelia could not believe her ears. 'Oh no!' she exploded. 'You don't get rid of me like that. If you're going to get Lindsay, I'm coming too. I will not be fobbed off with all this static. Either you take me along or I'm going to get on the phone to Lindsay's boss and tell him she's been kidnapped by one of your sidekicks. And everything else I know.'

'I can't take you with me,' he said.

'I'll follow you.'

'I'll have you arrested if you try it.'

It seemed like stalemate. 'I know about the tape,' said Cordelia. 'I know where there's a copy of the analysis of it, too,' she said, guessing wildly about Annie's involvement. 'Take me with you or the lot goes to Lindsay's paper. Even if you arrest me, I get to make a phone call eventually. That's all it'll take. And just think what a story it'll make – famous writer sues police for wrongful imprisonment.'

He shook his head. 'There's no point in all this blackmail, believe me. I give you my word, I'll get her back to you.'

'That's not good enough. Something's going on here. And I can't leave it in anyone else's hands. It's too important.'

He finally conceded, too worn out to carry on the fight. 'All right. You can follow me. But you won't be allowed to come in.'

'Why? Where the hell are you going? Where is she?'

'GCHQ Cheltenham, I think.'

'What?'

It was nearly midnight when they reached the main gates of the intelligence complex. As Rigano instructed, Cordelia parked as unobtrusively as possible about quarter of a mile from the brightly lit gate. She watched as Rigano drove up and, after five minutes, was admitted. Tearing irritably at the cellophane on the packet of cigarettes she'd bought at a petrol station *en route* Cordelia prepared herself for a long vigil. Rigano wasn't exactly her idea of the knight in shining armour. But he was all she'd got.

18

The chirrup of the telephone broke the stalemate in the smoky room. Lindsay was grateful for the note of normality it injected into what had become a completely disorientating experience. Harriet Barber frowned and picked it up. 'Barber here,' she said coolly. A puzzled look crossed her face and she turned to Stone, handing him the phone. 'You'd better deal with this,' she ordered.

'Yes? Stone speaking,' he said. He listened for a few moments then said, 'I'll be right down.' He replaced the phone and got to his feet. 'I don't understand this, I'm afraid. Are you staying here?' he asked.

'The situation down there is your problem, Stone,' she replied icily. 'Deal with it. Deal with it quickly.'

He left the room.

'I suppose a visit to the loo would be out of the question?' Lindsay asked.

'Not at all.'

'You surprise me.'

'Provided you don't mind my company.'

'What?' Lindsay demanded, outraged.

'We don't take chances with valuable government property,' Barber replied easily. 'Besides, I thought it might rather appeal to you. Given your . . . inclinations.'

Lindsay's face revealed her contempt. 'I'd rather eat razor blades,' she spat.

'That could be arranged,' Barber replied with a faint smile. She pulled a small black notebook from her jacket pocket and made a few notes. Lindsay glowered at her in silence. Long minutes passed before the phone rang again. 'Barber here,' the woman said again. She listened then said abruptly. 'Out of the question. No . . .' She listened again. 'He says what?' Anger clouded her eyes. 'Well, in that case, you'd better bring him up. I'm not going to forget this whole episode, Stone.' She slammed the phone down and stared at Lindsay. She lit another fragrant French cigarette then got up and offered one to Lindsay who accepted gratefully. 'We have a visitor, Miss Gordon,' Barber said, her voice clipped and taut.

'Who?' the journalist asked wearily.

'You'll see soon enough,' was the reply before Barber lapsed into silence again.

Lindsay heard the door open and swivelled uncomfortably round in her chair. A surge of relief flooded through her when she saw an obviously disgruntled Stone hustling Rigano into the room.

He stopped on the threshold, his face the stony mask that Lindsay had come to recognise as normal. But when he spoke, the concern in his voice was a distinct novelty. 'Are you all right?' he asked, moving slowly towards her. Before she could reply, he spotted the handcuffs and rounded angrily on Stone. 'For Christ's sake,' he thundered. 'She's not one of the bloody Great Train Robbers. What's all this crap?'

Stone looked helplessly at Harriet Barber, who responded immediately. 'Mr Stone is not in charge here, Superintendent. I am. and I have no intention of releasing Miss Gordon until we have the assurances from her that we require. I am under no obligation towards you, and you are here out of courtesy only.'

The tension between the two of them crackled in the air. 'We'll see about that,' Rigano replied grimly before turning back to Lindsay. 'Are you all right?'

'Considering that I've been kidnapped at gunpoint, threatened with a knife, transported in conditions that would be illegal if I was a sheep, and interrogated by assholes, I'm okay,' she answered bitterly. 'You got me into this mess, Jack. You shopped me. Now call off the dogs and get me out of it.'

'He doesn't have the authority,' Barber said.

'We'll see about that as well,' Rigano retorted. 'But I didn't shop you, Lindsay. That bastard Stone had my office bugged. I have proof of that, and it's already in the hands of my senior officers. You people, madam,' he said, turning towards Harriet Barber, 'had my men's full co-operation, but that wasn't good enough for you, was it?'

'As things have turned out, it looks as if that was a wise precaution. We haven't had your full co-operation, after all.'

'You don't get away with bugging a senior police officer's room, whoever you are, madam.'

'Your intervention at this juncture is tedious and utterly pointless, Superintendent. You have satisfied yourself as to the well-being of Miss Gordon and I suggest that you leave now.' Barber's tone suggested that she was not accustomed to being thwarted.

But Rigano refused to be intimidated. 'Where are we up to, Lindsay? What's the deal?'

'I would advise you not to reply, Miss Gordon. Superintendent, you have no standing here. I strongly advise you to leave.'

'You might not think I have any standing here, madam, but I'd have thought you'd welcome *any* intervention that might sort this business out. Now, will someone please tell me what the offer is?'

'It's simple, Jack,' said Lindsay. 'I sign away all my rights, promise to forget everything I know and Simon Crabtree gets to kill Debs.'

Exasperated by the situation spiralling out of her control, Harriet Barber got to her feet and said angrily, 'Don't be absurd. Superintendent, we expect Miss Gordon to sign the Official Secrets Act and to be bound by it. We expect the return of any secret material still in her possession. She will not refer to the events of this evening or to her theories about what has happened at Brownlow to anyone, on pain of prosecution. Not unreasonable, I submit.'

'That's the sanitised version,' interrupted Lindsay. 'What she misses out is that Crabtree stays free to take whatever steps he wants against Debs and that if I write the story I'll be silenced. Permanently.'

'No one has threatened your life,' Barber snapped.

'Not in so many words,' Lindsay agreed. 'But we both know that's what we've been talking about.'

Rigano shook his head. 'This is bloody silly. This is not the Soviet Union. People don't get bumped off because they possess inconvenient knowledge. You're both making a melodrama out of a molehill. Do you really think that any newspaper's going to print her story? For a kick-off, no one would believe her. And besides, you can easily shut up any attempts at publication.

'There's no need to threaten Miss Gordon with dire consequences because she'd never get any editor to take the chance of using this stuff. She's got no evidence except the computer tape and that means bugger all at the end of the day. All you need from her is her signature on the OSA and the return of the tape. You don't need threats.'

'But what about Deborah?' Lindsay interrupted. 'Crabtree's going to walk away from all this believing she knows something that can put him away. You can't protect her twenty-four hours a day for ever.'

Rigano looked puzzled. 'I still don't bloody see why you people want Crabtree free. He's a bloody spy as well as a murderer.'

Barber frowned. 'He has uses at present. He will eventually pay the price for his activities. That I can guarantee.'

Rigano jumped on her words. 'So surely until that happens you people can put Deborah Patterson into a safe house.'

Lindsay shook her head. 'I can't trust them to look after her. Their organisation's probably penetrated at every level already without Simon Crabtree hacking his way in. Besides, this lot would do a double-cross tomorrow if it fitted their notion of national security.'

'And there's the impasse, Superintendent,' Barber said. 'She doesn't trust us, and we don't trust her.'

Rigano thought for a moment, then said slowly, 'There is one way.'

Cordelia counted the cigarettes left in the packet. She fiddled with the radio tuner, trying to find a station that would take her mind off the terrifying possibilities that kept running through her head. She looked at her watch, comparing the time with the dashboard clock. He'd been in there for more than an hour. She lit another cigarette that she knew she wouldn't enjoy and stared back at the dark cluster of buildings in deep shadow under the severe overhead lights that led from the road. As she watched, a tall man came out of the main gate and started walking in her direction. She paid little attention until he stopped by her car expectantly. Wary, she pressed the switch that lowered the window until a two-inch gap appeared. She could see a blond head of hair above a windproof jacket. His eyes glittered as he asked brusquely, 'Cordelia Brown?'

'Yes,' she answered. An edginess in his manner urged her to caution.

'I have a message for you.' He handed her a note.

Cordelia recognised her lover's familiar handwriting and her stomach contracted with relief. She forced herself to focus on the words, and read, 'Give the copy of the computer tape to the man who delivers this if you've got it. It's all right. L.' She looked up at the man's impassive face. 'What's going on? Am I going to see her soon?' she pleaded.

'Looks like it,' he said. His voice was without warmth. 'The tape?'

She fumbled in her bag and handed him the unlabelled cassette.

'The note as well, please.'

'What?' she asked, puzzled.

'I need the note back.' Reluctantly, she handed him the scrap of paper.

Cordelia watched him walk towards the gate and gain admission. Unnerved by the brevity of the encounter she lit another cigarette and searched the radio wavebands again.

The digital clock on the dashboard showed 2:01 when the barrier at the gate rose. Cordelia stared so hard into the pool of light by the gate that she feared the sight of Rigano's car followed by Lindsay's MG was a mirage. She sat bolt upright in her seat, then hurriedly got out of the BMW. When the other two cars reached her, they stopped, and their drivers emerged. Lindsay and Cordelia fell into each other's arms. For once, no words came between them as they clung desperately to each other. Rigano cleared his throat noisily and said, 'You promised them I'd have the printout by ten. We'd better get a move on, hadn't we?'

Lindsay disengaged herself from Cordelia's arms and rubbed her brimming eyes. 'Okay, okay,' she said. 'And we have to work out the details of how you keep your end of the bargain. We'd better go back to London in convoy. I hope you're going to give us the benefit of the blue flashing light.'

'Is someone going to explain what's been going

on?' Cordelia demanded. 'I've been sitting here like a lemon half the night, going out of my mind with worry.'

'Later,' said Lindsay.

'No,' said Rigano. 'No explanations. That's the deal, remember.'

Dawn was fading the streetlights into insignificance by the time they reached Highbury. Cordelia drove off to garage her car while Lindsay went indoors to collect the printout. When she returned Rigano took the papers, saying 'What arrangements do you want me to make?'

Lindsay spoke abruptly. 'I need to make some phone calls. If the hospital say it's okay, then I'll act tonight. Unless you hear from me to the contrary, I'll expect your men to be gone by seven. And I don't want anyone following us.'

He smiled grimly. 'There won't be.' Rigano raised his hand in mock salute then turned and walked back to his car as Cordelia arrived at the door. After watching him accelerate out of sight, Lindsay buried her head in Cordelia's shoulder and burst into tears. 'I've been so bloody scared,' she sobbed. 'I thought I'd never see you again.'

Cordelia led her indoors and helped her upstairs. Lindsay's muscles felt like jelly and she was shivering. 'Tell me about it later,' Cordelia said as she undressed her and got her into bed. 'Sleep now and we'll talk later.' Lindsay fell back on the pillows and fell asleep almost immediately, sprawled across the bed like a starfish. Cordelia looked down at her exhausted face with pity, and decided to sleep in the spare room to avoid disturbing her.

Lindsay woke at noon to the sound of the phone ringing. She grabbed the receiver and was immediately deafened by a raging Duncan. She lay back and let him rant till he finally ran out of steam. 'So what've you got to say for yourself?' he yelled for the third time.

'I was in police custody till six this morning, Duncan,' she explained. 'I wasn't allowed to make a phone call. They had got it into their heads that I was withholding information concerning the Rupert Crabtree murder and they were giving me the third degree.'

The phone crackled into life again as Duncan's rage transferred itself to Fordham police. Again, Lindsay let the storm blow itself out. As he threatened for the fourth time to sue the police and have questions raised in Parliament, Lindsay butted in. 'Look, it's all over now, Duncan. It won't serve any purpose to jump up and down about it. Anyway, I'm on the trail of a cracking good exclusive connected to the murder. But I'm going to have to drop out of sight for a couple of days while I get some info undercover and look up a few dodgy contacts. Is that okay?'

'No, it's not bloody okay. What is this exclusive? You don't decide to fuck off chasing whatever rainbows you fancy just because you've had a lucky run with a few stories. Tell me what you're following up and I'll let you know if it's worthwhile.'

Lindsay could feel a headache starting somewhere behind her eyes. 'I don't exactly know where it's going to lead me, Duncan, but I've discovered that there's an MI5 man involved somehow in the fringes of the murder. I want to dig around a bit and see if I can find out what the intelligence angle is, see what it's all about. I think it could be a belter, Duncan. I've got that feeling about it. One of the coppers has hinted to me that there could be a security angle. But I'll have to keep a low profile. I might be out of touch for a day or two.' She kept her fingers crossed that the gamble would pay off. There was a pause.

'Till Monday, then,' he said grudgingly. 'I want a progress report by morning conference. This is your last chance, though, Lindsay. Piss me about like yesterday again and no excuses will do.' The phone crashing down at the other end nearly deafened Lindsay, but she didn't mind. She had got her own way, and Duncan was only indulging in office bravado in order to terrorise her colleagues.

Sighing, she got out of bed and quickly pulled on a pair of jeans and a thick sweater. She pushed her head round the spare room door to see Cordelia apparently sound asleep. It was good to be home again. The events of the last twenty-four hours had convinced her that in spite of her frequent absorption in her own concerns, Cordelia was still totally committed to her. Grabbing a pocketful of change on her way out, Lindsay headed across Highbury Fields. She was going to have to be careful. It was at times like this she could use Cordelia's help but it was too risky to involve anyone else unnecessarily. Lindsay couldn't justify to herself the act of confiding in Cordelia for her own selfish reasons. She put these thoughts to the back of her mind as she reached the phone box. She wanted to be sure these calls weren't going to end up on one of Harriet Barber's phone taps. She called Fordham General Hospital where, under the guise of a close relative, she eventually found a doctor who was prepared to admit that it would now be possible to move Deborah without untoward risk, though he personally would accept no responsibility for this.

There followed a series of phone calls including one to her parents in Argyllshire. She made the necessary arrangements with the minimum of fuss, then headed back home. She put some coffee on, then stripped off and dived under the shower. She spent a long time luxuriating in the hot water, putting off the moment when she would have to waken Cordelia and tell her she was about to go missing without trace again. It wasn't something she relished, particularly since the business of Deborah still lay unresolved between them.

She emerged from the shower and wrapped

the towel around herself. In the kitchen, Cordelia was staring moodily into a mug of coffee. Lindsay squeezed past and poured out her own. She reached across the table for a discarded packet of cigarettes and nervously lit up.

Cordelia picked up the morning paper and began to read the front page. Lindsay cleared her throat and said awkwardly, 'Thanks for last night. If it hadn't been for you, I don't know what would have happened.'

Cordelia shrugged. 'Least I could do. I do worry about you, you know. Ready to tell me about it yet?'

'I'd rather wait till it's all sorted, if that's okay. I've got to go away again for a couple of days.' Cordelia said nothing, and turned the page of the paper. 'We're taking Debs somewhere she'll be safe. Once that's done, I'll be able to tell you the whole story. It's not that I don't trust you – but after last night, knowing how heavy these people can get, I just don't want to expose you to any risks. I don't enjoy being secretive.'

'You could have fooled me,' Cordelia said with a wry smile. 'Okay, Lindsay, you play it your way. When will you be back?'

'I'm not sure. I'll call you when I know.'

Lindsay swallowed the remains of her coffee and went back to the bedroom. She dressed quickly, then she threw knickers, socks, shirts and jeans into a holdall, grimacing as she noticed how few clean clothes were left in her wardrobe.

Everything else she needed was in the car or Deborah's van already. She finished packing, and turned to find Cordelia standing just inside the room, leaning on the door jamb.

'You are coming back?'

Lindsay dropped her bag and hauled Cordelia into her arms. 'Of course I'm coming back.'

19

Closing the front door behind her, Lindsay felt weariness creep over her at the thought of the day ahead. She got into the MG, noticing how badly she'd parked only seven hours before. The memory of her ordeal threatened to overwhelm her, so she quickly started the car and shot off. Driving, as usual, restored some of her equanimity and she was fairly calm by the time she reached Brownlow. She went straight to the Red Cross bender and found Jane lying on a pallet reading a novel. Lindsay marvelled once again at the ability of the peace women to indulge in perfectly normal activities in such an outlandish situation. Guiltily breaking in to Jane's much-needed relaxation, Lindsay sketched out what she needed and why. Her sense of urgency transmitted itself to Jane, who agreed to the plan.

Lindsay waited until dusk, then borrowed a 2CV from one of the peace women. Going first to the hospital, she made a brief reconnaissance before heading back to the camp. She linked up with Jane as arranged and hastily they loaded the van with their own bags. Then Lindsay made up the double berth and got Cara ready for bed.

At twenty past seven, Lindsay got into the MG and shot off down the winding lane away from the camp, heading in the opposite direction from the hospital. A quarter of a mile down the road she spotted a set of headlamps in her rear-view mirror. Once she hit the outskirts of the town, she figured, her pursuer, this time in a green Ford Escort, would have to close up or risk losing her. Her calculations proved right. Thanks to her earlier homework she shook off the pursuit by doubling back down an alley and taking a short cut up a one-way street in the wrong direction. Then, driving in a leisurely fashion to a small industrial estate near the motorway, she tucked the MG into a car park behind one of the factory units. Jane was waiting for her in the van. Together they made straight for Fordham General. Lindsay directed Jane into a small loading area at the back of the main hospital building.

Lindsay crouched down beside Cara, who was lying in bed, drifting in and out of sleep. 'I want you to promise me you'll stay here very quiet till we get back. We won't be long. We're going to fetch your mummy, but she'll still be very poorly, so you've got to be very gentle and quiet with her. Okay?' Cara nodded. 'I promise we won't be long. Try to go back to sleep.' She stroked Cara's hair, then joined Jane outside.

They had no difficulty in reaching Deborah's side ward without arousing untoward interest since it was still during visiting hours. Lindsay quickly scouted round to make sure the area was not under surveillance before the pair of them ducked into Deborah's room. In the thirty-six hours since Lindsay had last seen her, Deborah had made a noticeable improvement. She was propped up on her pillows watching television, the deathly white pallor had left her skin and she looked like a woman in recovery mode. Even the drips had been taken out. When they entered, she grinned delightedly. 'At last,' she said. 'I thought you'd all forgotten me.'

'Far from it,' said Lindsay, going to her and kissing her warmly. 'Listen, there's no time to explain everything now. But we've got to get you out of here. The doctors say you can be moved safely, and Jane's promised to take care of you.'

Jane nodded, picking up the chart on the end of the bed. 'It looks as if your condition is quite stable now,' she remarked. 'Don't worry, Deborah, you'll be okay with me.'

'I don't doubt it, Jane. But what's all this about, Lin? Why can't I stay here? Surely I must be safe enough or the police wouldn't have left me unguarded?'

Lindsay sighed. 'I know it looks like I'm being really high-handed about this, but it's because I'm scared for you. You were attacked because Rupert Crabtree's murderer thinks you know something that can compromise him. I'll explain all the details later, I promise, but take it from me that the police won't arrest the person who attacked you. He doesn't know that, though. So you've got to get out of the firing line or he'll have another go.

'I've managed to arrange somewhere for you and Cara to stay for a while till the heat dies down, somewhere no one will find you. I don't trust the police to take care of you, so we're doing it all off our own bat, without their help. Will you trust me?'

'I don't seem to have a lot of choice, do I?' Deborah replied. 'But I don't know how you're going to get me out of here. I tried getting out of bed this afternoon. It turned out to be a seriously bad idea.'

It was a problem that hadn't occurred to Lindsay. But Jane had already found a solution. 'A wheelchair, Lindsay,' she said, smiling at the look of dismay on the other's face. 'We passed a couple outside the main ward, in an alcove. Can you fetch one while I get Deborah ready?'

Lindsay strolled down the corridor, trying to look nonchalant, till she reached the wheelchairs Jane had spotted. With all the subtlety of Inspector Clouseau, she wrestled one out of the alcove, struggled to release the brake, then shot off back to the side ward. Luckily no one saw her, for she would have aroused suspicion in the most naïve student nurse. Between them, Lindsay and Jane got Deborah into the wheelchair and wrapped a couple of hospital blankets round her. After checking that the coast was clear, they left the room. Jane started to push the wheelchair back the way they'd come, but Lindsay hissed, 'No, this way,' leading them in the opposite direction. During her earlier visit, she had reconnoitred an alternative route that was quicker and less public. Back at the van it was a matter of moments for Lindsay and Jane to lift Deborah in. Jane settled her into the double berth beside an overjoyed Cara.

Even so short a move had clearly taken its toll on Debs, who looked more tired and pinched than she had done a few moments ago. Jane carefully arranged the pillows under her to give her maximum support, but Deborah could not stifle a low moan as she tried to find a comfortable position for her head. Cara looked scared, but Jane soothed her and persuaded her to lie down quietly at the far side of the bed. Leaving the wheelchair where it stood Lindsay climbed into the driver's seat.

With perfect timing they left the hospital grounds in the middle of the stream of visitors' cars departing from the scene of duty done. Lindsay stayed in the flow of traffic for half a mile or so, then turned off to make a circuitous tour of the back streets of Fordham town centre, keeping a constant check on her mirrors. She trusted

Rigano to keep his word, but she felt no confidence that Harriet Barber would do the same. After ten minutes of ducking and diving Lindsay felt satisfied that no one was on their trail and headed back to the MG. She drew up beside the car and turned round to confer.

'We've got a long drive ahead. I anticipate about twelve hours, given the van. We need to take both vehicles so I can leave you the MG. Where you're going, you'll need wheels, and I think I need to borrow the van for a while. I suggest that we swap at the half-way stage, Jane, around Carlisle?'

'Okay, but we'll have to stop at every service area so I can check on Deborah's condition,' Jane replied.

'Just where are we going, Lin?' Deborah asked in a tired voice.

'An old school friend of mine has a cottage about ten miles from Invercross, where I grew up. She's a teacher and she's away in Australia at the moment, on a six-month exchange scheme, so I fixed up for you to use the cottage. It's lovely there, ten minutes from the sea. Electricity, bottled gas for cooking, telly, peat fires – all you could ask for. And no one will come looking for you there. Cara can even go to the village school if she wants. It's a small community, but they'll keep their mouths shut about you being there if my mother explains that you're convalescing after an attack and you're scared the man who attacked you is still looking for you.'

'My God,' said Deborah faintly.

'I'm sorry,' said Lindsay. 'I had to act quickly. I couldn't just sit back. There was no one else I could trust to make sure you were protected.'

'And how long do I have to hide in the heather?'

'That depends. Until Simon Crabtree is dealt with. It could be months, I'm afraid.'

'I'll stay as long as you need me,' Jane chipped in.

'I can't take all of this in. What has Simon Crabtree to do with me?' Deborah demanded, hugging Cara close. 'One minute I'm recuperating in hospital, the next I'm thrust into a remake of *The Three Musketeers* crossed with *The Thirty-nine Steps*.'

'I'll explain in the morning when I'm driving you, I promise,' Lindsay replied. 'But right now, we should get a move on.'

'I'll take the van as far as Carlisle, then,' Jane decided.

Lindsay nodded. 'That'll be best. And don't push yourself too hard. Any time you need a rest or a coffee, just pull off at the services. I'm used to driving half the night, working shifts like I do; but I don't expect you to do the same.'

'Cheeky so-and-so!' muttered Jane. 'Have you forgotten the hours junior hospital doctors work? You'll be flaked out long before I will, Lindsay.'

'Sorry, I forgot,' Lindsay apologised.

The journey seemed endless. Deborah and Cara

managed to sleep most of the way, only really waking during the last couple of hours. Lindsay explained the reasons for their flight to Deborah as she drove the last sixty miles down the familiar narrow roads with their spectacular views of the Argyllshire mountains and sea lochs on all sides. Cara was spellbound by the changing scenery and seemed not to be listening to the adult conversation.

Lindsay reached the end of her tale as they arrived in the tiny fishing village of Invercross. A cluster of brightly painted houses and cottages crowded along the harbour. 'So here we are,' Lindsay concluded. 'Right back where I started all those years ago. Only this time, on the run like Bonnie Prince Charlie and Flora Macdonald.' She pulled up outside a small, two-storey house on the harbour front. 'Wait here a minute, I've got to get the keys.'

The woman who opened the door before Lindsay reached it was small and wiry with curly grey hair and eyes that matched Lindsay's. She swept her daughter into her arms, saying, 'It's grand to see you. It's been a long time since the New Year. Now, come in and have some breakfast. Bring your friends in. Is Cordelia up with you?'

Lindsay disengaged herself and followed her mother indoors. 'No, she's busy. Listen, Mum, I want to get the others settled in at the cottage first, then I'll come back for a meal and a sleep before I get back to London.'

'You're not stopping, then?' Her mother's obvious disappointment stabbed Lindsay. 'You'll miss your father. He's at the fishing, he'll not be back before the morn's morning.'

'I'm sorry, Mum, I'm in the middle of something big. This was a kind of emergency. Have you got Catriona's keys?'

Her mother produced a bunch of keys from her apron pocket. 'I got them from Mrs Campbell last night when you phoned. I went up this morning with a few essentials and lit the fire, so they should be comfortable.'

Lindsay kissed her. 'You're a wee gem, Mum. I'll be back in a couple of hours.'

Her mother shook her head, an affectionate smile on her face. 'You never stop, do you, lassie?'

Ten hours later, Lindsay was back on the road south. Jane, Deborah and Cara were settled comfortably in the cottage, amply supplied with Mrs Gordon's idea of essentials – bread, butter, milk, eggs, bacon, fish, onions, potatoes and tea. Mrs Gordon had promised to take Jane to sign on the following Monday. If she lied about paying rent, they could fiddle enough to live on. So there would be no need for any part of the official world to know Deborah's whereabouts. Jane thought Lindsay's precautions extreme but she would not be moved.

Lindsay spent the night less comfortably than the three refugees. Her eyes were gritty and sore, her body ached from the jolting of the van's elderly suspension. She finally gave in when even the volume of the stereo couldn't keep her awake and alert. She parked in a lay-by off the motorway where she slept fitfully for five hours before hammering back down to London.

Somewhere around Birmingham, she realised that she'd felt no desire whatsoever to stay in Invercross with Deborah. That realisation forced her to examine what she had been steadfastly ignoring during the traumatic events of the last few days. It was time to think about Cordelia and herself. Why had she felt such an overwhelming need to sleep with Deborah? Did she subconsciously want to end her relationship with Cordelia and was Deborah just a tool she'd used? Until her kidnapping by the security forces, Lindsay had been confused and frightened about her emotions.

But there was no denying the fact that Cordelia had come to her rescue in spite of the problems there had been between them. Driving on, Lindsay gradually came to understand that her relief at seeing Cordelia outside GCHQ had been more than just gratitude. Her own behaviour had been negative in the extreme, and if she wanted to heal the breach between them she would have to act fast. As that thought flickered across her mind, Lindsay realised there was no 'if' about it. She knew she wanted to try again with Cordelia. Full of good resolutions, she parked the van outside the house just before noon and rushed in. The house was empty.

Stiff and exhausted, and having lost track of time almost completely, Lindsay ran a sweet-smelling foam bath, put Monteverdi's 1610 Vespers on at high volume and soaked for half an hour. Then, in sweat pants and dressing gown, she sat down at the word processor. Now that Deborah was safe, she had settled her obligations. There was even less honour among the Harriet Barbers of this world than among thieves and journalists, she had now realised. The promises they had made about leaving her alone had been shattered. They had tried their damnedest to follow her. There was only one real insurance left. So she wrote the whole story of Rupert Crabtree's murder and its repercussions, leaving nothing out.

She had barely finished it when she heard the front door slam. Alerted by the music, Cordelia superfluously called, 'I'm home.' Pink-cheeked from the cold outside, she stopped in the doorway. 'Welcome back,' she said. Linday picked up the sheaf of paper on the desk and proffered it.

'I promised you an explanation,' she said. 'Here it is. The uncensored version. It's probably quicker if you read it rather than listen to me explaining it.'

Cordelia took the papers. 'I missed you,' she said.

'I know,' Lindsay replied. 'And I've missed you, constantly. I'm not very good at being on my own.

I tend to get overtaken by events, if you see what I mean.'

Cordelia gave a sardonic smile. 'I've heard it called a lot of things, but that's a new one on me.' There was a silence, as they met in a wary and tentative embrace. Cordelia disengaged herself, saying, 'Let me read this. Then we'll talk. Okay?'

'Okay. I'll be in the kitchen when you've finished. The idea of cooking dinner in a real kitchen is strangely appealing after the last few days.'

It took Cordelia half an hour to work through Lindsay's account of her investigations. When she had finished, she sat staring out of the window. She could barely imagine the stress that Lindsay had been operating under. Now she could understand, even if she could not yet forgive what she instinctively knew had happened between Lindsay and Deborah. But the most important thing now was to make sure Lindsay's natural inclination to the defence of principle was subdued for the sake of her own safety.

Cordelia found Lindsay putting the finishing touches to an Indian meal. 'I had no idea,' she said.

Lindsay shrugged. 'I wanted so much to tell you,' she said. 'Not just at the end, but all through. I missed sharing my ideas with you.'

'What about Deborah?'

'It's not something you should be worried about, truly.'

'So what happens now? I don't mean with you and me, I mean with Deborah? Do we wait till Simon Crabtree is dealt with and then everything returns to normal?'

Lindsay shook her head. 'No. Those bastards didn't keep their word. They tried to follow me – you read that, didn't you? So as far as I'm concerned, I'm not just sitting back till I get the all clear from Rigano. The best way to make sure they deal with Crabtree is to force the whole thing into the open. Otherwise it could be months, years till one side or the other decides Crabtree has outlived his usefulness. I don't see why we should all live under a shadow till then. Besides, the guy is a murderer. He'll do it again the next time someone gets close to the truth. And next time it could be me. Or someone else I care about.'

'So what are you going to do?'

'I'm going to give the whole story to Duncan. And if he won't use it. I'll give it to Dick McAndrew. Either way, it's going to be published.'

'You're crazy,' Cordelia protested. 'They'll come after you instead of Crabtree. They've got your signature on the Official Secrets Act. And the first journo that fronts Crabtree with your story points the finger straight at you. If our lot don't get you, the Soviets will.'

'Don't be so melodramtic,' Lindsay replied crossly. 'I know what I'm doing.'

'And did you know what you were doing when you ended up in Harriet Barber's clutches the other night? I'd have thought you'd have learned more sense by now,' said Cordelia bitterly.

'Point taken,' Lindsay replied. 'But there's no use in arguing, is there? We're starting from different premises. I'm operating on a point of principle as well as self-defence. All you care about is making sure nothing happens to me. That's very commendable and I'd feel the same if our positions were reversed. But I think the fact that people who have committed no crime are hounded into hiding to protect a spy and a killer is too important to ignore simply because revealing it is going to make life difficult for me. I wish I could make you understand.'

Cordelia turned away. 'Oh, I understand all right. Rigano set you up to do his dirty work and you fell for it.'

Lindsay shook her head. 'It's not that simple. But I do feel utterly demoralised and betrayed. And I've got to do something to get rid of these feelings, as well as all the other stuff.'

Cordelia put her arms round Lindsay. 'I just don't want you to get hurt. When you get wound up about something, you completely disregard your own safety.'

'Well, I've learned my lesson. This time, I'm going to make sure my public profile is too high for them to come after me,' Lindsay retorted. 'Trust me, please.'

Cordelia kissed her. 'Oh, I trust you. It's the other nutters I worry about.'

Lindsay smiled. 'Let's eat, eh? And then, maybe an early night?'

In the morning, Lindsay smiled reminiscently about their rapprochement the night before as she gathered all her papers together and prepared to set off for an early briefing with Duncan at the office. Before she left, Cordelia hugged her, saying, 'Good luck, and take care. I'm really proud of you, you know.'

'Yes, I know. I'll see you later.'

'I'm afraid I'll be back quite late. I'm sorry, I didn't know you'd be home. I promised William we could work on the script rewrites for the new series tonight,' Cordelia apologised.

Lindsay smiled. 'No problem. I'll probably be late myself, given the importance of the story. I might even wait for the first edition to drop. I'll see you whenever.'

Outside the house, Lindsay hailed a cab and headed for the office. She had barely stepped into the newsroom when Duncan's deputy told her to go straight to the editor's office. His secretary had obviously been briefed to expect her, for Lindsay was shown straight in, instead of being left to cool her heels indefinitely with a cup of cold coffee.

Three men were waiting for her – Duncan, Bill Armitage, the editor, and Douglas Browne, the Clarion group's legal manager. No one said a word of greeting. Lindsay sensed the intention was to intimidate her, and she steeled herself against whatever was to come. 'I've brought my copy in,' she said, to break the silence. She handed the sheaf of paper to Duncan, who barely glanced at it.

Bill Armitage ran his hands through his thick grey hair in a familiar gesture. 'You've wasted your time, Lindsay,' he said. 'We'll not be using a line of that copy.'

'What?' Her surprise was genuine. She had expected cuts and rewrites, but not a blanket of silence.

Duncan replied gruffly, 'You heard, kid. We've had more aggravation over you this weekend than over every other dodgy story we've ever done. The bottom line is that we've been made to understand that if we fight on this one it will be the paper's death knell. You're a union hack – you know the paper's financial situation. We can't afford a big legal battle. And I take the view that if we can't protect our staff, we don't put them in the firing line.'

Armitage cut across Duncan's self-justification. 'We've got responsibilities to the public. And that means we don't make our living out of stirring up needless unrest. To be quite blunt about it, we're not in the business of printing unsubstantiated allegations against the security services. All that does is destroy people's confidence in the agencies that look after our safety.'

Lindsay was appalled. 'You mean the security people have been on to you already?'

The editor shook his head patronisingly. 'Did you really think the mayhem you've been causing wouldn't bring them down about our ears like a ton of bricks? Jesus Christ, Lindsay, you've been in this game long enough not to be so naïve. You can't possibly have the sort of cast-iron proof we'd need to run this story.'

Lindsay looked doubtful. 'I think I have, Bill. Most of it can be backed up by other people and I can get hold of a copy of the computer tape that clinches it all. The cops can't deny what has been going on, either. Superintendent Rigano should be able to back it up.'

'Rigano was one of the people who was here yesterday,' Browne said heavily. 'There will be no help from that quarter. The story must be killed, Lindsay.'

'I'm sorry,' said Duncan. 'I know you worked hard for it.'

'Worked hard? I nearly got myself killed for it.' Lindsay shook her head disbelievingly. 'This story is dynamite,' she protested. 'We're talking about murder, spying, security breaches, GBH and kidnapping, all going on with the consent of the people on our side who are supposed to be responsible for law and order. And you're telling me you haven't got the bottle to use it because those bastards are going to make life a little bit awkward for you? Don't you care about what they've done to me, one of your own?'

'It's not that we don't care. But there's nothing

we can legitimately do,' the editor replied. 'Look, Lindsay, forget the whole thing. Take a week off, get it into perspective.'

Lindsay stood up. 'No,' she said. 'No way. I can't accept this. I never thought I'd be ashamed of this paper. But I am now. And I can't go on working here feeling like that. I'm sorry. Duncan, but I quit. I resign. As of now, I don't work for you any more.' She stopped abruptly, feeling tears beginning to choke her. She snatched up the sheaf of copy from the table where Duncan had laid it, turned and walked out of the office. No one tried to stop her.

In the Ladies' toilet, she was comprehensively sick. She splashed cold water on her face and took several deep breaths before heading for the offices of *Socialism Today*.

Here there were no security men on the door to challenge her, no secretaries to vet her. She walked straight up to the big room on the second floor where the journalists worked. Dick was perched on the corner of his desk, his back to her, a phone jammed to his ear. 'Yeah, okay . . .' he said resignedly. 'Yeah, okay. Tomorrow it is then. See you.' He slammed the phone down. 'Fucking Trots. Who needs them?' he muttered, turning round to reach for his mug of coffee. Catching sight of Lindsay, he actually paled. 'Christ! What the hell are you doing here?'

'I've got a story for you,' she said, opening her bag and taking out another copy of her manuscript.

'Is it to do with the computer printout?' he demanded.

'Sort of. Among other things. Like murder, kidnap, GBH and spying. Interested?'

He shook his head reluctantly. 'Sorry, Lindsay. No can do. Listen, I had the heavies round at my place last night about you. It's a no-no, darling. It may be the best story of the decade, but I'm not touching it.'

A sneer of contempt flickered at the corner of Lindsay's mouth. 'I expected the big boys at the *Clarion* to wet themselves at the thought of prosecution. But I expected you to take that sort of thing in your stride. I thought you were supposed to be the fearless guardian of the public's right to know?'

Dick looked ashamed and sighed deeply. 'It wasn't prosecution they threatened me with, Lindsay. These are not people who play by the rules. These are not pussycats. These are people who know how to hurt you where you live. They were talking nasty accidents. And they knew all about Marianne and the kiddy. I'll take risks on my own account, Lindsay, but I'm not having on my conscience anything that might happen to my wife and child. You wouldn't take chances with Cordelia, would you?'

Lindsay shook her head. Exhaustion surged over her in a wave. 'I suppose not, Dick. Okay, I'll be seeing you.'

It took her more than an hour to walk back to

the empty house. She was gripped by a sense of utter desolation and frustration that she sensed would take a long time to dissipate. There had been too many betrayals in the last week. She turned into their street, just as a red Fiesta vanished round the corner at the far end of the mews behind. That unremarkable event was enough on a day like this to make her break into a run. She fumbled with her keys, clumsy in her haste, then ran upstairs. At first glance, everything seemed normal. But when she went into the living room, she realised that every cassette had been removed from the shelves above the stereo. In the study it was the same story. Lindsay crouched down on the floor against the wall, hands over her face, and shivered as the sense of insecurity overwhelmed her.

She had no idea how long she crouched there feeling utterly defenceless. Eventually the shaking stopped and she got unsteadily to her feet. In the kitchen she put some coffee on, then noticed there was a message on the answering machine. She lit a cigarette and played the tape back.

The voice sounded scared. 'Lindsay. This is Annie Norton. I've been burgled. My car has been broken into and my office has also been turned over. I suspect this may have something to do with you since all that has been stolen are cassettes. Whoever was responsible has probably got your phone bugged, so for their benefit as well as yours, for the record, they have now got the only data I had relating to that bloody tape you brought me. I wish you'd bloody warned me you didn't have the sense to leave this alone, Lindsay. You'd better stay away from me till this is all over – I need my security clearance so I can work. Look, take care of yourself. This isn't a game. Be careful. Goodbye.'

It was the last straw. Lindsay sat down at the table, dropped her head in her hands and wept till her eyes stung and her sinuses ached. Then she sat, staring at the wall, reviewing what had happened, trying to find a way forward for herself. As the afternoon wore on, she smoked steadily and worked her way down the best bottle of Burgundy she could find in the house.

By teatime she knew exactly what she had to do. She set off across the park for the phone box and started setting wheels in motion.

20

Lindsay waited patiently on hold to be connected, praying that the object of her call would still be at his desk. Even on cheap rate, the phone box was eating £1 coins at an alarming rate. While she hung on, she mentally congratulated Jane for forcing her to examine her conscience about doing something positive to support the peace camp all those months before. If it hadn't been for those features she'd sold abroad then, she wouldn't have built up the contacts she needed now. Her musing was cut short by a voice on the end of the phone.

'*Ja*?'

'Günter Binden?' Lindsay asked.

'*Ja. Wer ist?*'

'It's Lindsay Gordon, Günter. From London.'

Immediately the bass voice on the other end of the phone switched to immaculate English. 'Lindsay! How good to hear from you. How goes it with you?'

'A bit hectic. That's what I wanted to talk to you about. I've got a wonderful story for you. I'm having problems getting anyone over here to print it because of the national security angle, but it's too important a tale to ignore. So I thought of you.'

'Is it another story about the peace camp?'

'Indirectly, yes. But it's really to do with spying and murder.'

'Sounds good. Do you want to tell me some more?'

Lindsay started to tell the too-familiar story of recent events. Günter listened carefully, only stopping her to seek clarification when her journalistic idioms became too obscure for him to follow. Lindsay was glad she'd trusted her instincts about approaching him. As well as being the features editor of a large-circulation left-wing weekly magazine that actively supported the Green Party, he had spent two years working in London and understood the British political scene as well as having a first-class command of English. When she reached her kidnapping by the security forces, he exploded.

'My God, Lindsay, why isn't your own paper publishing this? It's dynamite.'

'That's precisely why they're backing off. They don't want a legal battle right now for business reasons – the publisher wants to float the company on the stock market later this year, and he wants to present a healthy balance sheet and a good reputation. Also, they've got no stomach for a real fight against the Establishment. If I was offering them a largely unsubstantiated tale about a soap-opera star having a gay affair, they'd go for it and to hell with the risks. But this is too much like the real thing. But let me finish the tale. It gets better, I promise.'

Günter held his tongue till Lindsay had finished her recital. Then there was a silence. 'What sort of price are you looking for?'

'If I hadn't jacked my job in today, I'd let you have it for free. But I'm going to have to feed myself somehow, and I can't imagine I'm going to find much work in national newspapers. Can you stretch to five thousand Deutschmarks?' Lindsay asked.

'Do you have pictures of this man Crabtree? And of Deborah Patterson?'

'I've got pics of Deborah, and you can get pics of both Simon and Rupert Crabtree through the local paper. I've got a good contact there. And you can do pics of me. What do you say, Günter?'

'How soon can I see copy?'

'I can fax it to you tonight. Have we got a deal?'

'Four thousand. That's as high as I can go. Don't forget, I've got translation to pay for too.'

Lindsay paused, pretending to think. 'Okay,' she said. 'Four thousand it is. I'll get the copy on the fax tonight and I'll bring the pics over myself.'

'You're coming over?'

Lindsay nodded. 'You bet. I want to be well

out of the way when the shit hits the fan. And besides, I won't believe it till I actually hold the first copy off the presses in my own hands.'

'So how soon can you get here?'

'I can get a night crossing and be with you by tomorrow afternoon. Does that leave you enough time?'

They arranged the rest of the details, then Lindsay hung up gratefully. Returning home, she picked up the bundle of copy she'd wasted her time writing for Duncan and left the house. She made for the tube station, not caring if she was being followed or not. It was already seven o'clock, and the rush hour press of bodies had dissipated. Emerging from Chancery Lane station she walked to the *Clarion* building. Her gamble that word of her departure wouldn't have yet got round paid off: she walked unchallenged into the building and made her way to the busy wire room on the third floor. After a quiet word with the wire room manager, he left her with the fax machine for the price of a few pints. An hour later, she left the building and headed back to Highbury. When she emerged from the tube station, she realised she wasn't able to face the empty house again just yet, so she walked slowly down Upper Street to the King's Head pub. Over a glass of the house red, she turned the situation over in her mind.

The chain reaction she had set in motion would blow Simon Crabtree's cover completely. She wished she could be a fly on the wall when it dropped on Harriet Barber's desk. The only question mark that remained in her mind was which side would get to him first. She suspected the Soviets would be the ones to terminate him; *glasnost* only extended so far. And it would be expedient for MI6 to keep their hands clean for once. But she knew she'd have to keep her head down till she was sure that Simon Crabtree had met the fate he deserved. And that might take a few weeks. A fatal accident following too closely on the heels of her revelations might seem a little too convenient even for the unscrupulous intelligence community.

The only problem that remained was how to find out when Crabtree was removed from circulation. Her first thought was to enlist Jack Rigano's help. He owed her one. As Cordelia had so forcefully reminded her, he had brought her into the frame when forces beyond his control prevented him from doing his job. But he had already stuck his neck out once for her, and the fact that it was he who had been despatched to put the frighteners on the *Clarion* demonstrated where his allegiance lay in the final analysis.

There was one other person Lindsay could ask. It would avoid the danger of providing an interested party with too much information. And provided the storm that the story was inevitably going to raise didn't make him lose his bottle, he'd also be happy to supply information when there was something in it for him. Lindsay searched through the pages of her notebook till she found the page where she'd scribbled Gavin Hammill's number. The pub phone was mercifully situated in a quiet corner, granting her some privacy.

She was in luck. The Fordham reporter was at home for the evening. After the formalities, Lindsay explained what she wanted. 'I'm going to be out of the country for a while,' she said. 'But I need someone to keep an eye on Simon Crabtree for me. I just want to know what he's up to, and if anything untoward happens to any member of the family. If you hear anything at all, especially if he drops out of sight for a few days, you can get in touch with me via a guy in Cologne called Günter Binden.'

She gave him Günter's office and home numbers and explained that Günter's magazine would pay him a generous credit for any material he supplied. 'They're very generous payers, Gavin,' she added. 'And they never forget a good source. If you do the biz for them, they'll put work your way. Oh, and if anybody asks why you're interested, don't mention my name.'

'Of course not, Lindsay. Thanks for thinking of me.'

'Don't mention it. See you around.'

The final phone call she made was to reserve a ticket for herself and the van on the midnight crossing to Zeebrugge. The train or the plane would have been more comfortable, but she wanted to be self-sufficient and mobile once she was out of the country.

She wished she could take Cordelia with her, turn the trip into a break for both of them. But she knew it wouldn't work out like that, even supposing Cordelia was able and willing to get to Dover for the midnight ferry. Lindsay knew that the divisions between them needed time and energy from both sides before they could be healed. A mad dash across Europe followed by all the hassles of getting this story on to the streets was no basis for a major reconciliation. Besides, Lindsay didn't know how long she would have to stay away, and Cordelia had other commitments.

It was a quarter past eight when she reached home. She would have to leave in three quarters of an hour. The clothes she had thrown into the washing machine earlier would be dry in half an hour, and it would take her only ten minutes to pack. She had half an hour to write an explanation of her absence for Cordelia. The word processor would be quicker, if more impersonal. But getting the words right was the most important thing.

She started by explaining where she was going and why. That was the easy bit. Now came the part where years of working with words were no help at all.

'I'm going to have to keep my head down after

this piece is published. The security services will want to bring charges, and I don't think it will be safe for me to come home till after Simon Crabtree is no longer a threat. I'm going to stay abroad for a while, but I don't know yet where I'll be. I'll let you know as soon as I've sorted things out and maybe you can join me for a while. I'm sorry – I really wanted to spend some time with you. I love you. Lindsay.'

She scowled at the screen, deeply dissatisfied with what she had written. But there was no time now for more. She got up and stretched while the letter printed out, then left it by the answering machine. The next fifteen minutes were a whirlwind of throwing clothes, books, papers, and maps into a couple of holdalls. She went through to the lounge to pick up some tapes for the journey, forgetting the raid that had left the shelves empty. When she saw the spaces where her music had been, she swore fluently. The shock gave her the extra kick of energy she needed to get out into the night and off to the ferryport.

Three nights later, Lindsay stood in the press hall in Cologne watching the massive presses flickering her image past her eyes at hundreds of copies a minute. Günter approached, clutching a handful of early copies from the run and an opened bottle of champagne. He thrust a magazine at Lindsay, who stared disbelievingly at the cover. Her own picture was superimposed on a wide-angled shot of the base at Brownlow Common with the peace camp in the foreground. A slow smile spread across her face and she took a long, choking swig from the offered bottle of champagne. 'We did it,' she almost crowed. 'We beat the bastards.'

EPILOGUE

Excerpts from the *Daily Clarion,* 11 May 198-.

MISSILES TO GO The Pentagon announced last night that the phased withdrawal of cruise missiles from Brownlow Common will begin in November . . .

DOUBLE TRAGEDY FOR SPY MURDER FAMILY The man at the centre of a German magazine's revelations about Russian spies at American bases in the UK died in a freak road accident last night.

His death was the second tragedy within two months for his family. His father, solicitor Rupert Crabtree, was brutally murdered eight weeks ago.

Simon Crabtree, who had been officially cleared by British security forces of any involvement in espionage, died instantly when his motorbike skidded on a sharp bend and ploughed into the back of a tractor.